NORTH WOLF

M.A. EVERAUX

ELLORA'S CAVE
ROMANTICA PUBLISHING

An Ellora's Cave Romantica Publication

www.ellorascave.com

North Wolf

ISBN 9781419954016
ALL RIGHTS RESERVED.
North Wolf Copyright © 2005 M.A. Everaux
Edited by Kelli Kwiatkowski
Cover art by Syneca

Electronic book Publication August 2005
Trade paperback Publication May 2007

Excerpt from *Dreams Eclipsed* Copyright © Kira Stone, 2007.

Content Advisory:

S – ENSUOUS
E – ROTIC
X – TREME

Ellora's Cave Publishing offers three levels of Romantica® reading entertainment: S (S-ensuous), E (E-rotic), and X (X-treme).

The following material contains graphic sexual content meant for mature readers. This story has been rated E–rotic.

S-*ensuous* love scenes are explicit and leave nothing to the imagination.

E-*rotic* love scenes are explicit, leave nothing to the imagination, and are high in volume per the overall word count. E-rated titles might contain material that some readers find objectionable—in other words, almost anything goes, sexually. E-rated titles are the most graphic titles we carry in terms of both sexual language and descriptiveness in these works of literature.

X-*treme* titles differ from E-rated titles only in plot premise and storyline execution. Stories designated with the letter X tend to contain difficult or controversial subject matter not for the faint of heart.

Also by M.A. Everaux

ଶ

The Claiming of Moira Shine

About the Author

ଶ

M.A. Everaux has never been to Canada, nor has she met a werewolf. Yet. She hopes to head an expedition soon, and in the meantime, spends most of her time at her computer, clacking away and putting the things that pop into her head on paper.

The author welcomes comments from readers. You can find her website and email address on her author bio page at www.ellorascave.com.

Trademarks Acknowledgement

ଶ

The author acknowledges the trademarked status and trademark owners of the following wordmarks mentioned in this work of fiction:

Daisy: Gillette Company

Formica: The Diller Corporation

NORTH WOLF

Chapter One

෨

Life was a playground, and he'd just been kicked off the swing set. Again. And then just for yucks, it'd given him a good kick in the balls. He was still reeling from that one.

Christian Tanner smiled slightly at the thought. Ordinarily, he wasn't one to get so melancholy. Usually, he was the happy type, fun to be around and ready to laugh. The kind of person others wanted to be around. It was in his nature to laugh and be joyful. It was who he was.

Except in this place, he thought. He'd come to the conclusion that a mental institute of any kind would be enough to make *anyone* mental. It was the whole purpose of the place. A conspiracy, even. The crazies went to get better, but in such an environment, regaining one's mental health was impossible. How could someone heal while eating mashed potatoes that tasted like paste? So, it was impossible. The crazies would stay crazy, and the doctors and nurses could dole out sedatives and stool softeners like they were going out of style, all the while fattening up their 401(k) plans.

And what did that say about the people who were employed in such a place? It was bad enough being committed and having no ability to leave, but to actually come to the place voluntarily, day after day — well, the poor saps had to be as crazy as their patients. He didn't care how well they were paid. The place was just plain miserable.

With a detached interest, he watched as one of the patients, a shriveled, gray gentleman with no hair and watery eyes, argued with the baby doll he held in his arms, accusing it of sleeping with his wife and stealing all his money. Christian cocked his head and listened more interestedly as the conversation got more heated, especially the parts about what the wife wouldn't do with the old man, but had no problem doing with the doll. He hoped to God if he ever got like that, someone would just shoot him and put him out of his misery.

He'd been lucky when they'd brought him in. The moon had gotten to him, a condition that was his own fault. He hadn't been changing enough, letting the beast free to roam. He'd get his ass kicked for his carelessness once he returned home. If he ever returned home.

As soon as they'd pinned him down, the orderlies knocked him out with a heavy-duty sedative. It was the only reason he was able to stave off the change, and even then, there'd been certain changes. It's just that no one had paid enough attention to notice the extra body hair he'd developed, or the heaviness of his brow and the sudden thickness of his jaw, nose and cheekbones.

He'd woken up two days later to tales of how he'd convulsed and yelled. But, he comforted himself with the knowledge that he hadn't been the only one. One urban legend that was true was that the crazies became even crazier during a full moon. The hospital staff had had their hands full with a naked, dancing old woman who insisted she was a mermaid, another man who was talking to the air, screaming that it was trying to kill him, and a multitude of other nuts, all of whom didn't have a chance in hell of escaping the joint.

And that was his current status — desperate. He needed a smoke. And he needed to get out before he became as crazy as the psycho who was quietly picking the erasers off all the pencils at the arts table and eating them.

Spying the head nurse, a rather dour, rat-faced woman with hair pulled back so tight it had to hurt, Christian leapt up and jogged over toward her station. She gave him a look that would have impressed Nurse Ratchet, then returned to giving orders to the doughy woman beside her.

Christian tapped his fingers against the Formica table top and waited. The nurse kept going on and on about bed pans and laundry collection. Finally, ten minutes later, she turned from the other woman and looked at him directly, her eyes so cold he was surprised his nuts didn't freeze and fall off on the spot.

"Can I help you?"

"I gotta call someone."

She lifted a superior brow. "You told Dr. Schneider that you didn't have any family."

"Lady," he huffed, agitatedly shoving his hair back from his face and pasting a smile on his face, just in case it worked, "The shrink spoke to me while I was still messed up with whatever shit you people gave me. I want my phone call."

His eyes were steely and demanding. The nurse stayed cold and collected, but he could smell the small, trace amount of fear that invaded her scent. He felt like howling with victory.

Slightly jerky, she pointed through the double doors leading to the hallway. "Tell Nurse Miller that I gave you permission to use the phone. But," she cautioned, recovering enough to hold up a finger, "Be aware that this is your only call this week. If you don't receive an answer, you'll just have to wait until next Wednesday."

He turned and uttered, "Blow me." He didn't care if she heard.

He pushed through the doors, which revealed a long hallway painted in the most unattractive piss yellow he'd ever seen. There were a few gurneys lying around, and your occasional crazy in a wheelchair, pushing along, but other than that, and the few nurses who kept coming through, it was quiet. The phone was just ten feet from the double doors, and being badly guarded by a woman wearing orthopedic shoes and paging through a fashion magazine. Nurse Miller, he presumed.

She was a round, plump woman in her early thirties, with thin blonde hair and a pasty complexion. She had that stationary look humans developed after sitting on their asses for too long. It always made him shudder when he saw someone like that. His brain immediately made the connection to plants, and he couldn't help but put the two together and picture a human with roots, which was just weird.

She sat at a cheap wooden desk that was little more than a TV tray, just a few feet to the left of the payphone, a panic button mounted on the wall directly behind her, as if management was really worried about someone holding the phone hostage. She didn't move, except to reach her hand into the bag of pretzels that was the only item on the desk. Watching her was a little like watching a lava lamp. Her hand motion was that smooth.

She didn't even notice him until he was standing in front of her, and she only took her nose out of the magazine then because he tapped on her desk.

Her large eyes blinked rapidly as she focused on him. Then her mouth widened in a smile and her pale skin flushed. With shaking hands, she set her magazine down and pushed away the bag of pretzels. "How can I help you?"

He flashed a smile and leaned his hip against her minuscule desk, but immediately straightened when the particleboard gave a groan. "Nurse Ratchet said I can make a phone call." She winced at his use of the name, but she didn't bother to ask him who he meant. It must have been a pretty common name for the bitch.

Nurse Miller pointed unnecessarily to the phone, her eyes becoming dewy and soft as she gazed up at him. She smiled dreamily, unconsciously sitting straighter in her chair, and then almost fell over as the wheel on the left side lurched, nearly tipping her sideways.

She caught herself in time, and shifted her weight to the other side, but her flush became tomato red and her voice was a little higher when she mumbled, "Right there."

Christian managed to keep any snickering to a minimum, but it was a close call. To make up for being rude, he winked at her before going over to the phone. He was desperate, the idea of staying in the hospital any longer making his skin crawl, but he still managed to keep the few steps to the phone as normal and sedate as possible, and his hand didn't even shake when he picked up the receiver.

He dialed the familiar numbers, his heartbeat suddenly increasing with both excitement and worry. Even before Connor took him in, Christian had always known to call him, for any problem, no matter what. But that didn't necessarily mean he wasn't going to get his ass kicked for this latest stunt.

The phone rang on the other end just three times before it was picked up.

"Hello?"

"I hope you're sitting down, man, because I am royally fucked."

"Christian, what have you done?" asked Connor, in that always-so-proper British way he had.

Christian leaned against the wall, relief flooding his system. "Get this—I'm locked up in a loony bin in Iowa. You need to come down here and break me out *pronto*." He rolled his eyes to the right to check on the nurse, and awarded himself ten points. She had turned slightly in his direction, and was watching him cautiously over the top of her magazine.

Never one to pass up a chance, Christian smiled at her again. She smiled back but with slightly less wattage, and actually looked a little suspicious, as if she had decided to humor his delusions. Oh well, fuck it.

Connor's tone was all business. "Give me your address. Eben is coming down tonight. Don't worry, he'll have any documents you need to get out."

Christian rattled off the address. On the other end, he could hear Connor scribbling the information down.

"Hold tight, I'm putting Eben on."

Christian switched the phone to his other ear and tapped his foot against the floor. He was usually calm, but being cooped up got to him. Unless there were a couple naked women around.

Eben came on, his deep voice a pleasant reminder of home. "What happened?"

Christian closed his eyes, leaned against the cool wall, and told his Alpha what happened, carefully, with no revealing words or phrases for human ears to catch.

"You were foolish. It'd serve you right if I left you locked up there until the next moon." There was a pause, and then slightly softer, "Are you all right?"

"I am now."

"I'll be there in the morning. Connor just got me a flight."

Christian sighed. "Thank you."

The phone clicked off. Christian hung up on his end and sighed. It was going to be okay. They'd come and get him, and it'd be over. As long as he could survive another night.

An hour later, he followed the directions of a nurse and entered the bathroom. Feeling jumpy with nerves, he ignored the urinals and instead selected the stall in the corner, shutting the door behind him. And that's when he saw it, taped up among a hundred or so other drawings, letters and pictures ripped out of magazines, all of them layered onto the door thicker than wallpaper.

"Fuck!"

Chapter Two

ৡ

Gwen liked to try and look at her stay at the St. Catherine's Hospital for the Mentally Ill in a philosophical light. She could hate her mother for having her committed, but in all reality it was probably the only reason she was still alive. She definitely would have tried to kill herself again if she was still in a confined space with only her mother's harping presence. And it wasn't all bad. She had her own room, complete with storage closet, a small desk to work at, plenty of art supplies and a window. Sure, it had bars on it, but she could overlook them for the most part. She could still see the sun outside, and the snow, and that was the important thing. At least she had a home, of sorts. Look how many people didn't.

But she still blamed her mother for lying. She'd *claimed* it was because Gwen had tried to kill herself. She'd *claimed* it was because she'd become unresponsive to her surroundings and the people who tried to help her through the death of her father. But Gwen knew better. She'd found the pamphlets from the hospital over a month before she'd cut her wrists. Her mother wanted her committed because Gwen had seen a werewolf.

In her mind, he was always the same — thick coppery pelt, angry wild eyes, and a threatening mouth filled with razor-sharp teeth. He certainly hadn't looked like a regular wolf, or at least, not like any wolf she'd seen. Instead, he was more of a man-wolf, as if someone had taken prime examples of both species, thrown them into a bottle and mixed them up, the end result being a weird mutation of the two—a great, hulking brute, armed with sharp claws and obvious intelligence, with the ability to stand on its hind legs but run faster than a rabbit on all four. With that fearsome combination, it would be nearly impossible for anyone to escape.

It would have been easier if she'd let the image go, like it was the dream her doctors kept trying to convince her it was. Except it wasn't. Her father had died that night in the accident, and she'd seen it happen. It was something she would always remember. Just as she'd always remember the creature, sitting in the road and eating the dead woman's body next to him. He'd growled as he went at it, tearing and ripping pieces of flesh from the poor woman who had probably had the misfortune to be in the wrong place at the wrong time. It was another memory that would never leave Gwen's head. It was too terrifying and disturbing. She'd closed her eyes through most of it, but the image of the werewolf with his head up, swallowing a large piece of the woman in one gulp, was locked in her brain forever.

Sighing, Gwen pushed her latest picture aside, feeling the heavy weight of the pill-induced sleep that was dragging at her. She'd slept a lot after the accident, taking comfort in it and the deep numbness that had taken over her body at the time. But she slept even more at the hospital. It had to do with the meds they kept pumping into her. And the food, and the people, and just the *place*. Since sleeping was what made the time go by the fastest, it was what her body wanted to do, all the time. Generally, she didn't fight it. But she needed to do one more picture to get the image out of her head, at least for a little while.

She took the top piece of paper from the pile sitting near the corner of her desk, and selected a piece of charcoal. In broad strokes, she put down the lines that would build the image, added shadows and depth, smudging the lines when needed. She didn't notice the scars on her wrists, each one running vertically about three inches, and she didn't notice the sun as it began to fall. Her eyes were locked on the paper, watching as the image came through.

She hated the werewolf. He caused the car crash that killed her father and crippled her for months afterward. But she mostly hated him because he was the reason she was in the hospital. Because once she'd seen him, she'd been forced to believe the fairy tales, and it scared her to think there may be others out there.

The night was passing at a snail's pace for Christian. He couldn't sleep with so many people howling and screaming. Not that he wanted to. With escape approaching, the last thing he wanted to do was sleep. He wanted to wait, see the sun as she approached her sister moon, the two kissing just as they changed places and the sun took over.

He stretched his legs along the decrepit sofa, and tried to forget the fact that it was only just after midnight. He was hanging out in the common room, which was one of the shared rooms between the male and female quarters. The television, though on, was muted. It seemed God hadn't completely forgotten him after all.

"Hey, that's your girl over there."

Christian jerked around and stared at where Jones, a schizo mother-killer, pointed. When he saw her, he kind of wished he hadn't.

"Seriously, that's who drew the picture in the stalls?" The picture he now had folded in his pocket. He drew a deep breath and pulled her scent into his lungs. He wanted to cough at first. The poor thing had so many drugs in her system she smelled like a pharmaceutical company. It altered her scent, making it musty and stale, like someone kept her in a box on a shelf somewhere. But underneath all that, was her. It was faint, but there.

Jones nodded his bald head. "Yup. That's her. She's probably the craziest bitch in the place. Get this—" He leaned his thick form forward. His eyes danced with the excitement of passing on a good tale. "She was in a car accident with her old man when she was eighteen. It killed him, left her lame, and through it all, she says it was a monster that caused the whole thing."

"No shit," Christian marveled softly. The girl was shuffling down the hall, past the common room, her movements agonizingly slow. She was a sickly thing, her form so spare it shouldn't have been able to hold her up, with lanky, pale-brown hair hanging in tangles and the most pitiful expression on her empty face that he'd ever seen. She was dead already. She just had to convince her body.

"Well fuck." He slumped down in the chair, shooting one last look at the girl before she moved from his sight.

"Of course no one believed her," Jones went on. "Her mom just excused her ramblings as stress. It wasn't until she slit her wrists that the old lady had her committed. And she's been here ever since. Near four years, now."

The visitor's area was just as ugly as the rest of the hospital. It was pink. Whatever idiot made that decision should have been shot and dismembered, because it was downright horrid. Especially with the wicker furniture.

The minute Eben came through the door of the hospital, Christian's worries flew out the window and he forgot about his appalling surroundings. Neither of them said a word or paid any attention to the nurses watching with interest as they greeted each other, but when Eben made the slightest gesture, Christian leapt at him, hugging him as tightly as he could manage.

"You smell like shit," Eben growled, releasing Christian and looking him over quickly.

Christian smiled. "I missed you too."

Eben would be pack leader, Lead Alpha, when it came time. Christian knew it, the whole pack knew it. Hell, Eben knew it. But that wasn't why he was so careful when dealing with him. Christian made sure he was careful because Eben was the one Were he truly feared.

He was a big man, and an even bigger Were. With thick arms, and a massive chest and back, he could uproot small trees with no problem. Christian had seen him do it. But his strength wasn't the scariest thing about him. Everything frightening about Eben lived in his eyes, and it was enough to make Jack the Ripper turn tail and run.

Eben was a bona fide killer, no matter how quiet and reassuring he appeared to the masses. It was a façade, a mirage, put on to fool anyone who wasn't Were, or shrewd enough to see the determination in his jaw and the strength in his eyes. Christian had witnessed the destructive force when Eben rose triumphant from a challenge with Andy Kaville. Andy was a strong Were, stronger than most any Christian had seen, and arrogant about it, using his strength to take the women he wanted and bully the Weres. Eben had killed him, and left the challenge ring with Andy's blood in his mouth and coating his muzzle. The whole thing hadn't even lasted five minutes.

No one knew what pack he came from, or who his parents were. Connor made no bones about finding him in Turkey when he was fifteen, but it was clear there was more than just Turkish blood in his veins. His eyes were pale blue, a blue so cold it made glaciers seem warm. The color came from somewhere, but if he knew, Eben never spoke of it.

With a slight shake of his head, Christian pulled himself back to business and led Eben past the wicker furniture, through the double doors, and to the quiet hallway just beyond. After making sure they were pretty much alone, except for the wacko screaming at the walls halfway down the hall, he handed the drawing over. It was a good sketch. With the wolf's lip lifted in a snarl and its piercing eyes, it was as accurate a picture of a Were as he'd ever seen.

Eben stared down at the picture and said only one word. "Who?"

Christian slid his hands in his jeans pockets and hunched his shoulders. "A girl, locked up in the women's ward. Gwen Branson. Everyone's sure she's crazy."

Eben's light eyes narrowed, but his voice came out cool and smooth. "I want to meet her."

Christian sighed. "Yeah, I thought you would."

Christian had a lie all ready to go as he walked up to the nurse's station to get buzzed into the women's ward. And it was a good one. A real work of art. But he didn't get to use it.

The nurse was young, obviously new, and was more than a little frazzled by the other three people who were already standing in front of her, two of them a set of parents, and the other a husband wanting to visit his wife. All of them were yelling at her, demanding to be let in even as she tried to dig out admit slips and verify identification. When Christian showed up she practically started crying, and with shaking hands, buzzed the door open.

Christian shook his head but followed the parents into the ward. The husband stayed and continued to bitch the nurse out.

"That was easier than I expected," Eben commented.

Christian nodded as he led the way down the hall. "No shit." Someone should complain about the lax security, but it wasn't going to be him.

The halls were quiet in the women's ward. Christian figured most of the occupants were in the common area, talking and watching TV. But like the men's ward, there were video cameras recording activity in the halls, and no doubt the nurses and doctors felt their safety and that of their patients was ensured by the technology. If he'd felt like hanging around longer, Christian would have loved to educate them on the fallibility of cameras.

Her door was wide open. Christian peered in, curious. It wasn't very large, but then none of the rooms were. There was a single window, barred, and a desk settled in front of it, the surface of which was covered with art supplies and paper. The door to the closet was open, revealing a tiny amount of space, just barely adequate for storing her meager collection of street clothes and shoes. Drawings were pasted to her walls. Some were sketches of patients and nurses, and others of unoccupied rooms filled with bare furniture and shadow. Some of the drawings were done as realistically as possible, while others were so abstract it was difficult to tell what the subject was. Not one of them was a picture of a Were.

The bed sat in the center of the room, the headboard butting up against the wall, and the girl lay in it, completely still. Eben inhaled sharply, and like a feral creature, zeroed in on the still form. Christian followed his lead, and studied her. She was tiny, appearing frail against the white sheets.

She would have been pretty if she was a healthy weight and actually saw the sun.

"They've got the poor thing so drugged up she can't tell what's what," he murmured, stepping into the room more and looking closer at her drawings. She had a good hand, and did especially well with the charcoals. It was too bad she was locked up, even if she was crazy.

Eben inhaled deeply again, his body so tense Christian was amazed it didn't fracture into a million pieces. "What?"

Eben rolled his eyes up, a snarl on his lips. As Christian watched, his eyes shifted from human to Were. "I want her."

"I hope you're kidding because that's really not funny. We're in a *hospital*. You can't just fuck a woman while she's out of it." Christian looked from Eben, to the girl, and back again.

"She's my *mate!*"

His voice was going guttural, but Christian still understood. And it nearly knocked him over.

He raked a hand through his hair, agitation running thick through his veins. *Mate?* This tiny human was supposed to be Eben's mate? The idea was as preposterous and crazy as the girl supposedly was. And mates were damn hard to find, but who in hell ever thought Eben's would be human? And insane? "She tried to kill herself. She slit her wrists, Eben. She's not exactly stable." He pinched the bridge of his nose, trying to come up with something. "Are you sure? Her system's so screwed up with the drugs, it's nearly impossible to get a good scent from her. Are you absolutely sure?"

Going completely still, Eben cocked his head and asked darkly, "Are you questioning me?"

Christian's blood jumped in warning. Solemnly, he said, "No Alpha. I do not question you."

His pale blue eyes, still canine in shape, followed every one of Christian's movements, and it made him even more nervous. For some reason, Eben had always been far more feral than most Weres. And that meant he was that much more dangerous.

"We're taking her with us."

Christian sighed. "Fuck."

They took her that night.

It was relatively easy getting in, mostly because the building itself was old, and no one had bothered with any security precautions on the basement level, where Christian broke in. The electrical system was as old as the building. It was housed in the back of the supply room, completely surrounded by boxes of medical supplies. Not a very safe place. It should have had its own locked room, and by the look of the fuses, it should have been overhauled years ago.

He took care of that gleefully. He smashed the metal housing, ripped out the wires, and then for good measure, broke the fuses.

Only when he was completely satisfied with his vandalism did he saunter back to the basement door and pull it open for Eben, who had absolutely no hope of squeezing through the same small, ground-level window Christian had.

"Do come in," he said regally, holding the door like any well-trained butler. "I believe we have an appointment for a kidnapping."

Eben glared at him but came in.

Even before they got to the steps, Christian could hear the sound of dozens of feet running overhead. With the electrical system ruined, there'd be no lights, the cameras would be out, and the security locks on the doors would be disabled.

When they came to the top of the steps, Christian smiled in satisfaction. It was just as he expected — complete and utter chaos.

The orderlies were running around like chickens with their heads cut off, patients scrambled to escape, and the rent-a-cops tried to find out what had gone wrong. It was beautiful.

"Well done," Eben murmured, stepping out of the stairwell and leading the way down the hall. When one of the orderlies stopped in front of him, demanding to know his business, Eben merely pushed him back. But just that little movement was enough to send the man flying. Wordlessly, they continued on their way.

The girl was still in her room, sleeping as deeply as before. Eben wrapped her in a blanket while Christian took all her pictures off the walls and shoved her things into a garbage bag.

"I'm assuming we're not going out the way we came," Christian muttered, grabbing the last of her drawings from the desk.

"We're leaving out the window."

"Of course we are." Christian dropped the garbage bag to the floor and leaned over the desk. The window was painted shut, but that was easily taken care of with one heave. The bars took a little more effort. He had to sit on the desk and kick them out.

He shoved the desk away, and then dropped the garbage bag out the window. He was all prepared to swing his leg through when a nurse popped her head inside the door, saw Eben with his arms full, and opened her mouth to scream.

They both reacted at once. Eben slammed the door shut with his shoulder and Christian crossed the room and slapped his hand over her mouth. He barely noticed her struggles as he held her off the ground and tried to come up with a plan.

"What should I do with her?"

A smile twitched at Eben's lips as he shifted the girl in his arms. "What do you usually do with them?"

Christian groaned. "What, you want me to fuck her until she falls asleep? This isn't the time, Eben." He glanced down at the nurse. "And she isn't the right woman for that. She's sort of...sour looking."

"It's kind of funny, isn't it? I don't often get to see you with a woman you don't know what to do with."

"Well let's be amused later. Right now, I have to figure out what to do with her."

They stashed her in the closet. Christian felt a moment of guilt, but then shoved it aside as he blocked the closet door with the bed. She was probably safer in there than out in the halls anyway, where patients were running amok.

He went out the window first, and then took the girl when Eben handed her down. There were no floodlights outside, since those too had been running off the main electrical unit. He felt kind of proud that he'd brought the place to its knees in such a completely simple and easy way. Maybe the assholes would think about updating their facilities now that they knew how vulnerable they really were.

Eben took Gwen Branson back once he'd squeezed through the window and landed silently beside them.

"Let's go."

Christian nodded and loped off, sticking close to the building as he went around the corner. Since the girl's room was located halfway down the left side of the building, and the SUV was parked in the back, near the stairs leading to the basement, they didn't have far to go.

Eben was already in the passenger seat and Christian was just slipping into the driver's side when the emergency door burst open and three guards emerged, heavy flashlights beaming outward. The man in the lead pointed his light directly at them, illuminating the interior of the car. And their faces.

"Shit." Christian slammed the door closed and twisted the key in the ignition. The engine roared to life.

"Go, go, go!" Eben ordered, staring at the men through the windshield. The one pointing the flashlight in their direction had a cell phone to his ear, and the other two were closing the distance at a run.

Christian threw the SUV into reverse and floored it. They squealed out, spitting gravel everywhere as he jerked the wheel left and threw the car into first without stopping. He drove the vehicle up onto the grass, across a ditch and took a sharp right onto the road. The hospital was gone from the rearview mirror in less than a minute.

"Well," Christian said, letting out a deep breath. "That was exciting. How are we going to get her home? She doesn't have any papers."

Eben was staring down at the girl. He held a lock of her hair in his hand and was rubbing it between two fingers as he answered, "Connor arranged it. Drive to the airport."

If Connor arranged it, then it was as good as set in stone. Christian shifted gears and headed for the highway. Home was only hours away.

It was far easier than expected. Once at the airport, Eben directed him not to the main terminal, but to a private hanger. They were met there by a small, wiry man. One whiff of him told Christian he was Were.

The man asked no questions, and barely gave the unconscious girl in Eben's arms a glance. "The cabin's ready. You may as well go and make yourselves comfortable. Throw the luggage in the back and we'll be out of here in ten minutes.

Not long after that, they were in the air.

Connor met them at the tiny airport near their home. He looked serious and regal, even with sixty-odd years under his belt. He was Lead Alpha, and wore the mantle of his power well, but in the last few years he'd started to feel tired. Weary of the responsibility, more than anything. Being leader was for young men with strength and energy. The strength he still possessed. It was the energy that he just didn't have like he used to.

His eyes nearly danced when he saw them coming. As Christian came around the corner, he gave a whoop, dropped the luggage he was carrying and threw himself at the older man. Connor's arms closed around him tight. "It's about time you came back to me, boyo. It's about time." He held on for a bit longer and then pulled away enough so he could get a good look at his son.

He'd been blessed in his life. He'd had a beautiful woman who loved him, and two sons. Though neither was of his blood, they were *his*, as much as any natural child could ever have been. "You look well. But you need a haircut."

Christian straightened to his full height and shrugged. "I don't know. The women like it long."

Connor laughed. "They liked it short, too."

Yeah, I know," Christian said, smiling cheekily.

Connor kept him at his side as they waited for his other son. He often marveled at how fate worked. Eben had been his first, a child so dark it had even scared him to take the boy on, but he'd done it all the same, and it'd worked out. It'd taken effort to make Eben trust him, to tone down his natural aggression, but eventually, Eben had relaxed. Now, he had the outward appearance of a respectable man, solid and steady. Hardly anyone ever realized how dangerous he was until it was too late.

Then, when he and Eben had moved up north, needing the space to run and live as Weres were meant to, they'd come across Christian, beaten and abused by his own family, and so pitiful it had been hard to witness. Connor had taken one look at the ten-year-old boy and removed him from his home, placing him in his. There'd been a bit of adjustment, mostly between the two boys, but it all worked out in the end, and he'd ended up with one dark son, and one so bright he was like the sun.

They had to wait a few minutes before Eben came out of the building, a bundle of blankets in his arms. He didn't seem to notice the cold or snow as he stepped outside, but he did tuck the blankets tighter around the woman bundled within them.

"Tell me what you know," Connor ordered Christian.

Christian lifted the luggage back to his shoulders. "I don't know much. She's in her early twenties, was at the hospital for four years, and she's seen a Were. Oh," he added, "and she's human to boot. Can you believe it?"

"My wife was human," Connor murmured, absently rubbing the ring he still wore in her honor. He hadn't removed it since the day she slid it onto his finger.

"I know. But you're you, and Eben is Eben. He's not exactly easy, especially when he's angry or feels threatened. How's a human supposed to deal?"

Connor's voice was sure and smooth as good brandy. "She'll manage, my boy."

Chapter Three

ဢ

Life floated along smoothly until the drugs wore off. Gwen blinked slowly, wondering if she was dreaming. She waited a minute, felt the softness of the blankets and the fluffiness of the pillow, and determined that she was indeed awake. Except she wasn't sure where she was. But one thing was definite — she wasn't in the hospital.

She felt groggy and slightly nauseous as she sat up. Her hair was a mess, and she was still in her nightgown. But her hospital room was gone. It made no sense.

Instead, she found herself lying on a gorgeous sleigh bed in a beautiful bedroom, with dark wood furniture, oatmeal-colored carpeting, and books on nearly every wall. Through the window, the only thing visible was snow and trees. *Lots* of snow and trees.

Not sure what else to do, she pushed back the heavy, deep brown comforter, slid from the bed and stood. Her legs were shaky, which was no surprise since she usually spent two-thirds of her days sleeping. Walking slowly to the window, she pressed her hand against the pane. It was very cold. Far colder than it usually got at home, which meant she was definitely *not* at home. So, where was she? It seemed to be the sixty-four-million-dollar question, and she had absolutely no idea. She didn't think she'd get to phone a friend, either.

"Ah," said someone behind her. "So you're awake. And not a moment too soon, either."

Not wanting to fall down and look the fool, Gwen turned carefully, keeping one hand clamped to the windowsill. In the doorway stood an elderly man. A gentleman really, with thick, silver hair and a full beard. His eyes twinkled and his mouth smiled. He seemed friendly, and, dressed as he was in dark wool pants and a high-necked charcoal gray sweater, he didn't look like a serial killer or rapist. But then, she'd never met a serial killer or rapist.

"Where am I? Did someone kidnap me?"

His smile faltered slightly. "No dear, no one's kidnapped you, in the normal sense. You're in northern Canada, actually. You were removed from the hospital because my sons thought you weren't receiving proper help there."

Proper help? It didn't sound right. Who in the world plucked someone from a mental institute because they weren't getting proper help? Unless…

"Are they doctors?"

"No," the man said, stepping into the room. "But they were extremely concerned."

Resigned, Gwen dropped the subject. There was no way it was going to make sense. "Can I go home now?"

"Do you wish to go home? Back to the hospital?"

She held her breath a moment as she tried to get her head on straight. Everything was still fuzzy, subject to the waning affects of the drugs in her system. Everything in her said she should be running away from the maniac, even if he did remind her of an older Cary Grant. Stealing someone away wasn't normal. For any reason. If only she had the energy to actually care.

"Like you'd let me. If you guys are holding out for a ransom, you picked the wrong girl. My mother doesn't have any money to pay a ransom with." She let her weight rest fully against the wall as her legs tired.

He sighed. "What would it take to make you feel safe here? Would you like to call your mother perhaps? Assure her that you are well and unharmed?"

"No," she said wearily, then seized on the one thing that no decent criminal would allow. "I want to call the cops."

He nodded regally and left the room. Seconds later, he was back with a cordless in his hand. He placed the phone on the bed and stepped away. "You can call information and get the number. I'll be in the kitchen if you need anything."

Gwen picked up the phone, half-expecting to find no dial tone. There was. With her breath held, she quickly dialed zero, and prayed it was as easy to get an operator in Canada as it was in the United States. When the operator came on, she let out her breath and asked for the nearest law enforcement office.

"Dawson Detachment," a rough, tired-sounding voice answered.

Gwen clutched the phone harder. "Uh, hi. This is the police?"

"Yeah. Can I help you with something?"

"Um, I just woke up and I don't know where I am. I think I've been kidnapped."

There was a moment of silence. "This some kind of joke?"

"No. No joke. I think you should maybe come and get me. Except you'd have to find me first. Do you have maybe caller ID? Can you figure out where I am by the phone number?"

He sighed. "Yeah—hold on. Oh. Sweetheart, you sure this isn't a joke?"

"No," Gwen repeated firmly. "This isn't a joke."

"Well, you're calling from Connor's place. And honey, if you're there, you haven't been kidnapped. Were you drinking last night maybe? Connor's a nice man. He wouldn't have brought you home if he wasn't worried. He's one of those types who like to help his fellow man. You want to leave, just tell him. He'll drive you himself, and probably hand over all his cash if you asked for it. Hey, you see him, let him know there's a big storm coming through. And tell him Dan says hi."

He hung up abruptly. Gwen numbly tossed the phone back to the bed, slightly dazed. When she looked up, the bearded man was standing in the doorway again.

"You're Connor?"

He nodded. "Yes."

"Police Officer Dan said to tell you a large storm is coming through."

He smiled and folded his arms over his chest. "Are you satisfied that you're safe here? That I'm not going to lock you in a closet and starve you until your mother pays an exorbitant amount of money?"

The way he said it, it certainly sounded ridiculous. And she couldn't imagine any respectable kidnapper condescending to steal someone from a county psychiatric hospital. "What happens now?"

"Your mother had you committed?" he asked carefully, going over and fluffing the pillows on her bed as if they weren't having an odd conversation at all.

"Yes."

"So you can't go back there. And your father is deceased. Do you have any friends or relatives you'd like to live with?"

Friends? Relatives? Not a one, or at least none who didn't believe she was crazy. And *how did he know this?*

"No." She could see her answer didn't surprise him.

"Well then," he said, straightening up and smiling. "Why don't you stay with us for a bit, just as a trial? If you're unhappy, you can go back to hospital, or we'll see about making other arrangements for you. If you're content, you're free to stay as long as you wish."

Gwen stayed silent, not sure what to say. Sane people didn't just stay with strangers because it was convenient. But where else could she go? She was twenty-two, with no job skills, and without even a high-school diploma. She had suicide scars, and that scared most people enough. Besides, she *was* crazy, so that was excuse enough.

"Why are you doing this?" she asked, curious despite everything else.

His smile became slightly melancholy. "I have been all over the world, and seen more than enough horror for ten lifetimes. I'd simply like to help." He cocked his head. "Are you scared?"

Gwen frowned in thought for a moment. "No. I don't think so. There're still too many drugs in my system to be scared."

He lifted his eyebrows but didn't comment on that. "Then relax, child. You've had a long journey. Bathe, dress and come to the kitchen. You're just in time for lunch."

"Lunch? But it's nighttime."

"This is the far north. It's dark most of the day during winter."

He left her with a smile, and Gwen was once again alone.

She did shower, and it felt divine. It seemed like forever since she'd been allowed to shower without someone watching her, waiting to see if she was going to kill herself with the pink Daisy razor that was so dull it was barely able to take the hair from her legs. She washed her hair twice, and her body, and used the man's razor that was already in the shower to shave.

The man had said for her to dress, but in what? She stood in the room, wrapped in a large towel and looking hopefully for anything to wear. There were no suitcases or boxes of clothes sitting around. Nothing was laid on the bed for her. In the end, she sighed and opened the dresser, hoping to find something.

What she found were her own clothes. All of them, not that she'd actually had that many at the hospital. Relieved, she threw on a long-sleeved undershirt and a T-shirt over it, and her favorite pair of jeans. She looked at herself in the mirror and stuck out her tongue at the reflection. She looked like a fifteen-year-old in the mall. With her hair hanging loose down her back, and her face scrubbed pink, she didn't even look old enough to drive, not that she had her license.

After pulling on her warmest socks, she left the room and headed toward the voices. There were two of them, one deeper and very British, obviously the gentleman Connor, and the other mellow and lighter.

She was passing a dining area, which was directly opposite the living room, when the voices stopped. She walked faster in the same direction, and halted at the doorway to the kitchen. Connor was there, cooking up a storm on a large gas stove. A large roast was steaming, sitting nearby on the granite countertop looking unbelievably juicy. A younger man leaned lazily against the cream-colored wall and watched Connor work, a smile on his face as he saw her.

"Hello," Connor greeted her, as he wielded a knife expertly, slicing thin pieces from the roast and laying them on a serving platter. He looked completely comfortable in his kitchen. And unlike her mother's, his wasn't all dolled up with doilies and decorations. In fact, his kitchen had little decoration at all. It seemed to be far more utilitarian, designed more for convenience than appearance, with little clutter, dark cabinets and lots of counter space.

Gwen clasped her hands together nervously and peered over her shoulder. The dining table was set with four places. "Hi," she replied nervously, turning back around, eyeing the younger man cautiously.

He was blond, tan and very handsome, and blessed with almost perfectly symmetrical, classic features. He reminded her a bit of Paul Newman. With his lean, muscular frame and shaggy hair, he was just plain beautiful. Like a model, but the bad-boy variety. He was dressed in jeans and a white silk dress shirt that somehow worked for him. He wore it casually, as if it was no big deal to be so stylish with such little effort.

"Dear," the older man spoke, "why don't you fill the glasses on the table with water. I'll be ready here in a minute."

Feeling slightly stupid, Gwen nodded. "Um, what're your names?" She pointed to the blond, her face flushing when they both looked over at her.

"Ah," Connor said, putting down the knife and wiping his hands on a towel. "Forgive me, Gwen. I forgot."

"You know my name," she pointed out.

"Yes, of course, just as you know my first name, although let's forget that fact right now. We'll start at the beginning, which is where we should have started. I am Connor Lowell, and this is my youngest son, Christian Tanner. I don't believe you've met my older son, Eben, but you'll be seeing him in a minute."

Gwen stared at the blond man, Christian. "Your last name is different?"

"I'm adopted." He gave her a cocky grin. "You didn't think these good looks came from him, did you?"

Adopted. It reassured her a little. Some people needed to feel they were helping others. It was obviously why they'd taken her. The two sons were older, so maybe they felt their father needed another project. Officer Dan had said nearly as much.

Smiling slightly in relief, Gwen nodded and went to the table to fill glasses. That, at least, was something she was qualified to do.

They were seated and dishing out food and neither of the two men suggested that they wait for the third. Taking the peas as they came her way, Gwen thought on that a minute, trying to figure out what it all meant. Her mother would have had a fit if everyone wasn't at the table within a minute of her declaring supper time. In fact, she had. Any time her father was stuck in the field or dealing with a cow that was sick.

But in this household, it wasn't anything. In fact, both Christian and Connor seemed perfectly content to start without the other man, and didn't give it a second thought as they cut bread, handed off bowls and platters.

Gwen filled her plate without even thinking, and passed everything on carefully. The house itself was lovely.

She could see the living area from the table, decorated elegantly and simply with little clutter and high quality leather furniture, made more for comfort than show. It would have looked too somber and dark if not for the bright, earthy-colored throw rugs covering the hardwood floor, and the handwoven blankets that were draped over the back of the sofa. A large fireplace dominated the room, a flickering fire already burning merrily.

"You've lived here long?"

"Oh, it must be fifteen years now," Connor said. "I moved quite a bit before, traveling the world and such, but this is my favorite place. It's why we settled here." He passed her a bowl of potatoes and smiled.

"You have a lovely home," she commented, setting the bowl aside.

"Thank you, child."

They were quietly talking and eating when another presence entered the room. Gwen stopped in mid-chew as all the hairs on the back of her neck stood up in warning. The other two men fell silent and turned. Connor smiled. "Come sit down. You're late."

There was no answer. Beside her, Christian smirked.

"I take it your project is going well?" Connor went on, oblivious to the tension in the air.

The chair across from her was pulled out by a large, dark hand, corded with heavy muscles. It was scarred in multiple places, with one scar obviously from an animal of some type. It looked like a claw, running vertically with three lines. The wound itself had to have been deep to leave such scars.

Gwen dropped her fork when the man sat down. She managed not to run away, but it was close. With his pale blue eyes locked on her, the urge was strong.

He wasn't perfectly handsome, like Christian. His beauty was far too savage and wild. If anything, he was scary, with a capital S, although she couldn't figure out why. Everything about him screamed out solid and dependable. But it didn't quite fit.

He was large and strong, with hugely wide shoulders and thick arms. Even without the muscles, she could tell he would have been large just from the thickness of his wrists. He was one of those people who were just built that way. While his size was threatening, it was his face that made him so attractive. It was rugged and as scarred as the rest of him appeared to be. His nose had a bump at the bridge, testament to the break that had caused it. His cheekbones were sharp, and with his coppery, burnished skin and black-as-ink hair, he was beautiful. Exotic. Far different than the usual Iowa farm crowd she was used to. With a blink, Gwen jerked her gaze away from him and stared down at her plate. Her hand shook as she picked up her fork again. She tried scooping up some peas, but they just fell off the tines. Agitated, she set her fork down and let her hands fall to her lap.

"Gwen," Connor said, "this is my eldest son, Eben."

Gwen barely nodded and kept her eyes down, desperately wanting to leave the table.

Christian leaned close to her and whispered, "Just breathe. He gets better after the first hour."

"Now," Connor said, oblivious to her anxiety, "isn't this nice?"

Christian snickered.

Their conversation flowed around her, smooth and comfortable. She could see how much the three men liked each other and enjoyed their time together. It was in their laughter and smiles, and the way Christian ribbed the other two men, who only shrugged it off. There were no petty insults, or complaints, or even punishing silences.

Her stomach gave a sudden, violent heave. Clumsily, she shot out of her chair, knocking it over in the process. "I'm sorry," she stuttered. "Excuse me."

They watched as she ran from the room, one arm clutching her stomach as she headed toward the bathroom. She slammed the door shut, and then there was silence.

"Well," Christian drawled, forking over another hunk of roast, "that went well. You should be proud of yourself, Eben. She's only going to be sick, not pass out. You're improving with age."

"Christian," Connor said sharply.

Christian ducked down. "Sorry."

Sighing, Connor picked up his fork again. "She becomes nervous easily. Eben, I hope you're prepared to be patient, because pushing her will only do more harm than good."

"I'll wait," Eben replied softly, his eyes meeting his father's.

Connor winced slightly. There was no mistaking the determination in his son's eyes. It was as strong as the man himself. But, it depended on the girl. And as Connor knew firsthand, it didn't always work out as it should.

Gwen woke the next morning more prepared than before. She had her clothes, her own room and some very nice companions. Now, she just had to settle down and relax. No one had made any comments or threatened her in any way. It was fine.

Her stomach hurt from the violent vomiting she'd gone through the day before, and as she stared in the mirror, she saw it wasn't the only consequence. Blood spots speckled her face, like she'd broken out in dark freckles overnight. They seemed to be especially concentrated around her eyes, and gave her a bit of a raccoon appearance.

"Bloody hell."

Disgusted, she hurriedly showered and dressed, making sure her hair was pinned up neatly in a coil before she headed toward the kitchen.

The house was quiet as she tiptoed along, hoping fervently that Connor was awake. She needed answers, and he seemed to be the one to ask.

With a sigh, she peeked into the kitchen and smiled in relief. "You're up."

Connor smiled over his cup of coffee. "Of course, dear. I'm an early riser. Christian you won't see before ten, but Eben wakes about this time. But, if none of us seem to be about, make yourself comfortable. Feel free to dig through the cupboards until you find something that appeals to you. Since you skipped dinner yesterday, you must be starving."

"Thanks." She slinked in and seated herself on a stool at the counter, relieved he was polite enough not to mention her digestive pyrotechnics of the previous evening.

He frowned and leaned closer, peering at her carefully. "Are those—spots?"

Blushing slightly, Gwen ducked her head. *Okay, so he's not that polite.* "Um, yeah. I kind of get them whenever I…well, when I become ill."

"Blood spots," he murmured, sipping.

"Yup." Smiling nervously, she laced her fingers together on the counter. "I've always gotten them. They drove my mother nuts."

"How so?"

"Well, she wanted me to do pageants. You know, those beauty pageants for little girls and teens. But I always got really nervous before. And during, and after," she amended quickly. "I would almost always throw up, and then I'd get spots and ruin everything for her. It was awful."

"You didn't like doing pageants, then?" he asked carefully.

She shook her head vehemently. "I hated them. But my mother really wanted me to do them, to coach me, you understand."

She fiddled with a spoon left on the counter and fell silent. She was wearing another long-sleeved shirt with a dark T-shirt over, reading *I'm a bitch. Deal with it.* in stenciled, red letters.

Setting his cup down, Connor asked, "So what will you have for breakfast?"

She looked up at him and shrugged. "Cereal is fine."

"You're easy then," he said, going to the cupboard and pulling a box down. "The boys tend to want a full meal, with eggs, bacon, potatoes and tomatoes." He handed the box to her and took down a bowl and spoon as well.

She took the items from him with a small smile. "Thanks."

"My pleasure, child."

She prepared her bowl of cereal and then sat and munched for a few minutes. She looked up to see him studying her intently. "What?" she asked.

As he refilled his cup, Connor said, "Go ahead. Ask anything you like."

Gwen choked on her cereal. Her hand flew up, covering her mouth as she mumbled, "Sorry?"

"Those questions buzzing about in your head. Why don't you ask what you want to know?"

Setting her spoon aside, she gulped and tried to get her thoughts together. After a minute, she said, "Okay. I'll ask. Where's your wife?"

He glanced down at the coffee cup in his hands, turning it gently between his fingers. The gold of his wedding band sparkled in the light of the kitchen. "She died. Many years ago, even before I had Eben."

"You adopted him, too."

"Yes. I found him when he was fifteen. I was touring Istanbul, and found him living on the streets. He's been with me ever since."

"So I'm number three then?" She concentrated on her bowl and waited.

"Three what?"

She shrugged. "Rescues. You said Christian was adopted too, and I just assumed…"

"You're correct," he mused, smiling over the fact. "That makes you number three, although you're over the age of adoption."

"So what are you doing with me?" she questioned, getting back to the main point. "I was on a regimen of medication. You don't even have my records, so how will you continue?"

He sighed and set his cup aside. "Child, all those medicines were killing you. Eben could see it, Christian could see it, and when they brought you here, I saw it. You *are* ill, Gwen. But there's nothing wrong in your head. Your illness is from the drugs, the environment and the lifestyle they were forcing you into.

"How do you know?" she argued, confused. "You know nothing about me."

"You're a good girl." His eyes dared her to argue. "And you'll do fine. My only worry is that your body will give out on you before I'm able to make you well. Now, finish your cereal."

Gwen frowned down at her bowl, but ate another bite.

"I'd like to ask a question, if I may."

She nodded, still chewing.

"Your wrists. I'd like to see them, please." He watched her, a small smile on his face as she almost fell off her stool in shock.

Her spoon clanged against the side of the bowl. She swallowed as she stared at him. "That's not exactly a question."

"Call it a request, then." He straightened in front of her, looking just how a king should look, or maybe a general when addressing his troops. "Come," he urged. "Lay them out so I can see." He patted a space on the counter.

A spot of cold rushed up her spine. Slowly, she pulled her sleeves up and laid her hands on the counter, palms up.

Connor fished in his robe pocket and pulled out a pair of glasses. After slipping them on, he turned first one wrist toward the light, and then the other, making little "hmmm" sounds as he did so.

When he was done, he removed his glasses and slipped them back in his pocket. He folded his arms across his chest and stared at her. "You did it very precisely, didn't you?"

Gwen pulled her wrists back and shoved her sleeves down. Picking up her spoon, she toyed with the mushy O's of the cereal and shrugged. "Can we talk about something else, please?"

His eyes refused to back down. "Are you going to try it again, Gwen?"

She stilled for a minute. Then, slowly, she shook her head. "Not that I know of."

He raised his brows at her answer. She sighed. "No."

"Good. I'd hate to be deprived of your company, child."

Silence overtook the kitchen. Gwen refused to meet his eyes as she methodically mashed the O's against the side of her cereal bowl.

"I'm going to leave you to finish your cereal and go get dressed. Afterward, I'll show you about the property and answer any other questions you have. All right?" He tipped his head to the side and looked directly into her eyes.

She nodded. Whistling a little tune, he left the kitchen, a slight spring in his step.

"So what is it you guys do here?" she asked, looking out over the trees and hills. "Or does everyone own hundreds of acres just for fun?"

So far, they'd viewed the house, all three floors—although they skipped the occupied rooms—the barns, complete with six horses, and another, smaller building where Connor stored his "stuff", which was everything from old bicycles to broken bird feeders. They skipped over the garage, and one other building that was farther from the house. Gwen hadn't bothered asking about it. Now, after a short walk through the woods, they had stopped at a small pond, frozen over and covered in a thick layer of snow, so she could rest and catch her breath. She inhaled deeply, reveling in the crisp fragrance of the cold air. It had a slight piney scent that reminded her of Christmas.

Smiling slightly, Connor replied, "We like the peace and quiet. And I'm a sculptor, if you're asking about my career. And I've had occasion to paint, when the mood comes on me."

Her eyebrows rose. "Really? I've never met an artist before."

"Now you have. Shall we return? I'd hate for you to catch a chill."

They walked back to the house companionably. He'd put quite a bit of effort into reassuring her and making her feel comfortable. And it'd helped. She felt almost as if she were visiting a family friend.

"I can't believe how big this place is," she said again as they stomped into the house.

"It's a vast area. Many families here own large parcels of land. And besides, the horses like it."

Gwen didn't point out that most people didn't buy so much land for their horses. "Can I see your studio?"

Connor took her jacket from her and hung it in the closet. "If you like," he replied easily.

Almost squirming with excitement, Gwen nodded.

He led the way to the second floor and opened one of the few doors he hadn't before. Gwen gasped.

"Holy shit." She clapped her hand over her mouth and stepped inside the room, twirling slowly, not quite believing what she was seeing. It was simply too marvelous for words.

"It's nice, isn't it?" Christian remarked from the doorway, wearing only a pair of boxers, obviously still waking up as he leaned against the doorway, his toothbrush in hand.

Gwen ignored him and stared at the walls, each one completely covered with beautiful mosaics of the forest, some with dark animals peering out, but mostly just the trees and undergrowth. But there were subtle changes— each wall depicted a different season, one blending into another at the corners of the room, so that the changing of the seasons was fluid and gradual.

"I can't believe you did this," she whispered in awe, eyes finally settling back on Connor. He just smiled and slid his hands into his pockets.

Christian wandered over, yawning and stretching, completely unconcerned with his bare chest, ever the lazy playboy. "I was just as shocked when I first saw it," he said with a slight smile, looking sexy and sleep tousled. "I do have to add that he didn't let me see it until I'd been here a month."

"You were unruly," Connor replied dryly. "I didn't want to take the chance that you'd take a marker to my masterpiece."

Taking another quick look at the scenes on the walls, Gwen gave her attention to the contents of the room. There was little furniture—a supply cabinet, a work bench flush against the wall on the right side of the room, and an old leather chair, made comfortable from years of use. A potter's wheel sat in the far right corner, and opposite was a huge block of plastic-wrapped clay. Two easels sat next to each other near the window at the back of the room, and the rest of it was bare space, just waiting to be used.

Gwen went to a stack of canvases leaning against the wall near the cabinet. Since Connor didn't stop her, she carefully picked up the first one. It was a woman, with beautiful chocolate-brown hair and a lush figure. She was nude, sprawled across the leather chair, and absolutely breathtaking.

"My wife," Connor murmured.

"She's beautiful." Gwen stared at it for a minute seeing the obvious love that had gone into the painting. It was a sensual picture, filled with shadows and angles that accentuated the woman. She set the canvas aside and picked up the next one. It was of the same woman, but she was standing near a window with her hair up, wearing a pair of overalls over a white shirt. Her hand rested gently on her distended belly.

"We lost the baby in the sixth month," Connor said, answering her unasked question.

"I'm sorry." It felt inadequate to say when looking at such a personal painting.

"As I said, it was a long time ago."

The next canvas was completely different. A young man, dark of skin and hair, and so fierce Gwen had a hard time looking at him, stood angrily against a wall, his displeasure obvious in every feature. She raised her eyes and frowned. "This is your son?"

He nodded. "Eben. Not long after I found him. We were still in Turkey at the time."

The picture made her uncomfortable for some reason, like he was staring at her from the canvas, accusingly. Feeling slightly foolish, she set it aside. The next one was worse.

She blushed when she realized she was staring at Christian, obviously recent, and completely nude. Much like Connor's wife, he was curled up in the chair, with his legs curved strategically so nothing graphic was exposed.

Christian laughed behind her. With a blush and a nervous laugh, Gwen set it aside. "I'm surprised you didn't let everything just hang out," she said, darting a glance at him.

Christian laughed even harder, and Connor smirked. "He wanted to, but I wouldn't have it. Women, I love to paint nude. I love their bodies. But I have no interest in giving intimate detail to a man's cock on my canvas."

Gwen dropped the next canvas in shock. Christian only laughed harder, slapping his hand against his thigh in mirth.

The rest of the paintings were relatively innocent, although they were obviously just as personal to Connor as the pictures of his family. One was a dead girl, lying in a street in some country, her body too thin and small. Another showed a mother breast-feeding her child in a park somewhere, her robes open and joy on her face at such a simple task.

"They're absolutely wonderful." Setting the paintings back, Gwen stood and turned to Connor. "Absolutely perfect. You're brilliant."

"He should be. He gets paid a mint for them," Christian said.

"And I'm sure they're worth every penny," Gwen retorted quickly, frowning slightly. There was something — something she was missing.

Her hand flew to her mouth. "Oh my God." She stared at Connor in shock, and then her eyes flew to the paintings against the wall. "I *know* who you are. I was supposed to go to one of your exhibitions in Chicago with my art class!" Embarrassment, thick and strong, rose to the surface and flushed her face. She was an idiot!

"Why didn't you go?" Christian asked.

"The accident—Dad...I can't believe I didn't even catch it," she moaned. "Everyone knows who Connor Lowell is. You're famous everywhere."

"Christ," Christian said, looking at Connor. "It took me three years to figure that out. All that time I thought all you did was walls."

"Really?" Connor said absently.

Gwen stared at Christian, horrified. "How could you have not known?"

"Hey, I was only ten at the time I came to live here. Give me a break."

"Besides," Connor argued, "I'm not truly that well-known. I've been lucky, and the museums and galleries have been kind to me."

He let her look through another, smaller stack of canvases. There was another of his wife, weeping, so sad it made Gwen unhappy, and another of Eben, just of his face, so close, with his eyes blazing out angrily. The rest were different scenes from his travels, some disturbing, some beautiful, but all perfect and moving in their own way.

"I'm sorry, but I don't have any of the sculptures here. I let the last one go about six months ago because I got tired of dusting it," he said apologetically.

Gwen did a quick view of the room and sighed. It made perfect sense. Connor Lowell was known to be an eccentric. His first sculptures were all based on his wife, each one sensuous and erotic, a celebration of women's beauty and sexuality, and as far as the art world was concerned, he was unique just for the fact that he'd been so in love with her.

"Now," Connor said, walking toward the cabinet. "Feel free to make use of anything you find in this room. I've seen your sketches, so I know you're comfortable with charcoals and pencils. I've got a lovely supply here on the third shelf. But if you're in the mood to experiment, you might want to try the ink, or even the paints. I've got extra supplies in the garage if I need them or if we run out of anything."

She stared in shock at the contents of the cabinet. It had everything from paints to erasers, any artist's dream. "Thank you."

"Hey, you never let me use any of your stuff," Christian pointed out, attempting to look pitiful.

"You have no talent," Connor shot over his shoulder.

"I'm feeling particularly creative now." Swaggering a little, Christian walked to the cabinet and plucked out a black marker. Turning to Gwen, he said, "Let's connect the dots." He leaned toward her face and held the marker right above her cheek.

"Don't you dare!" She took a step back and glared. "That's not even funny, you creep."

"Children," Connor said, with the tired patience of a mother, his mouth twitching at the corners.

Reluctantly, Christian replaced the marker and left the room. "What time tonight?" he asked over his shoulder.

"Eight," Connor replied. "And Christian, I expect you to be there on time."

Gwen looked at him, shocked. His tone was suddenly deep and serious, full of power and authority.

Christian stopped in the hallway and nodded. "I'll be there," he replied, solemn for the first time since Gwen had met him.

"What's going on?" she asked, once they were alone.

Connor closed the cabinet and turned the handle. "We're going to dinner at the pub tonight. There'll be neighbors and friends there. I thought it might be nice for you to become acquainted with everyone."

Nice wasn't a word she'd use. In fact, the whole idea was enough to give her nightmares. Gwen sent a silent prayer to the gods above that her stomach stayed calm for the next twelve hours. "Won't they think it's a little strange that you just adopted a complete stranger?" she asked.

"No."

Gwen glanced down at her hands and rubbed her thumb over one of the scars. "Do they know where I'm from? Where you found me?"

Sighing, Connor nodded. "They do. But none of them will look down on you because of it."

A shiver of unease slithered down her spine. What if she didn't stay? What would he tell his friends then? And wouldn't they wonder if she was just a little groupie, looking for a free handout from the famous artist?

They walked out of the studio. Connor made sure the lights were off and the door was firmly closed before he led her away. "Don't worry about dinner. The Noble Savage has excellent food. You'll enjoy it."

Gwen had her doubts, but she didn't speak of them. It would be enough to go through it that evening.

"Now then," he said, once they were on the ground floor. "I believe Christian will be feeding the horses in a few minutes. Why don't you go out and help him."

Gwen didn't argue. It would be nice to be around something that didn't make her nervous.

Chapter Four

ಸಾ

Connor waited until she was gone before seeking out Eben. He stepped out the back door of the house and headed for the one building he'd made sure to keep Gwen away from.

When he opened the door, he was immediately swamped with raging heat. A roaring fire was going in the pit, and it jumped about a foot with every work of the bellows.

Eben pulled strongly on the rope that controlled the air flow to the fire. With every movement, sweat gathered on his dark skin, dripping with every contraction of his muscles.

He let the handle go and removed the crude iron bar from the flames. It glowed orange in the dinginess of the building. Eben set it on an anvil, picked up a heavy hammer, and began pounding away, his movements smooth and methodical, timed so well it sounded like a metronome.

"I've called the pack together tonight," Connor said into the gloomy building.

Eben stopped his hammering and looked over at him. "Does she know?"

Connor nodded. "She's nervous about it. She doesn't like people staring at her or watching too closely. And she's embarrassed about the scars."

Eben nodded and went back to hammering. Every time the hammer struck, sparks flew, but he didn't seem to feel them.

"I'm also going to announce my retirement. Officially, it'll be at the next full moon, but I'll float it around tonight."

Connor watched as Eben tensed all at once. He stopped the hammer in mid swing.

"I'm too old to answer any more challenges," he continued, watching his son carefully. "I don't even want to. I want my art and grandchildren."

Eben let the hammer hang at his side. "Does Christian know?"

Connor snorted. "Lad, most of the pack knows you'll be taking my place. Even more, they expect it. You're a strong Alpha, Eben. I don't think I've ever met a Were to match you."

"Theron's going to challenge me for it." Eben turned and thrust the steel back into the coals.

"Yes, as well as some others. And you'll need to be careful. He doesn't fight fair, Eben."

"If he makes any move, I'm killing him." Eben's pale eyes connected with his, cold and steady.

It was stated evenly, with no emotion. Connor winced slightly but accepted it. Eben never left anything to chance, especially when lives were at stake. "I know."

"Call me when I need to get ready." He went back to the bellows and began pulling.

Connor walked toward the door and pushed it open, breathing in the cool air with relief. Just a few minutes in the shop and he was drenched with sweat.

Taking in another deep breath, he said over his shoulder, "She's stronger than I realized. All she needs is to learn to live and relax. That's going to be your biggest hurdle. Once she learns to relax with you, she'll be fine."

"I won't allow her to leave," Eben stated, pulling heavily on the bellows. Flames roared up in answer.

Connor sighed. "Hopefully it won't come to that. But, be prepared for her to be nervous, and a little scared. She's young, Eben. And being stuck in a hospital at such a tender age…" He shrugged. "It doesn't help, either."

"I won't let her leave." Eben repeated. "I won't."

Connor nodded. "I know." He silently left the building.

Gwen hardly even noticed the cold by the time they were done in the barn. She was warmed up from brushing the horses and hauling feed. She'd tried to lift the water pails and ended up splashing more on the floor than stayed in the bucket, but the hay she could handle. After the horses were fed, Christian instructed her on the proper cleaning of stalls, laughing the whole time as she struggled with the pitchfork.

"You need muscle," he said, smiling cheekily and taking the instrument of torture from her hands. She was panting too hard to reply.

But by the time they were done, the barn was spick-and-span, and she was acquainted with all six of the horses by name. She adored each one.

"Who rides them?" she asked, petting the older of the two mares. She wasn't as large as the others, and was a beautiful bay color.

"I used to, but haven't in a while. Eben and Connor never really learned. Plus," Christian added as he held out a piece of apple for a gelding, "the horses don't like either of them. They make them nervous."

"Huh." Gwen couldn't imagine Connor making anyone nervous.

They returned to the house after 6:00, both covered with snow and shivering. Gwen had snow leaking down her jacket in clumps, as well as snow frozen in her hair, thanks to Christian's overly enthusiastic push into a snowdrift.

For some reason, it didn't feel strange to treat him like a brother. He just naturally fell into that role with her, and Gwen appreciated it. She understood what kind of man he was, one who saw women as an enjoyment, indulging himself with them whenever he got the chance, and she liked the fact that he didn't look at her in that way.

Connor met them at the door, took one look at their disheveled appearance, and rolled his eyes. "To the showers. Both of you. And Christian, you had better be ready in an hour. I refuse to have a son who takes longer to dress than most women."

Christian flipped him the bird, and with a laugh, shot up the stairs. Gwen couldn't help but smile at his exuberance.

Connor sighed as he watched the blond head disappear. "He's always been a handful, that one."

She shrugged and slipped off her jacket. "He's funny. A little immature, sure, but funny."

Connor smiled at her. "I'm glad you had a nice time at the barn. Why don't you get cleaned up, hmm?"

With a little nod, Gwen handed her coat over and went to her room. After closing the door firmly, she did a quick inventory of her wardrobe and sighed. What did one wear to meet new people when there were severe wardrobe limitations?

She didn't have many clothes, and those she did have were mostly thin, long-sleeved undershirts. She generally wore a T-shirt over them, printed with something appropriately rude, but she wasn't really in the mood to insult a bunch of people she'd never met, especially since she didn't want to make Connor look bad.

She tapped her chin absently and considered her options. She was stuck with jeans, which sounded fine for a pub, and finally, after digging through what she did have, she settled on a thin, red shirt with long sleeves. She'd never worn it before. Her mother had presented it to her the second Christmas she'd spent in the hospital.

She just hoped the bar was nothing fancy, because fancy she definitely couldn't do. With a worried glance at her outfit, she grabbed a towel and hit the shower.

The drive was short, maybe ten minutes, and then they were pulling into a gravel lot and parking. The pub was a low building surrounded by trees on three sides, its rough exterior weathered to a dark gray. It didn't look fancy, which made her nervousness abate for a minute.

Christian jumped out first and held the door for her with a courtly bow. Gwen slid out and waited for Connor, needing someone strong and comforting beside her before she went in to face a bunch of strangers.

"Looks like most everyone's here," Christian commented, scanning the vehicles parked in the lot.

Gwen shivered again and tightened her arms around her middle. The drive had been bad enough, with Eben doing the driving and looking all dark and disapproving. And now she was here, and by the number of cars in the lot there were a lot of people inside.

Connor led the way in and held the door for Gwen. "Don't be nervous," he said softly as she passed through. "They're all very friendly."

Gwen took a deep breath and stepped inside.

Immediately, the smell of hot food and beer flooded her senses. It truly was a pub, with the same type of atmosphere as those found all throughout the United Kingdom. It wasn't lit too brightly, or decorated crudely with deer antlers. Instead, it was all wood, darkened with age. Something soft played in the background, and there wasn't a pool table or dartboard in sight.

It took her a second to grow accustomed to the dim light, but the minute she did, she noticed that everyone was staring at them.

Connor came up beside her and scanned the pub. He nodded to a group of men. "Gerard, Mike. How are you?"

The two men smiled and stepped forward, their hands out. Connor shook their hands and grabbed each man into an embrace.

They must be close, Gwen thought, watching the exchange, and then nearly stumbled back in surprise when what looked like half the crowd gathered around, greeting Connor by name and murmuring softly to him, almost always in French, tugging him deeper into the pub. Apparently the closeness extended to everyone.

It was a lot of people. At least thirty, and there were still more in the bar yet who were looking over at Connor and waiting.

Gwen stepped back, bumping into something large. She turned, saw Eben standing right behind her and nearly jumped away.

"Don't worry," Christian whispered in her ear, standing to her right. "Just hang out and no one will bother you. When he introduces you, just nod and you'll be fine."

He was right. She was acting ridiculous. It was just meeting new people, nothing difficult. Taking a deep breath, Gwen nodded. She could do this.

"Come on," Eben said, motioning for her and Christian to walk before him.

Christian looked left and broke out in a smile. "Hey, I'm going to go say hi to John," and with a wave, he was gone. Gwen's heart sank.

"Come," Eben ordered again, and slid an arm around her waist, moving her in the direction he wanted. "Connor's waiting."

Feeling a shiver of alarm, she let him lead her to a table and took the chair he indicated. Rather than sitting across from her, he took the chair next to her. Just seconds later, Connor joined them, taking the seat opposite. Another man sat next to him, and yet another pulled a chair over and sat at the end.

The man at the end was one of the first Connor had greeted, Gerard, Gwen thought. He was large and middle-aged, with kind eyes. She liked him immediately.

"You'll introduce me, Connor?" He smiled at her and winked.

"She's not his to introduce," Eben said smoothly, his eyes connecting with the older man's.

Gerard lost his smile. Nodding, he said with equal parts respect and wariness, "I apologize. Would you please perform the introductions, Eben."

Gwen watched the exchange, confused and astounded over the rudeness. Feeling a bit brave, more from irritability than anything else, she stuck out her hand. "Hi. My name's

Gwen Branson. I'm staying at Connor's for the week. Maybe a little longer."

Gerard took her hand, obviously a little uncomfortable, but he smiled anyway. "Nice to meet you, Gwen. You can call me Gerard." He dropped her hand and his eyes darted to Eben for a second.

"Eben, she doesn't understand," Connor said in French, watching the interaction between his son and friend. Eben appeared completely in control, as calm as anything, but it was a lie. His eyes were ice cold. "You're already confusing her with your behavior."

Eben's eyes were still locked on Gerard's, warning. "She's mine, Gerard. Be sure to tell the others."

Gerard's eyes dropped and he nodded. "Yes, Alpha."

Hoping to dispel the tension, Connor smiled at Gwen. "What would you like to drink?" he asked in English.

Gwen looked at the four men, trying to figure out what was going on. The other man, sitting next to Connor, was about his age, somewhere in his late fifties or early sixties, but shorter and thin. He wouldn't even look at her.

"Gwen," Connor prodded.

"Water with lemon, please," she said, slightly irritated. She hated when they switched to French. All the good conversation happened then, and she had no hope of getting any of it.

Smiling tightly, Connor left the table and walked to the bar.

"Christian seems well," the older man murmured, his eyes still downcast.

Beside her, Eben nodded. "He is."

"Will he be staying this time?"

"Yes. His wandering is over."

"Just in time for Connor's retirement, then," Gerard said.

A minute later, Connor came back carrying three glasses, with Christian trailing behind with three more. They set glasses in front of everyone and Connor sat down. Christian pulled over another chair and took the unoccupied end of the table.

"It's good to see you, Christian." The old man nodded to him and took a sip of his beer.

Gwen squeezed the lemon into her water and stirred it with the straw. She noticed the beers in front of Connor, Christian and Eben were so dark they were nearly black.

"What are you drinking?" she asked, frowning.

Christian held his glass up. "Guinness, hon. Wanna try it?"

"Um, no. Thanks." She would have rather drunk battery acid than the almost-black beer. Her stomach would have probably handled it better, too.

Christian took a sip and licked the foamy mustache from his upper lip. "You turned twenty-one while you were cooped up. You didn't even have a chance to enjoy becoming the legal drinking age. And here, the age is nineteen. Live a little."

"It's fine." Gwen pulled her water closer. "I'm good with this."

"You don't want that stuff anyway, Gwen," Gerard said with a grimace. "It'll make you sink to the floor it's so heavy."

"Are you insulting my taste in beer?" Connor asked with a smile.

"God, no. If anything, you've my respect being able to drink that stuff. I just can't figure out how you do it."

And the conversation progressed, moving toward more mundane things. Gwen tried to be inconspicuous as the conversation leaned toward hunting and the large buck that had been spotted in the woods. Carefully, she scanned the rest of the pub, watching as the people laughed and talked with each other, almost all in French. There was very little English, and what there was, spoken so low she could hardly hear.

There were a few women, but mostly men. She wasn't sure if that meant there weren't many women in the area, or whether they just chose not to frequent the pub. Whatever it meant, the people frequenting the establishment looked perfectly ordinary, most wearing faded jeans and boots and heavy tops that ranged from flannel to thick sweaters. There wasn't a single mountain man in sight, or at least none that she recognized.

"Gwen..."

"Hmm?" She frowned—there was something about them all that struck her as being slightly *off*. She just couldn't put her finger on it. Maybe—

She nearly jumped when a firm hand turned her head. Eben filled her vision, his face and eyes as unfeeling and calm as before. "What will you have for supper, Gwen?" His voice was deep and rumbly, like he needed a drink of water.

Swallowing, she shook her head slightly. "I'm not hungry."

His jaw clenched and anger crept into his eyes, but rather than warming them, it made them even more chilling. "What will you eat?" he asked again, the authority in his voice leaving no room for argument. "You *will* eat, Gwen."

With her mind in a whirl, she pulled back from him, and his fingers let her chin slip away. With no wish to fight in public, she whispered, "Soup will be fine." Soup was easy.

"Vegetable, beef or clam chowder?" the bartender asked, a pad of paper in his hand. His name tag said his name was Joe. He stood over by Christian and looked at her expectantly.

"Vegetable."

He scribbled it down and then looked at her again. "And?"

Christian rested his chin on his hands and smirked at her.

"Th-that's fine," she stuttered.

Eben fired off something terse in French. Joe nodded and scribbled something down before turning to Connor, who ordered salmon.

After everyone had their order taken, the men went back to speaking in French, and Gwen sat back and listened, happy to let their conversation flow around her. Christian didn't add anything, and seemed content to sit through it like her.

The food came, and Joe handed huge plates to everyone. He handed her a plate with a bowl of soup, and another with a huge turkey sandwich.

"I didn't order this." Gwen glanced down at it in question. A scoop of potato salad sat on the side, garnished with a large pickle.

Joe's eyes shifted to Eben. Cautiously, he said, "He got it for you."

"Eat it," Eben ordered, taking his own plates of food from Joe. He'd ordered a steak, gigantic, with potatoes, carrots and a lobster tail.

"At least try," Connor seconded, digging into his own meal.

Christian laughed silently into his arm. Gwen stuck her tongue out at him, which just made him laugh harder.

Sighing, she set the sandwich plate to the side and started on the soup. It was excellent, with a tomato-base broth and large pieces of vegetables. It was served with a slab of sourdough bread big enough to choke a horse. Gwen scowled resentfully at the sandwich as she ate.

"Theron's not going to like it and neither will his uncle," Gerard said, chewing vigorously.

Connor shrugged. "Then he can challenge, just like anyone else who feels they'll do a better job."

"You'll need to be careful of that one, boy." The older man next to Connor stared hard at Eben. "He's as likely to shoot you in the back as to challenge you directly. Or he'll get a few other challengers up first, hoping you'll get injured."

"Let him try," Eben murmured. "I can take it."

Gwen laid her spoon aside and raised her brow at Connor. He smiled back at her and took another bite of fish.

The conversation continued and became even more confusing once they began to talk about "clan rights", and "structure". Halfway through, they switched to French.

Sighing, Gwen pushed her bowl away and slumped in her chair.

"You didn't eat your sandwich," Eben said. The conversation around them came to a sudden stop.

She glanced from her soup bowl, to his plate, which was completely empty. He'd even mopped up the liquid from his steak with a piece of bread.

"Eat your sandwich, Gwen."

She looked at the sandwich, sitting so innocently on its plate. Was it right to resent a sandwich? Especially when the sandwich was an innocent bystander? For some reason, she felt like she was twelve and in her mother's kitchen, being forced to endure the pageant torture of makeup and curlers.

"No," she said finally, her voice quiet but firm.

His head turned slowly until he faced her. "Did you say something?"

He asked it calmly, as easily as he would have asked about the weather, but there was steel in it, and the expectation of obedience.

A frisson of fear surfaced, fluttering below Gwen's heart. Irritated, she pushed it away. Staring at him, with the barest hint of a waver in her voice, she said, "No thank you. I'm not hungry."

"Gwen..."

His tone annoyed her more than anything. It was commanding and dangerous, and strangely exciting. It made her want to be daring and aggressive for once in her life. Obeying orders had gotten her nothing except a free stint in the loony bin. Now, because she could, she let the anger bubble up, and welcomed it.

"You ordered it," she bit out, narrowing her eyes at him. "You can eat it."

Inside her chest, her heart was thumping a million beats a second, but her brain was doing a happy dance of victory. It felt so *good* to disobey, wonderful actually. So much she almost couldn't believe it.

"Of all places, you challenge me here," he growled, his tone so sinister she flinched.

Desperate to keep her courage, she grasped at the little that remained. "I don't want it."

The other men were all staring at the exchange, watching her like she was taking a knife to a kitten. "Alpha," Gerard said carefully.

Eben's eyes rolled toward him, and the other man immediately fell quiet.

Alpha? Who talked like that? And who was Eben to think he should be called Alpha? She almost snorted with disdain. Instead, because she couldn't quite help herself, Gwen pushed the plate in front of Eben, hoping no one would notice her hand shaking. "Enjoy."

For a second, she was sure he was going to pull her out of her chair and break her neck. But when he moved, instead of her neck, he grasped the sandwich and took a large bite, chewing smoothly.

"Well," Connor said drolly, "does anyone have any other worries or concerns?"

The men at the table all shook their heads in the negative.

He rubbed his hands together in satisfaction. "Then, I'm going to take Gwen with me and introduce her to the others. I'll see you all tomorrow."

Taking the hint and more than ready to leave the table, Gwen pushed away and followed Connor without a backward glance.

She fell asleep on the drive home, the sound of their hushed French lulling her. When she next opened her eyes, strong arms held her against a broad, heavily muscled chest.

Nothing made sense for a second, and then it all came back to her. She was in Canada!

She tried to jerk up and was immediately pinned tightly to a hard chest. Actually, it was quite nice.

"Don't."

She shrank against him, too tired to do anything else. The fighting was fun, but her bravery had long ago melted away and she was far too worn out to scare up any more.

Eben carried her silently to her assigned room, not bothering to turn on the light. When he placed her on the bed, he stayed leaning over her, his face heavily shadowed, looking almost demonic.

She was asleep before he removed her shoes.

Gwen got up early the next morning, even earlier than Connor. After dressing, she went to the kitchen and helped herself to cereal. All around her, the house creaked in the heavy winter wind. Normally, she would have been uncomfortable, but for some reason, she wasn't. It'd only been three days, but she was comfortable with them, or at least with two of them.

After she was done, she went to the studio room and helped herself to supplies. She hummed as she pulled out a large sketch pad and charcoals. And when she started with sweeping, heavy lines, she forgot about everything else for hours.

Connor knew where she was the minute he woke up. Her scent, now sweet and inviting with the absence of the drugs that were polluting her system, was heavy coming from the studio.

He gave her a few hours before he went up and knocked on the door. When he heard no response, he opened it silently and peered in.

"Gwen?"

She lifted her head from the bench and blinked at him, her eyes foggy with dreams and memories. "Hmm?"

Taking it as an invitation, he stepped into the room, leaving the door open behind him. "How's it progressing?" He thought pretty well, since both her hands were completely covered in charcoal. With her hair loose down her back and her pretty complexion, she looked lovely in a simple, unsophisticated way, much like the beauty of new snow, or a starry night. In just the few days she'd been with them, her weight was coming back, and the gaunt, lost look was no longer in her eyes.

She glanced down at the paper in front of her and frowned. "Okay, I guess. I'm not sure what it is, though."

Connor leaned closer and got his first look, and froze. "Where did you see this?"

She stiffened and shrugged. "I don't know. Probably dreamt it."

The Were didn't appear to be familiar, although it was difficult to tell, but the drawing was so accurate it was almost frightening. Although he'd seen her other drawing, the detail in this one left no doubt that the Were had gotten close to her. Far too close.

"Well," he said, keeping his tone light. "It's well done. Perhaps you should try painting it?" With paint there could be color, and with color, he had at least a hope of identifying the man behind the fur.

"I don't think so. I think I'm done for the day." She shoved it to the side and slipped off her stool, already cleaning up her supplies.

"If you wouldn't mind, I could use your help in the kitchen."

She nodded, and together they left the studio.

Once there, Connor set about preparing lunch for the boys. He pulled out a large chicken, already roasted and ready for slicing. As he cut and laid slices to the side, he told her of his travels throughout the world—Egypt, Jerusalem, Paris, every exotic place Gwen could even think of. He'd been to them all, and happily recounted silly stories or obscure facts that made her smile as she cut vegetables and sliced bread.

Methodically, they started building huge sandwiches of the fresh chicken and vegetables. By the time they were finished, they were thick and heavy, and far too large.

She eyed them warily. "Are you sure they aren't a little too big?"

Connor smiled over at her. "They're fine. Wrap these in plastic, would you dear?" He set three of the sandwiches in front of her and placed the rest of them on a plate. "And I'll fetch the potato salad and pickles. Eben's always favored dill pickles."

He rummaged around in the refrigerator and came out with a large jar of pickles and a vat of potato salad. After scooping what looked like a pound and a half into a sealable container, he slapped a lid on it and added it to the pile of wrapped sandwiches. He added a mound of pickles to the pile in a separate container, and after tapping his finger on the counter for a minute and staring, went back to the refrigerator and brought out an apple.

"That should do it," he murmured, shoving the whole thing into a zippered bag. "Now, would you be a dear and take this out to that building?" He pointed through the window to the building he'd neglected to show her.

He dropped the strap of the bag on her shoulder and turned away, already mumbling about supper and lasagna.

After donning her coat and boots, Gwen entered the freezing cold and promised herself that next time she'd refuse, except she knew she wouldn't. So far Connor hadn't made her angry enough to refuse him anything, and it seemed that she was too much of a pushover to be rude without the anger.

It felt like it took forever before she made it to the building. The snow was thick, and by the time she got there, her jeans were coated from her knees down. The small window at the north end blazed orange and the chimney belched out a continuous stream of thick smoke. Gwen didn't know what Eben did in there, but she had no doubt it was warm.

She was shivering by the time she pounded on the door. She waited for a minute and had her hand up, ready to pound again, when it was wrenched open.

He wasn't wearing a shirt, and he was sweaty all over. She blinked for a second, her eyes fastened to his chest, not sure she was seeing properly. For one thing, he had the most heavily defined chest she'd ever seen. It was thick and wide, and covered in ridged muscles.

After a moment of silence, she jerked her eyes to the side and blushed. She swallowed sharply and patted the bag hanging off her shoulder. "Lunch," she croaked.

His eyes narrowed, making her want to duck out and disappear. "Come in." He pulled the door wide and stepped back for her to enter.

She stayed outside for a second with the wind tearing her apart, chewing on her lip in indecision. Cautiously, she took a step forward, felt the heat coming from the open doorway and rushed in. He closed the door firmly behind her.

The building wasn't bright at all. There seemed to be no lights, only what was given off by the flames and coals in a pit that took up a huge portion of the space.

She stared at all the metal equipment—hammers, files and other things she couldn't even identify, wondering what it all was. "What is this place?"

He walked up behind her and slipped the bag off her shoulder. "A forge." He set the bag down and started pulling everything out, setting the food carefully on the nearest bench.

Gwen stood awkwardly, not sure what to do. She didn't want to stay, but he didn't seem like he was going to let her out yet, either.

"Is it okay if I—" She pointed toward the other end of the building and his eyebrows only rose in question. "Look," she finished lamely, her arm dropping to her side.

For almost an entire second, she was sure he was going to smile. Or half smile. His mouth actually moved, the corners almost tilting up. And then it was gone.

"Of course." He went back to the lunch items, and finished unpacking.

Curious, she walked around, examining the building and its tools. Most that were small enough hung on the walls. Some looked old, like they'd been used hundreds of years ago, and others looked fairly new. Toward the far end of the room was the fire pit, with a large bellows in the ceiling, a rope hanging off it. Thick pieces of twisted metal sat all over the building, leaned against walls, bundled together in a corner, and some even laid across the rafters in the ceiling. But what she found really interesting were the weapons hanging on the far wall.

There were five swords, each one elegantly made and as long as she was tall. They looked perfect, like they should be in a museum with other ancient weapons. Along with the swords were a few axes, knives, and even a pike.

"You challenged me last night."

She looked at him over her shoulder. He'd already finished the first sandwich and was leaning against the bench as he worked on the second, all muscle and sweat. And brawn. Big, muscular brawn. Menace was also there. She couldn't ever forget that. But he was so pretty, especially with so much skin exposed. Sometimes it was just hard to remember.

Turning back to the swords, she said, "I'm sorry." *No I'm not!* her conscience sang in her head, and she wasn't. It had been the most glorious point of her life. She actually *felt* alive. "Did you make all of these?" She pointed to the weapons.

"Through the years, yes."

"So that's what you do here? Make swords and knives and…other things?" She wasn't sure what to call some of the weapons.

After a minute, she heard him leave the bench and walk toward her. He stopped in front of her, blocking her view of the swords, and so close she had to back up a step just to feel comfortable.

"Don't," he ordered.

Gwen stopped in mid-step and stiffened.

"And yes. That is what I do here." His eyes glittered down at her, so pale it was amazing she could even tell they were blue at all.

"What?" she asked, frowning. It was unnerving, the way he stared at her.

"Next time you get your back up," he rumbled, "you *will* have to deal with me afterward."

The pub. He was talking about the pub. She nodded, and made a mental note to never challenge him again. Then she quashed it. Screw it. She had nothing to lose anyway.

"You can go." And he turned toward his food.

She left the building, her hands practically itching to sketch him.

Gwen was quiet through the lunch meal. Christian took one look at her, detected Eben's scent, and knew where she'd been. He visited the forge later that afternoon, after deciding to give Eben a few hours to cool off.

Unlike Connor, he didn't mind the heat of the place. He breathed in the smell of hot metal and sweat like it was a perfume, and stripped his shirt. He got an extra leather glove off the bench and waited for orders. Eben didn't waste any time.

"Man the bellows for me while I work on this."

For the next half hour, neither of them spoke. Christian pulled on the rope that operated the airflow to the fire while Eben pounded the shit out of the metal, alternating between two different pieces.

"Are you still sure she's your mate?" he asked, taking a break and wiping his brow. "Her scent's changed since she's been here."

Eben brought the hammer down a little too hard on the hot metal, and the sparks flew. "It's her."

Christian heaved on the bellows again. "Then what are you waiting for? She's at the house and you're always here. It's not exactly conducive to a burgeoning relationship."

Eben let the hammer bang down on the metal, flattening and shaping it. When the rod cooled a little, he shoved it back into the coals and pulled out the other piece. "She gets a month to relax. A month to not worry about what I want from her. After…"

Christian was so shocked he forgot to pull on the bellows. "Christ," he marveled, "I never expected you to be nice."

Eben shot him a dark look and nodded toward the pull. "It's the only freedom she'll have. After I take her, she'll be lucky to get ten feet from me."

Christian laughed and pulled.

Chapter Five

ɛᴓ

Gwen felt she understood what a true home was supposed to be. After being in Connor's home for several weeks, she finally grasped the entire concept, the comfort, the familiarity, the peacefulness. It was all part of what made it so nice. Maybe that was why she appreciated it so much—she'd never been in such a relaxed atmosphere before.

When she was a child, she'd lived in a nice house, but it had been anything but comforting. With her parents arguing all the time, her mother harping, and the farm always there requiring time and attention from her father, the house was more a place of perpetual discontent. Then, after her parents were divorced, she'd never been able to settle enough in either of their homes, feeling as if she didn't truly belong in either one.

But here, it was different. There was no one telling her to sit up straight, or complaining when she got dirty or tore a shirt, and because of that, she was able to relax, help Connor with meals when she wanted, Christian with the horses, and spend hours upon hours in the studio. Sometimes Connor was there with her, and sometimes he wasn't. It didn't seem to matter at all one way or the other since they worked well with each other, neither one of them intruding on the other's concentration. Plus, then she got to see him create.

She even became accustomed to the almost constant night, the snow, and the cold, and actually enjoyed the extremes of the northern winter. There was something savage about it, but beautiful, too.

She laughed more in the month with The Men, as she liked to call them, than in the last ten years of her life. Christian especially seemed intent on making her giggle, and was constantly whispering raunchy jokes in her ear, then smiling innocently when Connor or Eben caught him.

Even dinner was completely different from what she was used to. It was a fun, informal event. Eben often came to the table late. Connor never seemed to be bothered one way or the other about it, and generally started the meal without him, smiling at his son when he finally made it, dishing out food as if nothing was wrong. And to him, there *was* nothing wrong. That was perhaps what endeared him so much to her. Connor loved his children without trying to change them.

She even felt that she was getting used to Eben's dark ways, although it wasn't easy. He was large and scary, and sometimes he made her breathless, which she couldn't quite understand. He didn't like her much—she figured that out after two weeks. It was in his eyes and the way he avoided talking to her. It was hard to take at first, but finally she just shrugged it away. It wasn't that difficult. He spent his days out in his shop, pounding on hot metal and making swords, which she learned from Connor were often purchased by serious collectors and museums, and even occasionally used in movies. As it turned out, she rarely saw him except during the dinner meal, and then she had Connor and Christian to act as buffers.

The only dark spot in her new life was her mother, although it certainly wasn't a new problem. Gwen called her a few days after going to the pub. After listening to her mother's ranting for five minutes, she chastised herself for even bothering to try and explain her situation.

"*Do you know what people are saying?*" her mother screeched.

"No," she replied woodenly, clenching her hand around the phone. Connor looked over at her from the counter where he was rolling pie crust, clearly concerned.

"Margaret Miller is saying you went off with a boyfriend because you're *pregnant.*"

Gwen winced, knowing her mother's reaction to that one. She had been so afraid of her daughter becoming a teen pregnancy statistic, she hadn't even allowed her to date in high school.

Gwen listened for another few minutes, making no comment as her mother ordered, prodded, begged and yelled, insisting she come home and return to the hospital.

Gwen finally couldn't take anymore and interrupted. "I love you, Mom." She hung up the phone.

She woke later than usual one morning, several weeks later. When she went to the kitchen, Christian was there, wolfing down a huge breakfast. She helped herself to cereal and joined him at the table.

"Good morning." She carefully added milk, making sure not to splash.

"Is it?" he mumbled.

"What's wrong with you?" She scowled at him and set the carton down a little more forcefully than necessary.

"Shitty night." He shoved more food in his mouth and chewed viciously.

Gwen paused with her spoon just about to dip into her bowl. "I'm sorry. Is there anything I can do?"

His eyes slid over her for a second before returning to his plate. "No."

His tone rankled. Taking a deep breath, she decided the day would be best spent in the studio, preferably alone.

When she came downstairs hours later, loud voices were coming from the kitchen. Gwen stepped carefully down the stairs, keeping off the sections that squeaked, and listened. For once, they were speaking in English.

"You can't stay, Eben. You're taking over. I guarantee, boy, Theron will have convinced someone else to bring a challenge. And I'd expect more than one."

"She's my responsibility, Connor. Not Christian's."

"He likes her, and volunteered, Eben. Don't act like a fool when we're here to help you. She'll be fine."

Eben retorted with something too low and guttural for Gwen to catch. She stepped down a few more steps and waited. The conversation stopped for a second, then returned in French.

Sighing, she gave up and tromped down the rest of the steps. She didn't bother trying to be silent and actually dragged her feet and tapped on the walls as she headed for the kitchen, just to be irritating. It was uncanny how well they could hear, and terribly inconvenient. The tiniest little squeak of a floorboard and they switched to French. Any hope to eavesdrop was completely swept away.

Connor stood at the stove wearing a white apron around his waist. His eyes snapped to her briefly before returning to Eben, who looked perfectly calm, although his eyes glittered with emotion.

Deciding that directness was the right approach, Gwen said, "Don't worry about me. Go ahead about your business. If the three of you want to go hang out and do whatever," she gave a little shrug, "that's fine. I don't need a babysitter."

She tried to keep her voice light and unconcerned. Connor looked slightly worried, but he didn't interrupt, other than to pull open the oven and take out a pan of cookies.

Eben said something in French to Connor. Gwen couldn't tell what it was, but it didn't sound polite. Connor watched absently as the younger man turned and left, before reaching for a spatula and removing the cookies from the pan.

"What's his problem?" Gwen asked, eyeing the cookies. The smell was absolutely divine.

"He worries."

She selected one carefully and bit into the soft cookie, humming with pleasure as she licked the chocolate off her fingers. "Is that why he doesn't like me? Because he thinks I'm his responsibility, and therefore a burden?"

Connor stared at her in shock. "Where did you get that idea?"

Gwen shrugged and took another bite of cookie. "It's okay. It bothered me at first, but I'm okay with it now. Everyone doesn't have to like me, and I get that. But I'm really not his responsibility, Connor. I can take care of myself, mostly. You guys don't have to worry about going out together and leaving me alone. I'll be fine."

He didn't say anything as he stared at her, then went back to removing cookies, shaking his head slightly and muttering something like, "Stupid foolish boy."

"So, when are you guys going out?"

He took the last of the cookies off and went to the mixing bowl full of dough, and began filling the sheet up again. "Wednesday. We'll leave about noon and be back late."

It certainly wasn't the first time she'd heard of men doing an all-night poker party, or some other similarly manly activity. "Okay. Like I said," she smiled at him and took another cookie, "I'm a big girl. I can entertain myself for a few hours."

"I know." He finished the pan and slid it into the oven. "I know."

Eben didn't come to dinner that night. She almost asked, but the expression on Connor's face said that he wasn't in the mood for questions. She let it go, and hurried through the meal.

Christian was equally tense. He hadn't made any crude jokes in three days, and Gwen was starting to worry about it. They all acted like they were going off to an execution rather than a guy's night out. It was definitely strange.

Wednesday rolled around, and Gwen was relieved for no other reason than to get it over with. She was tired of the side glances from Connor, and the silence from Christian. It was unlike them and it made *her* uncomfortable, as if she were ruining their previously easy existence.

She got up early and went to the studio. She'd started working with a pen and ink the day before, and liked the results. Charcoals were still her favorite, but the clean line of the pen was a nice change.

At 10:00, she cleaned up and headed downstairs, ready to reinforce Connor's faith in her.

"I think it's going to—" She stopped speaking and inhaled sharply. "Sorry. I thought you were Connor."

Eben stood in the kitchen, leaning back against the sink with his head bowed. His eyes lasered in on her, heavy and cold, and for the first time she saw true emotion behind them, although she had no idea what it was. It was too cold to be anger, but too hot to be dislike. When she moved a step back, he traced it, like an animal watching prey and getting ready to pounce.

"I want to speak with you for a minute."

She stared at him, not quite sure she'd heard him right. Or heard him at all, to be exact. He hadn't said ten words to her in two weeks. What could he possibly need to speak about now?

Prepared to take some type of criticism, she nodded.

He moved closer, until he was just a few inches away, which forced her to tilt her head back, just so she could look him in the eyes. She wanted to take a step back, but didn't. He would probably just move forward again, anyway.

"You know we're leaving soon."

She nodded. "Yes. And it's fine. I'm okay by myself."

His jaw clamped for a moment. She felt sure he was going to say something scathing, but he didn't.

"Is that all?" she urged, wanting to get away. She felt that she was growing stronger and braver every day. But, she wasn't strong enough or brave enough to deal with Eben for any length of time. Short amounts of time, preferably under fifteen minutes, yes. Much longer than that, and she was out of luck. He was too imposing.

"No." He took a deep breath and held it, like he was trying to smell something. Gwen frowned at the action, thinking it strange.

"Don't leave the house after we're gone, for any reason. Don't unlock the door for *anyone*. There's an emergency number by the phone. If anything happens, call it immediately. The person who answers will get us a message. Do you understand?"

"I'm not a ch—" She snapped her mouth shut. After a minute, she just nodded.

"We'll leave in an hour." He turned away from her and left the kitchen.

Gwen watched him leave and scowled. Then stuck her tongue out at his retreating back. She wasn't that much trouble.

In all honesty, she was looking forward to them leaving. She was used to solitude, and in fact enjoyed it. It was one of the reasons why she liked the studio so much. It was quiet and peaceful, and even when Connor was there with her, she hardly noticed because both of them were so wrapped up in their work.

The house was going to be all hers and she was ready for it. She had chocolate, chips and sodas. All that was required was entertainment, and that was easy since the movie collection stored in the entertainment center was large enough to rival that of the local video-rental place. There were hundreds of movies, of every category, and it wasn't long before she had several she thought interesting.

The three men entered the room while she was going through the last drawer, muttering about "stupid Steven Segal". She looked up and saw them standing by the door. Christian carried a duffel bag, and all three of them were in their jackets.

"Leaving?" she asked, getting up from the floor.

"It's that time," Connor replied. "You won't be terribly bored, will you?"

"God, no. There are plenty of things to do here. Don't worry about it, and have a good time." She gave him a hug and smiled reassuringly.

Christian gave her a little wave and headed out the door, followed closely by Connor. Eben stayed and stared at her, hard.

She raised her brows and pursed her lips, wondering what else he wanted to harp about. Folding her arms over her chest, she said, "I think they're waiting."

His mouth tightened. "Remember," he ordered, stepping toward the door. "No one comes in."

She nodded and watched as he closed the door behind him. The lock sounded like a gunshot in the empty house.

Hours later, the night was cold and windy. Snow fell heavily, but she hardly even noticed. Harrison Ford called to her on screen, racing away from giant spiders and rolling boulders. Before that, she'd had Mel Gibson in *Braveheart,* and before that, *Ghost,* with Patrick Swayze. All in all, Gwen thought it a very successful night.

She was in the middle of switching DVDs when a sharp, pained cry broke the night, the sound alone enough to make her wince and run to the window. The creature cried again, this time louder and more desperate. She pushed the curtain away and searched, looking for any sign of movement.

There was another scream of pain before she saw anything, and what she did see infuriated and flooded her with such rage she couldn't do anything to stop it. Without a thought, she left the window and ran to the front door, unlocking and yanking it open with more anger than she'd experienced in the last ten years.

She didn't think to grab a jacket as she marched out into the night, walking into the cold with nothing more than her blind fury. She marched around to the side of the house, stopping when she spotted the man walking around the wounded creature. The animal was completely in shadows, hidden by the overhanging boughs of the trees, but she knew the sound of a wolf when she heard it.

"What do you think you're doing?" she yelled. She marched closer to them, not stopping until she had a clear view of the man's face. She memorized it, determined to give Connor a detailed description of the poacher. "This is private property. You're trespassing and better leave now. The cops are on their way." She wasn't sure where the lie came from, but it sounded good.

He was medium height, with what seemed like a slightly paunchy build, although she couldn't really tell because of his heavy winter clothing. He raised his face from the animal and smiled at her, his thick lips spreading into a creepy smile. "There you are, pretty girl."

He stepped away from the wolf and walked toward her. Gwen had a view of the creature's back, covered in a thick, pale pelt. It didn't move.

"There's someone who wants to meet you, pretty girl."

She jerked her attention back to the man, and for the first time felt a frisson of alarm run up her spine. She'd been fueled by anger when she'd seen the poacher, but now, with him approaching her in such a threatening manner, the word *stupid* ran through her mind on a banner.

"What would a pretty little piece like you be doing in this place, huh?" He stopped a few feet from her, and Gwen smelled the heavy odor of garlic on his breath. "Especially with stupid dogs like this?"

Cautiously, she took a step back, and then another. "Leave. The cops are going to be here any minute." The wind whined, blowing her hair into her face.

He sniffed at her and smiled wider, revealing crooked, yellow teeth. "Liar. I can smell it all over you. Plus," his smile widened, "I cut the phone line. Won't be getting no calls out of this place for a while." Suddenly, his smile disappeared and he licked his lips in a predatory manner. "I'm going to taste you, pretty girl. After I've had my fill, Theron can have you. What do you say to that?"

Gwen's breath froze in her chest. The snow was coming heavily, hitting her skin like tiny little darts. She exhaled slowly, everything suddenly seeming to still, and a second later, turned and ran, so quickly she almost slipped in the snow.

Her heart raced, thumping heavily in her chest as she rushed for the front door. She could see the door, so close. It was safe. All she had to do was get in and lock it.

She heard him breathing heavily behind her a second before he grabbed her and yanked her back. She went tumbling into the snow and his heavy body landed on top of her, smashing her into the cold, frozen ground.

She screamed and scratched at him. He slapped her hard, then again when she didn't stop struggling.

Gwen blacked out in a daze for a minute. Everything spun around her crazily. The sky was a sheet of blue velvet, tumbling in waves above her head. Occasionally, her attacker appeared in her vision, ripping at her clothes, squeezing her flesh painfully.

She gasped as he jerked at her pants, and came back to herself. She was nearly nude, wearing only shreds of her clothes, lying in the frozen snow. Above her, he reached for his zipper and pulled down his pants. His cock flopped out, red, pointed and dripping with pre-cum.

Gwen tried to leap up and get away, but he was on her in a second. Viciously, he grabbed her by the back and flipped her around, slamming her back into the ground. *"You will stay still, slut!"*

Tears ran down her face in hot streams. He was working his cock, trying to get closer to climaxing. At the same time, his other hand grasped her thigh, bruising her as he wrenched her legs apart.

With a last thought to survival, Gwen kicked her leg up, hitting him in the balls. With a short cry, his eyes rolled up and he crumpled, both hands going to his groin. With a single glance, she scrambled away, crawling on her hands and knees for the woods, no thought except to get away.

A streak flew past her, pale yellow against the snow. It growled and snarled as it launched itself at her attacker. It was huge, six-and-a-half feet and covered in a thick pelt. It growled low in its throat, and her breath froze—she was staring at her nightmare all over again.

Through her haze of pain, Gwen watched as the creature tore and ripped at the skin of the man. Her attacker was suddenly growling and changing before her, his bones and skin popping and reshaping, reminding her of too many horror movies. Hair sprouted all over his body as his clothes tore away, until his form was changed into that of the other, the werewolf. Her terror.

She stayed where she was, collapsed in the snow, unable to tear away from the horrible sight before her. The pale werewolf was already bleeding, already hurt. It flinched and screamed as the darker one aimed and bit down, tearing a large piece of flesh from its side.

Then it seemed to get a second wind, and seeing an opening, it went for its opponent's neck, pinning the darker werewolf to the ground. With a fatal shake of its head and a tearing of flesh, the darker wolf howled in pain, a small geyser of blood splashing across the snow and gurgling in its throat.

Gwen lay still in the snow, watching the creature's death spasms. It died jerking and yelping, its legs twitching.

The other werewolf collapsed with a cry, its back arching in pain. Even in the dark, its blood was visible on the pristine snow.

She couldn't tell how much time passed as she huddled in the snow, that old and familiar numbness strong, making it possible for her to survive. Her shirt was in shreds, and her jeans were gone. She had to warm up or she'd die in the cold.

Stumbling, she moved closer to the house, watching both forms cautiously, on guard for any sudden movements.

She was close to the house when the pale form turned toward her, its clawed hand/paw reaching for her.

"Gwen," it groaned through vocal chords not meant to speak.

She stilled, new fear flooding her bloodstream. With disbelief and horror, she crawled toward it. *It couldn't be.* "Christian?"

Its huge head rolled and foreign, feral eyes blinked up at her, clouded with pain. Its mouth opened, revealing rows of jagged teeth as he gasped, "*Call Connor, Gwen.*"

Her shivering suddenly became violent. Pressure exploded in her chest, demanding to be released.

Her cry broke the night, full of hurt and confusion.

The Christian creature inched closer to her, and she scrambled back. Its lips lifted in a growl of warning. "Don't."

She cried silently with her arms wrapped around her chest. How could this be? How could she not *know*?

"Gwen," he growled again, his voice weaker.

She sucked in her tears and looked around her. She was outside, nearly naked, and hurt. Feeling as if she was waking up from a long nap, she tried to get to her knees and immediately fell down again.

"Go. Now."

She tried again, and fell again, sprawling even closer to him. For a second, she lay there, unable to move. "I don't think I can," she whispered.

"Get up!"

She scrambled away, fear giving her strength. The house was there, she could make it.

Falling every few steps, she pushed herself to the door, agonizing and crying the entire time. When she finally touched the handle, she could hardly feel it, her fingers were so cold. She had to try three times before it opened properly and she was able to pull her body inside. She locked the door immediately.

She lay in the hallway, panting and crying until she was warm. She had no idea how long it took, and hardly even thought about it. Her mind was empty suddenly, giving her time to heat up before dealing with other issues. The numbness was still there, protecting her from the terror, and she let it take hold, thankful.

She stood up on shaky legs finally, slightly dazed. As if it were any other day, she glanced down at her body, seeing the bruising and blood. She studied it, and then pushed it out of her mind, too. Later. She'd deal with it all later.

Humming slightly, she walked to her room and pulled out sweatpants and a shirt. After getting dressed, she went and sat in the living room, shivering. And she waited.

Her mind stayed pleasantly empty as she stared at the shelves of books. So many, all different colors. She could look at them forever and not get bored going over the differences. Maybe she would do that.

The clock struck midnight. Gwen jerked her head up and stared out the window, as all those thoughts she didn't want poured into her head. Christian was a werewolf, like the monster she saw the night her father died. He was a monster.

She absorbed the information, trying to get a handle on everything. But it didn't feel right. Monsters were things that only destroyed and killed, with no thought to the pain they caused others. She'd been alone with Christian, joked with him, laughed with him, and he'd never tried to hurt her. He hadn't even made a pass at her, and liked all women, short, tall, thin, thick. He loved women.

And he was lying out there in the freezing cold, bleeding and hurt. Possibly dying.

Jerkily, with fresh tears running down her face, Gwen stood up. Call Connor, he'd said. She could do that.

But when she got to the phone, there was no dial tone. Her attacker hadn't been lying about cutting the line.

With that avenue taken from her, she went to the door. If she helped him, she'd have to get him inside. He couldn't stay in the cold while hurt so badly.

Knowing what she was going to do, she put on her boots and pushed the door open. Christian was exactly where she'd left him, covered with a light dusting of snow.

He didn't move as she stepped close to him. Carefully, she kneeled next to him and with a shaking hand, reached out and laid it on his thick neck where his pulse would be if he were human.

He groaned. Scared, she jerked her hand back and stared down at him. His eyes slitted open, revealing his canine eyes.

"*Go*," he groaned roughly.

Her breathing was too fast and froze in the frigid air, looking like little clouds. She wasn't sure if she'd be able to do it. But somewhere, she found the strength. "I can't lift you," she shivered. "You need to stand and hold onto me to get inside."

His claws scraped at the frozen snow as he realized what she was saying.

"Can you do that?" she asked, her voice quavering.

His muzzle moved in the dark. "Yes."

She reached out, but stopped just shy of touching him. His body was covered in a thick pelt of pale, blond-colored fur. It got shorter on his stomach and around his cock, which was embarrassingly visible. His body was heavily muscled, but it wasn't human muscle, just as his altered bone structure was also foreign and had similarities to wild canines.

Taking a deep breath, she abruptly set her hands on his chest and moved them up to where his front legs/arms met at his shoulders. She tugged and brought him up to a half-reclining position. "Come on," she urged, grunting with strain.

He snarled at her, but she held on, and together, they managed until he was sitting, with his awkwardly bent legs in front of him and his clawed hands wrapped around hers for support.

"Okay," she huffed. "I'm going to pull, and you have to stand. On the count of three."

He howled with pain when she got him up. His weight immediately crashed down on her, and she nearly fell over with it. He had a thick gash across one of his legs, and it bled freshly as he put weight on it. Gwen also got a look at the wound on his side.

It was a bloody mess—the muscle across his ribs and stomach was torn, and strings of tissue hung loosely, dripping blood into his thick fur. The wounds bled sluggishly, but what shocked Gwen was how some of the flesh was already knitting together at the top. Astonished, she realized he was already healing.

"Move!"

She forgot about his wound and concentrated on their most immediate threat, which was the cold. Gwen walked awkwardly with his huge frame pressing down on her like a ton of bricks. He groaned and whined with nearly every step, clearly pained from his wounds.

They made it to the house finally. She had to reach for the door with one hand while she kept the other around Christian's furred middle. Once the door was open, they limped inside.

They walked through the foyer and headed for the living room. Once there, Christian released his grip and fell to the floor. Gwen stared down at him in a daze, noting the blood covering his side and muzzle. In the dark, he could easily have been the creature that caused the crash.

Her legs gave out on her and she slid to the floor, leaning against the couch. Her eyes went over the creatures form, looking for any sign of Christian. In the end, it was his eyes that reassured her, and she held that thought tight, repeating it again and again in her head.

Chapter Six

ഔ

She woke up suddenly, her body screaming in pain. For some reason, her head felt like it was three times the normal size and filled with bricks. Large bricks.

"You look terrible."

She squinted in the dark and saw Christian, lying on his stomach and slightly curled inward. In a flash, the night's events tumbled through her mind and she groaned.

He was no longer covered in fur, but back to his normal form. A deep gash was still evident on his side, but it looked like it was days old, already covered in scabs and healing skin.

He was nude, but didn't seem to be the least bit embarrassed. His eyes were open, and they were plain chocolate brown, just as she remembered.

"Eben's going to have my head when he comes back and sees you like this," he remarked tiredly. "Why the fuck didn't you call them?"

"Phone's out." She tried to sit up and cried out from the pain. For some reason, it felt like someone had taken a whip to her back. "Is that man," she choked over it for a second, "dead?"

"Yes." There was no apology in his eyes.

"Do I really look that bad?" she whispered, lifting her hands to her face. They were bruised, scratched and shaking violently, so she shoved them down into her lap.

"You do. Plus, you're bleeding. I can smell it."

She flinched, thinking about that strange ability, which in turn made her think about what *he was*. Hastily, she reached behind and pulled a blanket off the couch. She spread it across her body and huddled beneath it.

"Yeah," Christian drawled, "that'll make a difference. They'll never notice now."

"Shut up," she breathed.

They both fell silent, waiting. Connor had said they'd be back late, and by Gwen's calculation, it was way past late.

The time crawled by, both of them tense and hurting, anxious for Connor's return. The clock struck 4:00. Minutes after, Christian stiffened, and then Gwen too heard the sound of the front door opening. Her head lolled against the couch cushion and her eyes closed. It was a relief to know help was coming.

"They're like you, aren't they?" she asked on a whisper.

"Yes," Christian replied, just as quietly.

It was a thought that should have frightened. It did frighten her, especially Eben, but it also explained so many things.

There was no sound of running feet, but suddenly they were both there. Connor took one look and kneeled next to Christian with a quiet, controlled, "Damn him to hell." Gwen couldn't tell who he was damning and wasn't in the mood to ask.

"Who?" Eben asked, standing over them. His voice was soft and detached, but his eyes were filled with blazing fire.

"It was Tom," Christian said, his eyes closed and grimacing as he shifted slightly to allow Connor better access to his wounds. "Don't worry, I got him. He's behind the house."

"Is that a bullet in your back?" Connor asked, frowning at the hole in his skin.

"He shot me first." Christian groaned, shuddering as Connor pressed his fingers to the area.

Eben stood over them, breathing far too slowly. He stared into Gwen's eyes as his changed, turning to that of a creature, a werewolf.

"We need to get the bullet out," Connor was saying, worry creasing his face.

"Don't worry about me right now. You need to check on Gwennie. She's bleeding."

Connor's eyes flew to her. "I thought that was you, Christian."

Christian winced and met Eben's eyes. "I failed you, Alpha. I was out for a little while after the bullet got me. He was trying to rape her."

"Was he?" Eben walked around the room, his pale, werewolf eyes moving from his brother to the small, huddled form of Gwen.

Christian smiled in memory. "She kicked him in the balls. He was rolling around screaming when I got him."

"You saved me, Christian," she argued weakly, trying to sit up against the sofa. "He would have gotten me if not for you." And that was something she'd always be grateful for.

Connor moved to her side, his face creased with worry. "I'm going to lift you onto the sofa, and then I need to remove your clothes, okay?"

She was already shaking her head. "He didn't do—" She sighed and tried again. "He didn't finish. I just need help getting up and then I'll be fine."

"I don't know." Connor looked at her worriedly.

"Really," she insisted in a whisper. "I'll be okay as long as I can get to a shower."

Sensing that Connor was going to argue with her, Gwen pushed herself up, hissing from the pain. Places she hadn't realized were hurt suddenly stood up and shouted with pain. Especially her ribs, which she couldn't figure out at all.

She took another deep breath and pushed until she was on her feet. She wobbled a bit before stabilizing herself with a firm hand on the couch.

"I want you to take a sedative before you take a shower," Connor ordered, standing and taking her arm, leading her from the room. "Then you'll sleep, and hopefully escape without any nightmares."

She nodded and let him help her from the room. At the doorway, she turned and looked down at Christian. "Thank you."

He smiled at her weakly. "My pleasure, princess. Now, let Connor take care of you before he has a conniption fit."

Christian waited until they were gone before questioning Eben. "How many challenged you?"

"Three."

"Deaths?"

His eyes slid to his brother. "Two."

He'd been injured. Christian could see the cuts from claws across Eben's cheek, and he could smell the fresh blood on him, even though he'd showered. It didn't matter.

He'd be healed in two days anyway, the wounds no more than a memory.

"What happened to Eben?" Gwen asked, as Connor helped her sit on the toilet in the bathroom. "How'd he get those wounds on his face?"

He turned the shower on and adjusted the temperature. "As you've figured out, we're not exactly human. Eben has taken my place as Lead Alpha of the pack, and he had challengers."

Challengers. Gwen knew he wasn't talking about chess. "Did he win?"

"Sweetheart, Eben doesn't know how to lose." He pulled the curtain closed and turned to her, his face lined with worry. "Do you need help?"

She shook her head. The last thing she wanted was someone taking her clothes away. "I'm fine."

"Just shout if you need anything. I'll hear you."

He closed the door on his way out, and she was finally alone.

The water burned when she first got in. After she got used to it, she scrubbed her body furiously, so hard she was red when she got out, but she needed to clean that man's touch from her body.

After slipping on a heavy set of pajamas, a gift from Connor, she slid into bed, feeling the effects of the sedative he'd insisted on. Her eyes drooped and she let sleep take over.

Chapter Seven

ೲ

Gwen woke up early, feeling groggy from the pills and achy all over. She took another shower and examined her body in detail. Every inch seemed to be covered in a bruise or scrape of some kind, and each one hurt. Her face was a disaster, but her back gave her the most problem. It burned every time she moved her arms.

"I think there's something wrong with my back," she told Connor after finding him in the kitchen. He looked worn and tired, and ten years older than usual.

He nodded and set his coffee cup aside. "You'll need to remove your shirt," he said carefully.

Her heart thumped noisily in her chest. Turning, she hesitantly pulled her shirt off and held it against her chest. With her ribs and back hurt, she hadn't bothered with a bra.

She didn't hear Connor step close, but suddenly he was touching her, his fingers gentle as he felt the tender areas. Even so, it was agonizing, especially when he pulled at the edges of the wound.

"That son of a bitch," he murmured finally, stepping away from her.

"Well?" she asked, turning to him.

"You saw him change, didn't you?" He stood back and stared at the pale expanse of skin revealed to him, crisscrossed with multiple furrows from sharp claws.

Gwen nodded. "When Christian knocked him down, he changed."

"Child," Connor said softly, "he was already partially changed when he was hurting you. He ripped your back up pretty well with his claws."

She paled and gulped. Her voice came out wavering and weak. "Am I going to be like you now?"

He suddenly looked offended. "It's not a communicable disease, Gwen. We're a different species, not a virus. There's nothing that could happen that would change you and make you Were."

"Not even if I was bitten by one of you?"

He snorted. "Of course not. But," he held up a finger, "the wounds need to be cleaned and disinfected. And you could probably use some stitches."

Her breath whooshed out in relief. "I don't care. Do whatever." She smiled and wilted against the kitchen counter, feeling as though a weight had been removed from her shoulders. *Thank God!*

Connor patted her on the head and went to get his supplies.

Twenty minutes later, Gwen was thankful for the local he'd given her and definitely not smiling. She'd had stitches once before when she was ten. A new bike from her father resulted in a deep cut on her chin along with her mother's never-ending wailing and complaining about scars. Gwen did have the scar, but that emergency room visit, where her father had held her on his lap the entire time, was one of her fondest memories. He'd made her laugh even when the doctor came near with the needle.

She winced and sucked in a breath, returning to the present when she felt Connor jab the needle through her skin and pull the threads. "Ow."

"Sorry, dear. Just another few — I'm actually quite good at this, you know. Between the two boys, I've had quite a lot of practice."

"What, you guys don't like hospitals? There all sorts of funny stuff in your blood that would raise the proverbial red flag?" She shifted slightly in the chair, and felt the tug of the thread again. Ick.

Connor's fingers moved nimbly against her back. "We don't exactly have a local emergency room around here. We're a bit far out for that. And since we do keep our existence unknown among the humans, obviously it's quite a bit easier to do without putting evidence in the hands of those who would most like to know. Scientists, doctors. That type. Wouldn't you agree?"

"Why do you do that?" she asked curiously. "The hiding thing, I mean?"

"There was a time, just several hundred years ago in fact, when our kind was unfairly persecuted. Along with others, I might add. Our numbers decreased substantially. It's safer for us this way. We blend well with humans."

He snipped the last of the thread and set the needle aside. "You'll need to be careful not to pull it," he ordered, taking out a stack of gauze pads and tape and covering the worst of the wounds. "We can remove the stitches in a week and a half or so, and then you should heal as good as new."

Gwen nodded. She slipped off the stool, her shirt still held over her chest, and turned to question him about showers. Instead, she saw Eben standing in the doorway, and her questions died in her throat, forgotten. She immediately flushed and turned her back to him. "Do you *mind*?" She jerked her shirt over her head and shoved her arms through, trying to hide as much as she could manage.

Connor lifted his head from his medicine supply bag, but said nothing. Eben left the doorway and walked into the kitchen, his body relaxed and flowing with the movement. "I told you to stay in the house."

With all her parts covered, she turned around and glared, not even bothering to hide her irritation. "If I hadn't, Christian could very easily have died."

"I gave you an order, Gwen." he said softly, leaning down so she couldn't avoid him. "And you agreed to follow it."

"I'm not your responsibility." She folded her arms over her chest and moved her eyes to the refrigerator. It was pale, beige maybe, and it wasn't towering over her angrily, so it was a big improvement over Eben. "And I'm not a child." She looked over at Conner, who was standing helplessly, a slightly worried expression on his face. "Tell him."

But Conner only shrugged. "He is Alpha, Gwen. By that alone, you are his responsibility."

"Traitor," she muttered.

He smiled and left the kitchen, his supplies in hand.

Eben moved in front of her, and again filled her line of vision. He was so still and silent it was alarming. He leaned in, his mouth so close to her ear she felt the warmth of his breath. "You're wrong," he whispered.

His response only served to increase her ire. "I'm twenty-two years old," she spat at him, glaring because she shouldn't have to deal with him. "I'm smart and capable, and I *don't* need anyone else telling me what to do! I'm sick of that shit."

He straightened and backed up until he was leaning almost lazily against the counter, with his arms crossed over his chest and his head lowered slightly, staring at her from under his brow.

"You don't know what you're doing, little girl."

Feeling mutinous, Gwen tossed her hair over her shoulder and flipped up her middle finger. "Kiss my ass. I'm out of here."

She was all prepared to stomp off from her first honest-to-God fight, with Eben, no less, gloriously triumphant. And she would have, if he hadn't grabbed her and dragged her back, anchoring her back gently against his chest.

"What are you doing?" She pulled away, or tried to, and didn't budge an inch. He growled. She stilled her struggles the moment the animal sound came from his chest. She'd almost forgotten, and wanted to kick herself for it. She *had* to remember they weren't human, weren't even close. They were werewolves, monsters, known to kill and destroy without a thought, even if none of them had hurt her.

"I want to leave," she said stiffly.

His arms tightened around her, pulling her lower body tighter against him. "Where's the fear, Gwen?" he asked in his crisply accented voice. "You should be scared, baby girl, because you're not going to like this one bit."

She stiffened against him, and suddenly her blood ran cold. "Don't hurt me."

He smiled against her hair, inhaling her scent deeply. "I'd never. That's not what I want from you."

She looked over her shoulder at him, and shuddered. He was so close, close enough to see the way his eyes were liquid blue and changing, close enough to see the fine lines in his dark skin, and close enough to see the slight points of his canines when he spoke. "I don't think my disobeying you warrants this type of punishment. Can't you pretend I'm sorry and go on your way?"

He actually smiled, and it was devastating. Devilish. Wicked. Sexy. "Don't you want to know why I chose you? Chose you from the hospital?"

She shook her head. "No. Not at all."

He ignored her refusal and continued, a bitter smile tingeing his words with resentment. "Christian was locked up there, caught in a park when the moon was near full. He found your drawing, and I needed to see you, to know if you were a threat to my people. And you are, Gwen."

She remained silent against him, completely unmoving in his arms but her heart going a hundred miles an hour. It was beating so hard she could feel the pulses in her neck. "I'm not a threat. I promise I won't tell anyone."

"But you already did." Languidly, he splayed his palm across her stomach, kneading her flesh gently, and it only made her nervousness worse. She wanted to wiggle away from it, and did for a second, but stopped when she felt the large bulge at her back, hard and insistent in his jeans. "Um, Eben…"

His voice dropped an octave. "You told as soon as you were found and taken to the hospital. You told your mother, doctors, everyone. You even drew pictures to show them, and that I can't have. My people's lives depend on secrecy, and you were destroying that."

She began panting as she realized what he was saying. "So you're going to kill me?"

"I wish I could," he murmured, lowering his mouth to the side of her neck, letting his lips brush her soft skin in a small kiss. She shivered in reaction, and he smiled. "I wanted to, but there's another problem."

She waited on tenterhooks, wanting him to finish, but he just stood behind her, his hand lowering gradually over her tummy. His hips arched against her, and he groaned, making her twitch in his grasp.

"What are you doing?" she whispered harshly, her fear dropping back for a minute as she tried to figure him out. He looked like an axe murderer, all dark and dangerous. He could probably even use one of the ones hanging on his wall. "Eben..."

His mouth stayed against her skin. "I want you, baby. Badly. I wanted to fuck you the second I saw you in the hospital. You were sick and weak, and I still wanted you, even then."

Her eyes widened in shock and her knees almost gave out. Her head snapped around. "You don't even *like* me!" she hissed. "You can't stand even being in the same room with me!" It couldn't be. *It made no sense!* She tried to turn her body, and he let her, although he still kept her pressed against him. Facing him, she shook her head slowly. *"What's wrong with you?"*

He took her hand in his and jerked it down his body, pushing her palm flat against the thick ridge in his jeans and holding it there. She tried to tug away but he held her firm. He spoke through clenched teeth, his voice deep and lethal. "I get hard every time I'm near you, Gwen. And it *hurts.*"

She shook her head again, not wanting to believe him. "So, what? You're mean to me? You're rude? Eben, people don't do that!"

"It's not easy for me," he bit out.

Gwen clamped her mouth shut, her eyes narrowing slightly. It wasn't an answer. It was an excuse, and a bad one. Finally, she asked, "What do you expect of me?"

He dropped her hand and let his palms rest on her hips, tucking her right against his swollen flesh. Gently, he rolled his hips and moaned at the sweet agony of it. "You're mine, Gwen," he growled, letting his head fall toward her as he manipulated her body. "Christian and Connor know, my pack knows, and I know. You *are* mine." He punctuated his words with a hard pull of her hips, thrusting in time with them.

Gwen's breath stopped in her lungs with the movement. A coil of heat like nothing she'd felt before pooled low in her groin, and she wanted it to stop, needed it to stop. "So you want me to have sex with you."

His dark hair rested against his forehead, blue-black and slightly wavy, so thick she wanted to run her hands through it. "Not sex, Gwen. I want to fuck. Hard, soft, any way I can. I want to lick you everywhere. I want your lips around my cock. I want it *all*."

His words made the heat worse. It built in her and mixed with the fear, sending little waves all through her body. Her legs were weak, and her breasts ached. Her nipples felt like small, burning points. She gulped for breath and looked at him steadily. "What if I don't want any of that?"

His smile was mocking. "I can smell your arousal. You can't lie to me, Gwen."

"Oh God." Blood flooded her face in embarrassment. "I need to go. Please let me go."

"You disobeyed me," he whispered against her ear. His tongue darted out and swiped against her lobe, the motion so quick she wasn't quite sure she'd even felt it. "You destroyed any trust we were building, and you will pay for that."

His arms loosened. Panicked, Gwen darted away and leaned against the wall, her chest rising and falling rapidly. As she watched him, Eben reached down and adjusted the large bulge of his cock within his jeans. He gave it a firm caress before walking around the counter and pulling a bottle of water from the fridge.

He swallowed and she watched the thick line of his throat, saw his muscles flex. He finished the bottle in a few more swallows and set it on the counter. Then he turned back to her.

His pale eyes blazed, and she realized how angry he really was. He was dangerous, vengeful and just plain pissed. "I'm moving your things into my rooms. You'll spend your nights there, in my bed. I want your scent thick there, Gwen."

She looked away from him, needing to focus on something inanimate. She picked the basket of fruit, arranged artfully by Connor just that morning. "Like I said," she breathed, trying to keep her voice steady and methodical, "I'm not your responsibility, and I don't belong to you. If you'll excuse me…" She stepped from the room, every muscle in her body shivering and twitching. She was absolutely terrified. At least, she hoped that's what it was.

Connor looked up from his book when he heard Gwen exit the kitchen. She went right past and didn't even see him.

When Eben followed a minute later, he stared in the direction Gwen had gone. He didn't look pleased.

Conner asked, "Did you tell her?"

"No."

He sighed and laid his book aside. "Are you going to?"

Eben turned and came into the living room. He sat in the chair across from Connor and leaned forward, his elbows on his knees and his head bowed. He sighed and said quietly, "No."

"She has to know she's your mate."

His head rose. He stared at Connor, his eyes filled with angst, guilt and determined ruthlessness. "Not until I've had her."

Connor shook his head. "Eben—"

"She'll run from me," he said sharply, angrily. "If I tell her before, she'll try and leave me."

"She may try that anyway," Connor said simply, but he gave up and went back to his book. "Just be honest, Eben. You'll gain more from that than from withholding the truth."

"I'll try," was all he said.

Gwen hid out in the barn. It seemed like the safest place, considering, and she figured the horses would give her the heads-up if he tried to corner her there.

Christian was already busy feeding the horses. He moved stiffly, especially when using his right arm.

"How are you feeling?" she asked, closing the door firmly behind her. Two of the horses raised their heads in their stalls, saw her, and went back to munching contentedly.

He leaned on the pitchfork he was using and studied her. "Christ, I'm fine. How the fuck are *you*? You look like hell."

She smiled and shrugged. "Connor gave me an ibuprofen, and that helped with the swelling. We did stitches this morning, but otherwise I'm okay." She shrugged again, the resulting pull of the stitches reminding her to be careful.

He shook his head and went back to slowly cleaning stalls. "I'm surprised Eben let you out of the house like that. Thomas is lucky he's dead. Eben would have ripped his spine out and skinned him alive."

Somehow, Gwen didn't think Christian was teasing. "Actually, I kind of left the house without telling. I needed to get out."

He looked over at her, one eyebrow raised. "He's going to kick your ass when he finds you." He tossed a forkful of soiled straw toward the wheelbarrow, then halted for a minute. "You need to be careful with him, Gwen. He's not like the rest of us."

She studied her hands carefully, noticing the jagged edges of her nails. "Do you mean like a human, or like what you guys are?"

"We're Weres. Not monsters or werewolves, but Weres, and judging by the pictures you've drawn, you've seen at least one of us before. Not many of us would do what Thomas did to you."

"What's wrong with werewolf?"

He narrowed his eyes at her. "Would you like to be named after some silly creature that has no sense or intelligence, and seems to always chase after the pretty, vapid girl and get nailed with a silver bullet, which by the way, doesn't work at all. Have you seen any of the movies, or read the stories? Each one of them makes us either into a cannibalistic beast, or a paranoid freak covered in lots of hair, with a perpetual hard-on."

"So you call yourselves Weres," Gwen intoned. "Isn't it just semantics?"

Christian raked fresh straw into the stall as he continued. "So what if it is? We are what we are, and we'll be called what we want to be called. We're pretty simple creatures, Gwennie. We like a good hunt, a good run and a good fuck. In our pelts, we're likely to chase you down if you run, but after that you'd probably be left alone, if a little bruised. That's the animal instinct in us, so remember that if you're faced with one of us after the change. We're like humans in a lot of ways, hon. There are bad Weres, just as there are bad people."

"Which one is Eben?"

He looked over at her, his eyes darkening slightly. "He's a bit of both, and that's what makes him so strong."

She groaned and dropped her head into her hands. "I'm in trouble, then."

Christian smiled at her sadly. She was such a young, inexperienced woman. "Yeah, you are."

She made Christian go to the house first and call the barn, just to make sure Eben was in his shop. He laughed at her, but she ignored him, more interested in avoiding another confrontation than anything else.

It wasn't that she wasn't interested in his offer, because there was a part of her that definitely *was*. Actually, a large part. But what would she do once she was in his bed? Her mother had accused her of being a slut from the time she had her first period. The last thing she wanted to do was prove her right.

She skipped dinner and spent the time in the studio drawing scenes of Christian, his body reshaped into that of his Were form. She also drew a sketch of the man who'd attacked her, Thomas, in the middle of his change, with his bones at awkward angles and his face frozen in pain.

When she went downstairs a few hours later, all was quiet. Connor read in his leather chair, every now and then reaching over for the glass of brandy at his side. He didn't even look up when she came down the stairs.

She was more than ready for bed. Her jaw throbbed, her back ached, and all she wanted was her own personal sanctuary of peace and quiet. And sleep. Lots of sleep.

When she got to her bedroom, her jaw flopped open. She couldn't even manage to gasp or shriek as she stared at her empty room, devoid of even proper sheets and blankets.

"That bastard," she finally whispered. She rushed through the room, pulling open drawers and cabinets, each one empty of her possessions. He'd even taken her shampoo from the shower.

She did a small twirl around the room. It was like it had never been hers. Not even a sock was left behind.

She stood in the room for several minutes fuming, unsure what to do, her hands clenching over and over again. She couldn't confront him, he'd have her hauled into his bed in a minute flat, and that wasn't something she was ready to tackle. She was best off avoiding him completely and handling the situation on her own.

She said nothing to Connor as she crossed the living room and stole a towel from his bathroom, but his eyes twinkled as he followed her march through the living room, which only made her irritation worse. Just to be bitchy, she also picked up the blanket from the sofa, daring him to say anything.

She showered quickly, afraid Eben would barge in at any moment. When she was done, she wrapped herself in the stolen blanket and lay on the bare mattress. It felt strange and a little scratchy, but she clenched her jaw and made herself relax. She was getting stronger, day by day, and she refused to give in. Minutes later, she fell asleep with the image of Eben, shirtless, in her mind.

Connor wasn't surprised when Eben came downstairs after midnight, a scowl on his face.

"Where is she?"

He nodded his chin toward her room. "There. She snagged the blanket from the sofa." He smiled at the memory of Gwen stomping through the living room, her jaw set.

Eben ran a hand over his hair, pushing it back from his forehead. He was shirtless, but wore a loose pair of pajama bottoms that hung around his muscular waist, hanging off his hipbones. He slept nude, but he was obviously making an effort not to scare his human mate.

He sighed and scratched absently at his chest. "Hell, she's becoming more rebellious every day."

Connor flipped the page of his book, his eyes sparkling merrily. "She's comfortable, Eben. Probably for the first time in her life."

Eben turned toward her room and halted. His shoulders stiffened as he asked, "Am I wrong to want her so badly?"

Connor's book lowered as he too remembered what it was like, finding the woman that both parts wanted, the man and the beast, with equal measure. It was a need, violent and pure, but so strong it was frightening at times. Especially when it was for a human. "I don't know. I truly don't know, Eben."

A minute later, Eben came through the living room, holding Gwen's blanket-wrapped form. She snuggled into his bare chest, completely oblivious to the tension she was creating.

"Good night," Eben murmured, going up the steps as silently as he'd come down.

"Good night," Connor whispered. "And sweet dreams."

Chapter Eight

ဢ

Gwen woke with a stretch and a happy sigh. Any night without nightmares was a blessing, and she took each one as a gift from God. She'd feared that after the attack, her nightmares would return with a vengeance, the two memories merging together to create an entirely new and terrifying version, but they hadn't.

She blinked her eyes open and stared up at the ceiling. After a few seconds, she cocked her head and stared harder. She didn't have a ceiling fan in her room, yet one was above her head.

Sitting up slightly, she studied the room. It was larger than hers, and there weren't any bookshelves lining the walls. There were two windows in this room, both large and looking out onto the forest. A wooden rocking chair sat next to one of them, and a heavy wooden dresser next to the other. The bed dominated the room—it was huge, with tall posts at each corner and thick, fluffy blankets covering it, which only made it seem even bigger. Eben lay beside her, sprawled out on his stomach, all dark skin and muscle. And tattoos, she noticed.

They were thick and black, Celtic in design. They ran around his upper arms and joined in the center of his back, running down his spine in a spiraled pattern, and eventually tapering midway down. She missed them in the forge because it was just too dark and dingy.

Bloody hell," she muttered, scrubbing her hand over her face, then wincing as she rubbed too hard across her

111

jaw. She'd been so proud of herself, outwitting him at his own game. And in the end, it turned out she hadn't.

She moved the covers and prepared to slip out, the rustle of them sounding noisy in the quiet of the room.

"Going somewhere?"

She halted with the sheets pulled up partially. Her eyes closed and she pursed her lips, sighing. "I'm getting up."

He rolled toward her, dragging the blankets and sheets with him. He rested against the pillows with his hands behind his head, his chest bare in the weak light. She immediately felt breathless.

"You slept well." His eyes traced the bare skin of her shoulders and back.

With a huff, she leaned forward against her knees and wrapped her arms around them, hiding her nudity as best she could. "Where are my clothes?"

"Here," he rumbled. "Some in the closet and the rest in the dresser. Why are you nervous, Gwen?"

She shook her head over the quick subject change. "I wake up in a bed that's not mine, nude, with a man I don't know very well who until eighteen hours ago, I thought didn't like me very much. Gee, I wonder what could possibly make me nervous. I want my clothes."

He blinked lazily, his lashes looking impossibly dark against his pale eyes. "Then go get them." A slow, lazy smile bloomed on his face, and she suddenly became breathless. Good lord he was beautiful.

"I don't have anything on." She glanced down at her bare skin, flushing slightly.

He rolled to his side and propped himself on his elbow. His other hand came over and latched around her neck, pulling her face down toward his. "I'll bargain with you," he whispered, his lips against her neck. "I'll get your robe, but I want something in return."

Gwen shivered at the determination in his eyes and voice. "I'm not having sex with you for my robe," she said stiffly, trying to pull away from him.

He laughed softly, the sound low and smooth. It soaked into her skin and left her hot and agitated.

"No, baby. That will come later, after your stitches are out. What I want right now, is a kiss." He pressed a soft kiss to her neck and brushed his nose against her skin, the caress so soft Gwen couldn't help closing her eyes and shuddering. "Will you do it?"

She opened her eyes and looked around the room again. There were no shirts or clothes left on the floor or hanging from the door knob, so she'd have to scramble until she found something she could throw on, which could take several minutes, and that would be embarrassing. *Dignity is everything when that's all you've got.*

"How old are you?" she breathed, the question popping out of nowhere.

He stopped moving against her for a second, his hand flexing around her neck. There was no seduction in his voice as he asked, "Why?"

She nervously shrugged and kept her eyes glued on the darkness of the far wall. "I'm twenty-two. I was wondering because I think you're probably a lot older than me, and I'm not really sure if this is such a good idea. The differences..." She shook her head slightly, rather dramatically, she thought, and cut off her rambling. The "a lot older" comment was harsh, but she was in trouble. This was a war, after all, and she needed to bring out the big guns.

"Do you think I'll let you go because you find my age unacceptable?" His eyes grew chilly as he stared at her, one eyebrow raised. "I won't, Gwen."

She looked away from him.

"Now," he said, "answer me on our bargain."

She opened her mouth for a second, and almost backed down just from the tinge of bitterness in his tone. But she was a new woman, a strong woman, learning new things every day and living a new life. She refused to give up the precious little bravery she actually possessed.

It came out soft and breathy, more from wariness than true fear. "How old are you, Eben?"

His jaw tensed and the temperature in the room seemed to drop ten degrees. Gwen had to exercise restraint just to keep from rubbing warmth into her arms.

The tension was terrible in the silence, like waiting for a bomb to explode.

"Fuck it," he muttered, tugging her toward him, the movement angry. "I deserve this." And his mouth crashed down on hers.

He wasn't gentle as his lips opened and his tongue plunged into her mouth, petting and licking, determined to wring a response from her.

She gasped and pushed at his shoulders but he didn't budge. Instead, he pulled her more tightly against him, rubbing her nude body against his chest. His hands softly traced her spine down to her buttocks, and rolled her hips against his blanket-covered groin. He rolled to his back and pulled her on top of him.

Gwen was in a daze, not sure what to do, not sure what she could do, but sure she didn't want it to stop. His mouth was magic, driving thoughts from her head and making her so wild she wasn't sure it was healthy. He growled and nipped at her, traced the interior of her mouth with his tongue, and forced her to give more.

He pulled his mouth away, just enough to growl out, "Put your tongue in my mouth, Gwen."

He dragged his tongue from her collarbone up her throat, laving little circles into her skin. She groaned and arched her neck, wanting more. At her jaw, he gave special attention to the bruises before returning to her mouth and plunging in.

She responded in kind and tried to follow his movements. Embarrassment wasn't even an option for her, he simply didn't give her any time for it to catch. She was too busy sucking on his tongue and licking over his bottom lip.

"Do you want me to stop?" he asked, panting heavily. His hands cupped her breasts, kneading and brushing against her nipples which seemed to send fire straight to her groin.

She rolled her head back and tried to think and breathe at the same time, but it was so hard. Every movement he made against her was torture. It was like having a rubber band in her abdomen, pulled taught and just waiting to be released, and the tighter it went, the less air she was able to suck into her lungs.

"No," she breathed.

His hand drifted from her right breast, down over her stomach, and slid between her legs for just a minute. His finger rubbed gently on her clit, making her want to scream.

"Now you know how I am, every day, waiting for you," he growled, pressing a quick kiss to her forehead and rolling her carefully off him.

She lay on her side, panting and in need. *He was stopping now? The son of a bitch.* She was dying. She had to be, because there was no other explanation for the heat that was racing through her body, burning her alive.

"That was cruel." She sat up in the bed. Glancing down, she jerked the blankets up, covering her breasts.

Eben stood in the room, completely nude and so beautiful it almost hurt to see him. His legs were long and smooth, thick with muscle at the hip and thigh. His stomach was corded and ridged, full of tension. He had no body hair, except what was on his head. It made Gwen pause in her examination of him—he was completely smooth, all over. But it was his cock that finally took her attention.

It bobbed heavily in the cool air, the tip deep purple and shiny with his fluids, slightly bulbous compared to the thick length below. He was long, dark and thick, and the sight of it scared the lust right out of her.

Eben's nose flared slightly, scenting her fear, and then his eyes warmed slightly. "It'll fit, Gwen. I promise."

"Are you sure? That doesn't look quite...normal." She winced.

"For a Were, it's normal."

He went to the bathroom and came out holding her terry cloth robe. She extended her arm from the covers and took it from him, making sure to keep her eyes politely downcast. "Thank you."

He stayed by her side and ignored her discomfort. His hand cupped her jaw and turned her face toward him. "I want you to look at me," he said darkly, his eyes pale and intense. "I need it, Gwen, just as I need to look at you."

"No. I don't think so."

He bent toward her. "Let me convince you." His mouth touched hers again, this time gently, coaxing her to respond with each thrust of his tongue. It took disgustingly little.

She moaned and dropped the robe, shuddering as his mouth went to her neck, sucking and biting at the soft skin there.

He pulled away finally, staring with satisfaction at the marks on her neck. He pulled the blankets from her body and picked up the robe, holding it out toward her. "Come," he ordered roughly.

She shivered in the chilly morning air. Seeing no way to win, she slipped from the bed, her whole body flushed with embarrassment.

He held the robe open as she slid her arms in, then pulled her hair away as she knotted the tie at her waist.

"You're very lovely."

She shrugged and kept her back to him, wishing she could be modern and strong about this rather than embarrassed. Maybe she'd get there eventually. No doubt, he'd offer her assistance in the endeavor.

He turned her around and tilted her chin up. Gwen refused to meet his eyes, instead choosing to stare at his chin.

"I'll be in the forge. I'll see you tonight." He pressed a kiss to her forehead and went to the dresser, pulling out clothes and dressing quickly. Just before he closed the door behind him, he turned back and bit out, "Thirty-five."

She stayed where she was for nearly ten minutes after he was gone. Then, with a sigh, Gwen collapsed onto the bed and admitted to herself that she was in serious trouble. And why didn't that scare her quite as much as it should?

She stayed busy the entire day. She volunteered to clean all the horse stalls herself, ignoring Christian's arguments about her stitches. She needed the activity, desperately. It was either get drop-dead tired, or lust all day after a man she wasn't even supposed to like.

After the stalls, she swept the barn and scrubbed water pails. When everything was done in the barn, she moved onto the storage shed, rearranging and organizing everything, throwing out old paint cans and boxes that were wet with frost and mold.

"What is she doing out there?" Connor asked Christian, staring through the window at the old shed where all the activity was occurring.

Christian sighed and watched through the window as she rolled an ancient bicycle through the door, leaning it against the wall. "She's trying to forget about Eben."

"This should be interesting," Connor commented. .

Christian agreed wholeheartedly.

When she came in later, Connor didn't waste any time in admonishing her.

"You tore your stitches," he complained heatedly, glaring at her from the kitchen. "I can smell the blood all the way over here, Gwen."

"Like I care," she muttered under her breath, throwing her jacket down.

He raised his eyebrows and folded his arms over his chest. "Come in here. I'll be with you in a minute."

She glowered but stomped over and hunkered down on a stool. Shaking his head, Connor went and retrieved his bag of medical supplies, and came in to find her glaring at the sink.

She winced through the process of cleaning the wounds and reapplying bandages. "It's your own fault," he grumbled. "I don't have to re-stitch them, but you pulled the threads." He finished bandaging and taping everything and then stood back to admire his work.

"Since I can't trust you, you're going to have to stay in the house until this properly heals m'dear. I'm sorry, but you don't want the mess torn stitches can cause. It's a nasty business, and I'd like you to have as few scars as possible."

Connor watched as she hopped from the stool and clomped toward her room. A minute later, a loud "*Damn it!*" echoed through the first floor.

Christian came to the door of the kitchen and looked in. "What happened?"

Connor smiled as he tossed the pieces of bloody gauze into the trash. "She forgot he moved her things into his room."

Christian laughed.

The next week went by too quickly for Gwen, mostly because she was so busy avoiding Eben. She kept to herself, staying mostly in the studio, working on anything to keep her mind occupied. As he'd promised, Connor refused to let her go to the barn, or anywhere else unless she gave him a full report of her activities. It was irritating, but she didn't grumble about it, excusing his behavior as a byproduct of worry.

She saw little of anyone, and she liked it that way. There was too much tension in the air, and it only gave her a stomach ache. The only part of her day she was forced to interact with everyone was during dinner, and that was chaperoned, although it did little good. Eben wasn't shy about his lust and desires. They were there in his eyes for anyone to see.

In an effort to avoid any more embarrassing confrontations, Gwen fell asleep on the couch every night after dinner. Her original hope was that he'd leave her there for the night. When that didn't pan out, she took comfort from the fact that she slept through him gathering her up and taking her to his room. And her mornings ended up being okay too, since he got up earlier.

With that major worry out of her hair, she devoted her extra time to the computer Connor had in his studio. It was a small laptop hooked up to a satellite online service. It was filled with graphics programs, as well as word processing and other office tools, but what interested her most was the Internet.

Although she certainly wasn't going to admit it to anyone else, it bothered her that she hadn't finished high school. She felt stupid not having that little piece of paper, even though she knew that was silly. So, she looked up GED programs, and then online college courses and vocational schools. In for a penny, in for a pound, and all that. Besides, she needed to be self-sufficient and independent, and school was the only way to get that done. After all, she wouldn't be able to accept Connor's charity forever.

"You're thinking about something," Connor murmured, as he carefully snipped the stitches from her back.

Gwen rolled her shoulders and winced as he pulled the threads out. "I was looking up stuff on getting my GED."

He paused and stared at her over her shoulder, a smile wreathing his face. "I think that would be marvelous. I'm quite sure I still have some of the materials from when Eben did his. They should be in the den somewhere." He frowned in thought, "Or maybe the basement," and went back to pulling stitches.

"Eben didn't finish school either?" she asked curiously.

"Dear," he said, finally finishing up and dabbing the small holes with alcohol. "He was fifteen when I found him, and hadn't attended school a day of his life. I couldn't see enrolling him in a normal school. He had difficulties adjusting to just having a home and wouldn't have fit at all well into the regimen of school, so I hired him a tutor. When he was ready, he took the exams and he passed." He smiled at her as he closed his supply bag and set it to the side. "I'm surprised you didn't take the test in the hospital. Don't they encourage that sort of thing?"

Gwen tugged her shirt down and stood in front of him awkwardly, trying to come up with a way to explain her situation without making herself appear stupid. "Actually, they did, but I had another problem. I don't read very well." She smiled uneasily. "And with the drugs and everything—well, it was difficult."

He folded his arms across his chest. "Explain about the reading."

"I'm dyslexic. I've had problems all my life so." She shrugged again, at a loss. "Dad had it too. It drove mom nuts because she had to go over pageant speeches with me and read everything until I memorized it."

He tossed the soiled gauze in the trash and wiped the counter. "I think one of the pack members is a teacher. I'll ask him and see if he can help."

Gwen's eyes widened in alarm. "God, please don't do that. I'd kind of like to keep it private, if that's okay."

"Gwen," he sighed, exasperated. "These are very nice people. Any one of them would be pleased to help you in any way they could."

"Please," she begged softly, desperate. "I'm not ready to go for help yet. I'd like to try by myself for a little while."

His eyes were steady, letting her know he didn't like it. "You'll ask *me* for help if you need it," he said sternly, the picture of a concerned father.

She nodded and breathed out a sigh of relief. "Absolutely."

Later, at dinner, Connor said to Eben, "Do you remember where your high-school equivalency materials are?"

"In the office, I think. Why?"

Gwen dropped her fork and wanted to melt under the table as Connor cavalierly replied, "Gwen wants to get hers, and I thought your materials might help her study."

Eben's eyes swiveled to her. Gwen prayed for death.

"I'll find them," he promised.

They went out running after dinner. Gwen raised her head from the couch to see Christian and Eben at the door, both of them just wearing jeans.

"We'll be back later," Christian called, giving her a little wave as he went through the door.

Eben only stared at her before ducking out, his eyes heated.

She waited for a minute, letting the quiet close over her and Connor, who was reading beside the fire.

"Are they going to—change?"

"Yes." He flipped a page.

She watched a movie and for the first time in over a week, felt relaxed enough to enjoy her evening. There was no thought to avoiding Eben's advances or ignoring her own feelings. She was able to just sit back and enjoy her movie with no concerns.

Halfway through, a loud howl split the night. Connor raised his head, his eyes getting a faraway look as he stared through the window at the woods just beyond.

"Why don't you go out?" she questioned, the look of wanting in his eyes hitting her hard.

He smiled at her and raised his book again. "One of us needs to stay with you, Gwen. There are some out there who will try to hurt you just to get to Eben."

She absently ran her fingers over the buttons of the remote, feeling the difference in texture between the smooth plastic and the rubber buttons. "Is that why that other man hurt me?"

He looked over at her. "We don't know. He was dead by the time we got home, remember?"

She pursed her lips, going over that night and wondering if she should ask the question flying through her head. After peeking a few glances at him, she finally did, making sure her voice stayed light and absent of worry. "Who's Theron?"

His book slid down again, but this time there was no mistaking the demand in his eyes. "Why do you ask?"

"You guys say his name a lot and I was just wondering." She stared at the carpet and hoped she sounded convincing enough.

Connor didn't relax and tilted his head to the side. "You're lying," he murmured. "I can smell it."

"Who is he?"

Connor's eyes became just as cold as Eben's just before he went back to his book. "He's a Were who thinks to challenge Eben for control of the pack."

Gwen mulled over the information, chewing her lip in thought. Eben had told her everyone knew she belonged to him. Apparently, he wasn't kidding.

"Where did you really hear the name, Gwen?"

She could see how much he wanted the information, but it worried her. Christian had killed Thomas, protecting her from his attack. Theron, even if he'd convinced the other man to take her, hadn't really done anything wrong, and she wasn't sure if she could live with his death on her hands, all because of something she possibly could have misinterpreted. "From you guys," she said finally. "Really."

His expression said he was skeptical. "I'm going to tell Eben you asked. He'll insist on questioning you," he warned.

Her heart plummeted but she didn't back down. "I'm not lying."

He smirked at his book, the hard look in his eyes finally dissipating. "Sure you are, love."

She fell asleep with no difficulties, but woke up just a few hours later, starved.

She tiptoed downstairs, checking carefully to make sure there were no threatening, furry bodies prowling around. When she was sure the coast was clear, she went to the kitchen and started digging.

Connor had plenty of goodies in his cupboard, along with some stuff that was just gross. Caviar? Goose liver pate? She'd rather carve out her own eyeball. After careful consideration, she went with the chocolate, marshmallows and graham crackers. She hadn't had a s'more in years, and they were suddenly calling her name.

She weighed the advantages and disadvantages of both the microwave and the stove as heating options, and settled on the stove so she could have a crispy, golden-brown marshmallow rather than just a melted one.

In one of the drawers, she found a beat-up fork and stabbed her two marshmallows down on the tines firmly. Connor insisted on using real silver at meals, and she hated to use one of his pretty forks for heating up her marshmallows on the stove, not sure how the silver would react to the gas stove's flame.

The first marshmallows went up in flames and became a sticky, charred mess. But the second set didn't do so badly, although it took a little bit of maneuvering to get all sides properly browned. Getting the marshmallows onto the graham proved equally as tricky, but she managed and only burned her finger once. She added the chocolate and gently pressed down with the other graham.

She took a bite and moaned in joy. Although it was a slightly juvenile treat, it was terribly good, far better than something as simple as cracker, marshmallow and chocolate had a right to be.

She was in the middle of roasting the next batch when the front door pushed open. Christian came in, a sleepy smile on his face, followed closely by Eben.

It took her a second to spot the difference in him. He was relaxed, his movements slow and lazy even, like a cat waking up from a long nap. The whole week he'd nearly hummed with pent-up energy, and now it was gone, leaving just him, lethargic and at ease.

They both turned toward her at the same time. "Marshmallow's burning," Christian blurted.

She returned her attention back to her roasting marshmallows, only to find them flaming.

"Damn it!" She pulled them away from the flame of the stove quickly and blew out the fire. A small trail of smoke rose up from the charred lumps, heading right for the smoke alarm. "Shit!"

Grabbing the nearest towel, she started waving it through the air, biting her lip and praying. *Please, please, please, don't go off!* Not like this, not in front of him!

Christian glanced sadly at the charred marshmallow. "Well, since there's no chance I'm eating that, I guess I can go to bed. Good luck." He smiled and winked at Eben before loping off toward the stairs.

Gwen abandoned her towel, feeling relatively certain she'd made a big enough fool of herself. Plus, the alarms weren't blaring, which was the *only* thing going right for her. With her jaw clenched, she cleaned up the mess she'd just made and tried not to feel nervous with Eben watching her so intently. After throwing the other lumpy mess into the trash, she stabbed another set of marshmallows onto her fork and held it over the flames of the stove. She didn't take her eyes off them for a second.

"I take it you had a nice time out there." She pulled the marshmallows up and made sure everything was golden brown before turning off the stove.

Eben leaned against the doorway of the kitchen, his head tilting as she slid the marshmallows off the tines and onto a graham cracker. Like a chef admiring her work, she gave them a little pat with the top graham, squishing them just slightly before sliding a piece of chocolate in between.

"You know," Gwen said as she turned toward him, her s'more in hand, marshmallow oozing out from the crackers. "It's really your fault the other one burned, which is why I'm not going to give you this one. That's your punishment." She took a big bite out of it and chewed thoughtfully. "The marshmallows wouldn't have burned at all if not for you." She popped the rest of it in her mouth and dusted off her hands. Excellent.

"Sweetheart," he stepped fully into the room and poked at her s'more supplies, "what is it you're eating?"

"A s'more." She chugged down half a glass of milk which she'd had on the counter, handy whenever eating anything with chocolate. When she set the glass aside, he was still looking at the marshmallow and crackers as if he didn't quite get it. "Please tell me you've had one."

"I haven't."

Which should have been impossible, except he hadn't grown up where she had. In fact, he'd lived on the streets until he was nearly an adult, she reminded herself. He'd probably nearly starved more than once and had to steal his clothes. Deprived — that's what he was.

Businesslike, Gwen flipped the stove back on and reopened the bag of marshmallows. "This, I can fix."

She laid the two marshmallows out on the counter, got the pieces of graham cracker and the wedge of chocolate ready, and put everything down in order. "The proper way to do it is over a campfire or grill. However, a good stove will work in a pinch. Why don't you come and stand here, and I'll coach you on the proper way to roast marshmallows."

"There's a proper way?"

"Of course. You do it wrong and you have melted marshmallow all over." Her skin prickled as he moved closer. When she saw that he was smiling, her heart sped up. "You're laughing at me."

He dutifully took the fork and marshmallows from her. "I like it when you're bossy," he said, his voice all deep and gravelly. "What is it I'm to do with this?"

"Like you don't know. Put the marshmallows on the fork. But do it through the ends, so they don't slip off when they're melted. Let me tell you, there's nothing worse than trying to clean scorched marshmallow off the stove burner."

"Nothing worse, is there? Then I take it you've had the pleasure."

"My dad and I," Gwen said, smiling a little over the memory. "We used to do this at the stove. We had more than one accident." Seeing Eben had the marshmallows mashed down on the tines of the fork a little more than necessary, she got back to the business of proper roasting. "Now, this is the tricky part. Since you've never experienced the absolute perfection of a good s'more, then we're sort of operating with a disadvantage. You may very well be one of those sick and twisted individuals who actually *likes* burned marshmallows. I know," she said, her hands raised, "it sounds impossible, but let me assure you there are people out there who prefer them quite charred. And there are more of them than you'd think."

Eben looked at his squashed marshmallows skeptically. "I think you give this too much thought."

"Probably, but wait 'til you've tried it. Only then can you mock. Now, go ahead and hold that over the flames a little, but not too close or we may as well dig that mess out of the trash and slap that on a cracker." While she had time, she went to the refrigerator and refilled the glass of milk.

She came back to the stove to find him staring at her quizzically, his marshmallows not even close to the flames. Slowly, his head lowered toward hers, and Gwen knew he was going to kiss her. She didn't move a muscle, too entranced watching as he came closer and closer. She closed the last few inches herself, and leaned up on her tiptoes to press her lips against his mouth. Slowly, carefully, she moved against him, letting her tongue come out and dance against the seam of his lips.

His hand came up and gently cupped her jaw, tilting her head just so as he widened his mouth. When his tongue flicked between her lips, Gwen clutched at him and felt that same familiar heat burst through her loins.

After a minute, Eben lifted his head, his tongue licking across her lips at the last second just before he pulled away. Gwen leaned against him, her head resting against his chest as she fought to get her breath. His skin was all warm and smooth against her cheek, the muscle hard but not uncomfortable to lie against. She could even hear his heartbeat just below her ear.

"Marshmallows," she reminded him, lifting her head and staring at the stove. "Remember?" She pulled him directly in front of the stove. His discarded fork was sitting on the counter. She grabbed it, shoved it into his hand, and moved his arm an appropriate distance from the flame. "See? Not too close, so it won't burn to a crisp."

He leaned down and kissed her again, quick and hard, and then turned his attention to the marshmallows, his unoccupied arm curling around her waist and keeping her at his side.

"And how do you know when it's done?"

Gwen breathed in his scent and sighed. He smelled lovely—like the outdoors, all piney and manly. "Everything is golden brown. Generally, that means the center is done, as well. But be warned, it doesn't always work out that way."

The silence grew while he finished the marshmallows, but it wasn't uncomfortable, and Gwen wondered idly why she'd been so nervous the last week. It was easy to be with him like this.

"Okay," she said, breaking the quiet. "You're done. Now you have to slide everything off the fork without burning yourself, yet still manage to get everything on the square of the cracker."

Almost so easily it was disgusting, he slid everything off, using the top cracker to direct the flow of the marshmallows. When he had it perfect, he looked up, his eyebrows raised. "Chocolate?"

"Yeah." Her eyes followed the movements of his hands, scarred and callused from his hours in the forge, as they delicately placed the chocolate on top of the marshmallows. Then he pressed the top cracker down, just as he'd seen her do.

"Now you eat it," Gwen said unnecessarily. When he just looked skeptically at the s'more, she sighed. "Eben…"

It looked positively tiny in his large hands, but he managed to pick it up without breaking either of the crackers. In fact, he didn't even get any marshmallow on him when he bit into it.

He chewed thoughtfully, and then popped the rest of it into his mouth. Gwen wordlessly handed him the milk. He drained it in two swallows and handed the glass back. She rinsed it out in the sink and then looked at him expectantly. "Well?"

"If we had more time, I'd make another."

"We have more time." Gwen looked at the supplies, still out on the counter. The stove was off, but that was easily taken care of,

"No, we don't." He placed his hands on her waist and effortlessly lifted until she was sitting on the counter, her legs pushed apart by his waist. "We have other things to do." He captured her mouth, pushing his tongue deep into her mouth for a minute before pulling back. "Don't we?"

She closed her eyes and gave up the fight, knowing it was useless. "Don't you ever stop pushing?" she whispered, barely keeping a groan back as he flicked his tongue against her neck.

"Never," he breathed, pulling her hips closer to the edge and rubbing against her. "Not when there's something I want."

Gwen tried to blink the fog of desire out of her eyes, but it stayed. Desperately, she said, "I want you to leave me alone."

"Liar." He stepped away and waited.

She sighed and slid off the counter. "I wasn't going to do this, you know. But you're just too pretty to resist."

He tugged her forward and linked her fingers with his. "Come on. It's time for bed, Gwen."

Climbing up the stairs, he asked, "*Pretty?*"

Chapter Nine

❧

Her nervousness mounted as they entered the room and she realized what was going to happen. Then the nervousness turned into full-fledged apprehension.

His jeans were already unsnapped when he closed the door to the bedroom and turned, leaning against it. "You're scared."

"Yes," she answered, her voice quavering. "Anyone would be." She twisted her fingers together and tried to look anywhere but at the bed.

He walked toward her, stopping only when his chest brushed against her robe. "I'll be gentle," he promised, as he untied the belt at her waist and pushed the robe off her shoulders, letting it fall to the floor.

His fingers trailed down the front of her pajamas, releasing each button along the way until they hung open. "Take off the bottoms," he directed.

She stiffened, not sure if she could. He waited a minute, then slid his hands down and tucked his fingers into the waist. Slowly, he pushed them down until gravity took over and they dropped, puddling at her feet.

"Beautiful," he murmured, his accent thickening slightly. His hands came up and pushed the sides of her top open. "Absolutely beautiful."

He leaned in and inhaled her scent, the motion a reminder that he wasn't human. "You smell divine." He leaned closer and licked her collar bone.

"Oh God." Her head fell back on her shoulders as the desire roared back. His head moved lower, licking and biting at her skin, drifting to her breast, then lower to her nipple. Gently, he lapped at the little point of nerves, finally taking it into his mouth and suckling.

Gwen trembled, the sensation too much. She thrust her finger into his hair, holding him there even as she said, "I don't think I can stand anymore."

He lifted his head and his eyes had switched, gone to Were. "Then don't." He returned to her breast, switching over to the other one and giving it the same attention. His arms closed around her waist, rubbing and massaging until she felt as pliant as a wet noodle.

"I want you on the bed."

Gwen blinked, confused as her brain tried to muddle through the *something* that was said. "I'm sorry?"

His wild eyes switched to the bed. "There. Now."

His voice was so low and guttural she couldn't understand him. But the push he gave her was unmistakable. Slowly, she went to the bed, lying down on her back as she watched him.

He nearly ripped his jeans away, shoving them off his body with a snarl, the movement so violent she was afraid he'd hurt himself. As soon as he was nude, he came for her, each step a predatory movement.

He crawled onto the bed and leaned over her, his eyes tracing her body. "I want to *taste*."

Her hands gripped the comforter desperately. "Eben?"

"Hush." Slowly, he lowered his body to the bed and grasped her by the thigh, pulling gently until she parted her legs. His fingers traced the bruises there for a moment, then he leaned down and licked the dark marks on her skin.

Gwen closed her eyes as his tongue wove its way up her thigh, tracing patterns only he could see. *Oh God!*

Deep inside, low in her stomach, her muscles clenched spasmodically, desperately trying to grasp something, anything. "Eben," she begged.

He laughed, the sound low and deep. "How does it feel, Gwen?"

"It hurts," she breathed, even though that made little sense to her.

"Where? Here?" His hand slid up and rested right above her clit, rubbing gently through the crisp curls on the point of her pelvis.

Her body arched. "*OhGodOhGodOhGod…*"

He smiled and let his hand lower to her pussy. "How about here, my beauty? Does it hurt here?" He ran a finger into her folds, spilling her syrupy juices all over until her whole cunt glistened with need.

"*Yes!*"

He leaned up, letting his fingers slip away from her. "I'm going to kiss you now, Gwen love."

She mewled, her hips thrusting toward him. He laughed again even as he crushed her mouth beneath his.

Her hands wandered over his chest, unable to be still. She brushed her fingertips over his nipples, and at his indrawn breath, did it again.

His mouth suddenly grew more aggressive as a low, vibrating rumble rose from his chest. His hand dragged hers down his chest, across his stomach, lower, and finally wrapped her fingers around his cock.

She held him and went perfectly still. His hips thrust against her hand, and getting the idea, she slid her fingers up and down his length, happy with the feeling of so much hard, silky flesh.

"Like that?" she whispered.

He grunted and nodded briskly, his eyes closing as she made her hand go faster, up and down. He jerked against her, groaning, and pulled away, breathing heavily. "Enough."

Gwen raised herself on her elbow as he moved away. "You're done?"

He pressed her shoulders back down to the bed. "Lie down, baby."

She watched as he slid down her body, pressing kisses along the way to her shoulders, her breasts, and then her belly. Nervousness again coursed through her as he slid his torso between her legs, pulling them over his shoulders. "Uh, Eben, are you sure—"

His tongue darted out, passing over her clit repeatedly. Gwen fell back with a moan, her back arching off the bed. *He was definitely sure.*

He lapped at her, sucking, licking and occasionally even biting at her pussy. Sometimes quick, sometime so slow she was ready to scream.

"Do you want more?" he asked, biting the inside of her hip with just the right amount of force. He licked the area after, washing any twinges of pain away with his tongue.

"I want more," she breathed.

He thrust inside her. Deeper than a tongue should have been able to go, and Gwen went crazy. Her body arched. She couldn't seem to keep still.

"Come," he ordered hoarsely, letting his tongue dive deep into her again. "I want your cream on my tongue, down my throat. Come, Gwen."

She gave a little scream when his tongue dipped into her cunt, again and again, and couldn't hold back the small explosion that released deep in her womb.

He watched her through it, his tongue fucking her gently through the convulsions. When she was done, he only said, "Again," and continued eating her up.

It seemed to go on forever. Gwen tried to hold back each orgasm, knowing it wasn't right that she benefited from his ministrations alone, but he dragged them from her. Through each one, her body shuddered more, breaking out in a light sheen of sweat as she tried to recover enough to take control. But it didn't happen.

She was so out of it, she didn't even notice when he pushed himself to his hands and knees, staring up the line of her body like she was his last meal. He gave her pussy one more lick, and crawled back up her body, his cock swinging heavily with need.

She lay there, panting and trying to figure out when her body had stopped obeying her.

"I'm going to fuck you." His eyes dared her to refuse him.

Gwen let her head loll and her eyes close. *Thank God.* "Eben..." she panted. It was the only thing she could manage to say.

He positioned the head of his cock at her entrance, rubbing it against her slightly to get more of her moisture. "Wrap your legs around my waist, love."

She did as he ordered and held her breath as the first inch of him slid inside her. It was tight, and pinched a lot more as he pushed forward. He clenched his jaw and pulled out slightly, his eyes rolling to meet hers. Then, in a forceful push, he slid fully inside.

Gwen's back arched as she screamed from the invasion. All the breath suddenly was pushed from her body as a wave of pain washed every bit of the pleasure he'd given away.

He halted with his cock buried deep inside her. His eyes were far gone, so much the animal she had a hard time seeing the man inside. "You haven't done this before," he bit out, breathing heavily.

"No," she whispered, breathing hard as he moved inside her.

He closed his eyes and surged into her again, smoothly, and there was less pain. She gave a little yelp of surprise, but didn't object.

"Good?"

She nodded and closed her eyes, absorbing the feeling of him inside her, so large and deep, hitting nerves and caressing muscles that had never been touched before. *This,* she thought, *is going to be good.*

His rhythm began as a simple one-two motion, but after a few minutes, it changed. It turned into something Gwen couldn't figure out, but it was good. Really, really good. His hips pumped forward faster, harder. Sweat gleamed on his brow as he clasped her hips and tilted her pelvis higher, getting deeper penetration. It felt as if he was inside so deep he could touch her heart. He could steal it, if he was so inclined. Take it away and never give it back. She wasn't even sure she cared.

The tension built deep inside, ten times stronger than before. Panicked, she opened her eyes to see claws clutching her tightly, the nails rasping against her skin. Sharp teeth glittered in the dark, no longer human as he flung his head back and howled into the night, the sound so loud Gwen screamed as the tidal wave took her, too.

It seemed like it took forever, but it still wasn't long enough. He shuddered over her for a minute, his head back and his mouth open. Through a cloud of satisfaction, she saw his claws slip back and his teeth recede, leaving only his human face and hands. He pulled out slowly, and immediately Gwen felt a little river of liquid leave her body. Embarrassed, she turned on her side and clasped her legs together. "I need to get up."

He stared down at her. "You didn't tell me this was your first time."

She rolled off the bed and hobbled to the bathroom as quickly as possible. She closed the door firmly behind her.

She cleaned up as quickly as she could, blushing furiously at the seed and blood she found on the insides of her legs. What a mess. No one ever spoke of how messy sex was. Certainly not in any of the outdated magazines the institute had received as donations. All that had ever been in those were articles about achieving orgasm. And that definitely wasn't a problem. At least not with Eben.

When she came out again, he was lying on his stomach at the foot of the bed, obviously waiting for her. "Why didn't you tell me?" he asked.

She rummaged around on the floor until she found her pajamas. She pulled them on, her fingers shaking slightly as she buttoned the top.

"Gwen," he said warningly.

"I thought you knew," she answered finally.

"How? You went to school. People have sex in school, especially in America."

She paused in her buttoning to glare at him. "I wasn't allowed to date in school, and I was committed just after I turned eighteen. There wasn't time for me to fool around on the side. And I really wasn't in the mood at the hospital."

He watched as she finished up the rest of the buttons. "I've never been with a virgin before."

"Congratulations. Now you have." She finished up and slid onto the bed. He was lying on the covers so she didn't try pulling them up.

He turned his body toward her, curling around her feet like some giant cat as she lay stiffly. "Did I hurt you terribly?"

She tried to glare at the ceiling, but she just couldn't do it. Her body still hummed with afterglow, and she simply felt too good to glare at anything. And then her mother's accusations entered her mind, repeating over and over again. *Slut. Whore. Tramp.* With little effort, she managed to glare. "No."

His hand slid up her ankle, ducking into the leg of her PJs and caressing her skin. "What's wrong, Gwen love?"

She stayed silent, her abdomen still twitching from the aftermath.

"Gwen?"

She bit her lip. "I'm a slut."

He stopped his petting and leaned forward. "I beg your pardon?"

She smiled through the tears that were forming, hearing Connor's years of proper etiquette in the phrase. "I said," she repeated slightly louder, "I'm a slut, whore, wanton. Pick your phrase. That's me because toward the end there, I was pretty much begging for you. And if I wasn't, I would have."

He crawled to the pillows and pulled her stiff body toward him. "I don't like those words," he said bitingly. "I've known whores, and you aren't one. Do you understand?"

"Not according to my mother," she said, deliberately trying to make her voice lighter than she felt.

"Your mother," he over-enunciated, "should shut the fuck up. Sex isn't wrong, Gwen. With two consenting adults, it's fun and good, and everything it's supposed to be. I want you to take pleasure from fucking me, baby. I want you to scream with it every time you come. I get off from it. It makes me hot. If you don't get wet when I lick your body, I'll stop. I won't ever touch you if you don't want it."

"How do you really know?" she asked, studying him carefully. His face was filled with determination of another kind, the knowing kind people get when they've seen too much, or experienced things they shouldn't have. "About force, I mean? The way that you talk about it, well…"

"I've seen women forced." His eyes darkened slightly, but enough to warn her away from the topic. "Now, go to sleep," he bit out.

Gwen studied his face for a minute before rolling to her side. "Good night."

He was silent, then she felt his hands on her body, tugging and pulling at her pajamas. "Get these off," he ordered, his hands getting rough enough to tear the material. Buttons flew in every direction as he wrenched the two sides of her top apart.

"Hey," she argued, trying to hold her top together. "Your *father* gave these to me. I love them."

"I want them off. Next time I rip them from your body."

He tugged the bottoms off next and finally relaxed against her back, content with her nude body. Gwen tried to pout. If he was so determined to rip pajamas, he should tear apart his own, not her very special flannel pair. But then his hand drifted across her stomach in small circles, occasionally cupping her breast and rasping her nipples on the rounds, and she couldn't keep it up. It was nice. Comforting, but still intimate.

"You know," she said into the silence, snuggling closer to him, "I expected to feel different afterward."

"How so?"

"I don't know. Just different. But sex doesn't really change you, does it? I mean, yes it's lovely and everything, but the end result is I'm still me and you're still you. I guess I still had that teenage view of it, as if I'm supposed to feel changed. But I don't." She turned her head just enough so she could look into his eyes. "Did you feel different the first time?"

"I was relieved." He smiled slightly. "After wanking off so much, it was a relief to simply have someone to help me with the whole mess."

"Busy in your teen years, were you?" With his body, and his sex drive, she didn't doubt it.

"You have no idea."

Later, when she was on the verge of sleep, she muttered, "Well, I guess old age is good for something because you definitely knew what you were doing."

He shifted against her back and leaned over her shoulder. His teeth were white against the dark as he smiled. "Go to bed."

She smirked as she fell asleep.

Chapter Ten

୬

She headed downstairs at mid-morning after waking up late. She took extra long in the shower, letting the water work out the kinks and soreness from her body. It was shocking to go to bed a virgin, and wake up...not. Like going to bed a brunette and waking up a blonde, although the process for losing one's virginity was a whole lot more enjoyable than getting a good dye job.

"What are your plans today?" Connor asked, as she came into the kitchen. He lowered the Toronto paper an inch and stared at her over the top.

"I don't know. Maybe clean the barn." Rather than pull down the cereal right away, she climbed onto a stool and leaned against the counter. The reach for the cereal scared her a little bit. Her legs weren't quite feeling right after her night of sin.

"I could use your help with something." He raised his brows. "Would you mind?"

"Of course not. What do you need?"

He smiled pleasantly. "It can wait until you've finished breakfast. Now, what would you like *this* morning?"

An hour later, she stood in the studio and stared at Connor, hoping she hadn't heard him correctly. "You want what?"

He walked around the room, pulling out a large canvas and propping it on the easel, arranging paints, and moving lights so they fell just right. "I can hardly paint you in that," he said, pointing to her *Orgasm please!* T-shirt. Very appropriate, considering her activities of the night before. "Don't be such a prude. Strip."

She shook her head vehemently. "I'm sorry, no. I'm not the nude type. Are you *insane?*"

He sighed like a martyr and glared up at the ceiling as if to ask *Why me?* "Wait here. I'll be right back." He loped out of the room, muttering under his breath.

Seeing no other choice, she waited, and was right where he'd left her when he returned carrying an elegant white dress shirt. He handed it to her and turned his back. "Put that on, please."

Gwen held the shirt like it was a used tissue. "I don't think this—"

"Gwen," he begged, "I'm an artist, it's what I do. It's either the shirt or nudity. Either way, I'm painting you."

Feeling particularly sacrificial, she shed her clothes, trying to give herself a little pep talk. After all, he was an *artist*. And they were known to be crotchety and egotistical about their work.

"Okay," she announced once she had the buttons done up. "You can turn around."

Connor stood back and studied her, his hand tapping against his chin lightly. The shirt was one of Eben's, and on Gwen, it hit her just above the knee. "Unbutton the top three buttons, child."

She glanced down at the buttons, and with shaking hands unbuttoned the top three, revealing the slight swelling of her breasts and the start of cleavage. "Okay?"

"Now," He dragged the brown chair to the light and positioned it, leaving it slightly skewed. "Sit here and get comfortable because this is going to take days and days."

At first, she slumped into the chair, with her legs held tightly together and her hands anchoring the shirt down.

"Gwen..."

In the end, she curled her legs behind her and laid her head on her arms, which rested on the thick arm of the chair. It was a large chair, and she fit in it easily all curled up and content. Connor pushed her hair so it fell in a long sheet, then stood back, a slow smile growing on his face. "I think this is perfect for you."

Satisfied, he retrieved his sketchbook and started on the preliminary sketches. "So tell me how you feel," he ordered, as his hand moved furiously across the page.

She wriggled a little. "Comfy. I'll be fine."

They let the silence reign for the next hour as Connor transferred the image he wanted to the sketchpad. Gwen was content with the silence, and actually closed her eyes and napped lightly for part of the time.

After an hour, he insisted she get up and stretch. When she was ready to continue, he carefully resettled her in the chair, making sure her arms were just so, and then went to the canvas and started to delicately add guide lines. "Tell me about your father. Tell me about the night he died."

Gwen lifted her head slightly. "Why?"

He rubbed a line gently with his thumb, smudging it, and scowled at the canvas. "I'm interested in you, and I want to hear what happened that night."

A huge wave of melancholy swept up and took her over. It was painful looking back at that memory. The Were creature was always in her mind, threatening, but the despair of losing her father was almost too much.

"We were a lot alike, my dad and me. Best pals even." She smiled at the memory. "Mom didn't like it. I was the daughter she'd always wanted, but it was Dad I adored. He always said I looked like my grandma. His mum. I saw a picture once. I guess we look a lot a like. Mom didn't like that either."

"Why?"

She shrugged. "Grandma apparently didn't like my mom. Said she was a city lady and that she'd drive dad nuts on the farm. And she was right. Mom hated the farm. Why they ever married I'll never know."

He smiled sadly. "Sometimes people marry for the wrong reasons. They don't realize it at the time, but it happens. My own parents were one such case. They were miserable together."

"They divorced when I was thirteen," she told him. "But you know what? It was kind of a relief. They fought so much. I remember listening to them late at night, when I was supposed to be asleep, but couldn't because of all the yelling. When they finally split, I didn't say a word."

He nodded in understanding. "And that night? When you were eighteen? What happened then?"

"We were driving," she said finally. "Dad liked to take the back roads when we were going to Mom's house. Sometimes we'd see deer or raccoons, you know, the usual stuff."

"It sounds nice."

She nodded. "It was. But that night, we didn't see any animals. We were talking, and the next thing we knew, a huge creature was there, sitting on the side of the road." She shivered in memory, wanting the image to dissipate, but it stayed strong in her head, as always. "I couldn't tell what it was. But I saw the woman. He was dragging her by one leg. She was dead already, bloody and broken so it wasn't hard to tell. After the truck hit the tree, he ate her in front of me."

Connor stopped drawing as he listened to her voice, soft and far away, filled with memories and sadness. "What did he look like?"

She lifted her head and blinked, wiping hurriedly at the few tears that escaped to trail down her smooth skin. "It was dark. I think his coat was reddish brown. I know it was a guy because…well…" She shrugged and smiled nervously.

"Because everything hangs out after we shift," Connor supplied, going back to the canvas.

"Yeah."

He kept his tone as soothing as he could manage. "I'm sorry you had to go through that. Most of us don't prey on people, although I admit there are a few. But with every human brought down, the risk of our discovery goes up. It's a dangerous pastime to pursue if you're Were."

"Is that what we are to you?" she asked curiously. "Prey?"

He tilted his head in thought. "Well, there is certainly that aspect." He set his pencil aside and frowned. "But I don't think it's because you're human. I think it's more in the way you react when faced with a threat. Prey runs — rabbits, deer, elk. They all run from us. When humans do the same thing, our instinct is to chase. When we chase, we want to take something down." He raised his brows and pursed his lips. "It's how we're programmed."

"So I shouldn't ever run from someone if they're in their Were form." She nodded smartly, trying to make light of it. Christian had said exactly the same thing. "Okay. Got it."

Connor pulled over the paints and began digging, only stopping after he held the tubes he wanted. "You shouldn't have to worry about it. None of us would ever hurt you, in either form, and the rest of the pack wouldn't consider approaching you without one of us at your side. Besides, the urge isn't only there in Were form. We still have it when we're bipeds."

She smiled at his terminology and laid her head down again, feeling lethargic in the peaceful room. The wind howled outside, but it made the warmth and security in the house that much more relaxing and lavish. "I worry about it, sometimes."

He looked up. "About what?"

She shrugged. "About the Were I saw that night, if he's going to find me and kill me. Sometimes I was even sure I saw him at night, pacing around the hospital. I know it's silly because I was on so many meds, but it's there, in the back of my head."

"You know you're safe here, Gwen. There's no one in this house who wouldn't die to protect you." His eyes were silvery in the pale light of the room, and suddenly so powerful and aggressive she had to fight not to cringe.

"I know," she assured him. "And I thank you for that comfort. I don't want any of you to die, though, for me or anyone else."

He picked up a paintbrush, squirted a few dabs of color on a palette, and stood in front of the canvas. "I will endeavor to meet your demands. Now, you will have to close your mouth and let me paint. I am an artist, you know."

"Yes," she murmured, "I've heard."

When they broke for lunch, Gwen was prepared to make a break for it.

"You stay here," Connor insisted, wiping his hands on his once-pristine jeans, spreading a streak of slate blue across his leg. "I'll bring something up."

"I think I should get lunch." She sidled closer to the door, her freedom in sight.

Quick as a snake, Connor had the handle in his hand and smirked. "Stay here and relax. I'll be back in a few minutes."

Gwen watched as her escape slowly crumbled before her eyes into a pile of ashes. When the lock clicked in place, it disappeared altogether.

"That man!" She stomped her foot and waited.

Several hours later, after a lengthy discussion on the sexual appetites of Picasso, which Gwen just nodded her head through, curious and appalled at the same time, Connor finally pulled away from the canvas, wearing more paint than the painting, but pleased. "It's going well," he decided finally. "Definitely time to stop."

Gwen uncurled from the chair, her back screaming at her. She now knew firsthand what a chick felt like just coming from its egg, uncurling its body for the first time.

"God, I'm tired. This is ridiculous—I haven't even done anything today." She made a little squeaking noise as she stretched her arms over her head and slid out of the chair. "Is it really going well, or is that just an excuse because you're tired enough to stop too?"

"It's an excuse." He methodically swirled his brushes in the mineral spirit solution and smiled. "Eben's coming up the steps and I doubt if he'll let me keep you cooped up in here all day."

Gwen stopped in mid-stretch and looked at him. "How do you know?"

Connor raised his brows and tapped his ear. "Remember?"

The door popped open and they both looked over to see Eben step into the room, his shirt unbuttoned down the front and flapping at the sides of his chest, his jeans work-stained and worn. If Gwen hadn't known he was in the forge, she would have the minute she saw him. He was still sweaty and flushed with heat from the coals.

She looked away, embarrassed. He'd seen her last night, panting and screaming for him, completely naked and shameless. How was she supposed to act? How did he *expect* her to act? She only prayed Connor didn't know.

Eben nodded to Connor solemnly. "You're done?"

"For today. She refused to pose nude so I borrowed one of your shirts. I hope you don't mind."

Eben's dark eyes stared at her, pale and expressionless. "Actually," he drawled softly, watching the blush that covered her cheeks, "it looks better on her than me."

Connor finished with his brushes and carefully laid them out for the next day. "Precisely what I thought."

Gwen thought it a good time to leave. Jerking her head up, she turned away and grabbed her clothes, still in a pile where she'd left them. "I need to get dressed." She scurried around Eben and headed for the door, ducking her head lower as she passed him. Her breath whooshed out in relief once she was out the door and in the hall.

"I'm making meatloaf tonight, Gwen," Connor called after her. "I'll need your help, if you don't mind."

Gwen bit back the retort that almost burst out of her mouth and continued to Eben's bedroom. Their bedroom, now, although it still felt strange to say that.

She dressed quickly and wore the most unrevealing clothes she had, which were her overalls. They were pale and worn, but so comfortable. Over an old shirt, she thought she looked quite cute in them.

Pleased with her little outfit, she hummed a tune as she went downstairs.

After dinner, rather than hang out and listen to idle conversation, Gwen went to the studio and ended up staring at a blank sheet of her sketch pad, not sure what she was doing. No pictures came into her head, no images that were just begging to be put down. Her hand didn't even move on its own, knowing what it wanted to draw. Instead, all she had were questions. And almost all were about Eben.

Behind her, the door opened. When she looked around, Eben was standing in the room, his back to the now closed door, and his arms folded over his chest. He didn't look pleased.

"You disappeared on me."

Gwen turned back to the paper, and with a sigh, closed the sketch pad. "I'm sorry. I didn't think it would matter. I wanted to go somewhere and just be quiet for a while. I didn't realize I needed your permission."

He actually snarled. And it wasn't at all a nice sound.

Gwen stood up and put the sketchpad back in the cabinet. When she closed and latched the doors, he was standing just to the side, his eyes searching her face.

"You regret last night."

"I don't regret it," she said immediately. "But I don't know exactly what it is you want from me. I don't understand this...thing, you have for me at all."

"I want you. That should be enough." He moved closer, crowding her against the cabinet.

It should be enough, but it wasn't. "For how long? Do I get any say in this? And what about female Weres?" she went on determinedly, giving voice to the thoughts that had been circling through her brain. "Don't they exist? Isn't there someone in your little group who has first dibs on you?"

"There are females."

She waited for him to continue, and when he didn't, she asked, "Then why aren't you with one of them? You're thirty-five. You should have kids and a wife. Why in the world are you messing around with me?"

"So it has come to this." He sighed and moved away, his back arching for a minute. He sat down in the battered leather chair and stared at her, his eyes narrowed. Finally, he said, "You won't like it."

She slid her hands in her front pockets and shrugged. "You said you wanted me when you saw me in the hospital. I was a mess there, Eben. You can't claim to have suddenly been overcome with rapture, because that doesn't fly. And if you decided I would be an easy catch, well, I can't really disagree with you there. But you could have picked someone a whole lot more healthy, a lot more stable. There's something you're not saying, and I don't like it. I want to know."

"I didn't want anyone else. I wanted you."

"Right." She rolled her eyes. "And you figured this out after taking one look at my unconscious body. I may be insane, but that doesn't make me completely gullible."

A low growl came from his throat, and even as she watched, his eyes altered, changed and reshaped to that of his other form. "I don't like it when you say that, and there is no other woman for me. Only you."

"Only me," she repeated softly, shaking her head and folding her arms over her chest. "Eben, what are you saying?"

"Come. Sit with me." He crooked his finger at her and pointed to his lap. "Sit."

Gwen let out her breath and inched forward. His eyes were the only things that had changed, but it still made her nervous. His eyes alone were almost as scary as seeing the full package of the Were the night her father died.

She stood over him, biting her lip and avoiding looking into his eyes. "Um, what am I supposed to do here?"

"Sit. And we'll talk for a while."

"Just sit," she mumbled, climbing into his lap clumsily and settling against him. It felt strange. Awkward, actually. The feeling of intimacy they'd developed the night before was completely gone. At least for her. Eben didn't seem to have any problems as he pulled her higher against his chest and played with the end of her braid.

"You were going to answer some of my questions," she reminded him, laying her head on his shoulder.

"Which would you have first?"

"Why aren't you married?"

"I am."

"You are," she repeated, abruptly straightening and pushing away from him. She stopped immediately when a warning growl came from his throat. "I'm leaving."

"*Don't you ever say that to me.*"

She didn't even dare to blink or take her eyes off him. "Eben," she said carefully, her voice completely even. "Let me go."

He bared his teeth in a vicious grin. "I'm Were, Gwen. We, like wolves, mate for life. That's why I took you. That's why I have no woman from my clan. That's what you are to me. *Mate.*"

She let out her breath and dropped her eyes to his chest, which was moving up and down as slowly as before, as if there hadn't just been a tense moment. *Mate.* It echoed in her head, over and over again.

"Look at me," he ordered.

She did, but she didn't want to.

"You *are* my mate."

She wanted to laugh. Long and loud. *Lord, what a joke.* "And they thought I was insane," she quipped softly, shaking her head. "I wonder what they'd think now if I told my shrink any of this? He'd probably shove a needle in my arm and lock me in one of the safety rooms. They're padded."

"Don't say that to me," he hissed. "And don't tell me what I know. You are for me. In the eyes of my people, already you are my wife."

"And that's *it?*" she suddenly railed. "What, you just declare it, and the whole thing is over? Don't I get a say in this?"

His mouth widened in a cynical smile. "You made your choice. Last night, when I took you. If you didn't want me, then you should have said so then."

"Which is why you didn't say anything to me before. Jesus!" She hopped off his lap, half expecting him to stop her. "This is absolutely crazy. I can't believe it." She walked in a brisk circle around his chair, thinking, plotting, figuring it all out. All of a sudden, she stopped in front of him again. "Eben, this is really bad."

"From where I'm sitting," he said softly, "this is incredibly good."

"No, this *is* bad. Very bad. To just arbitrarily be partnered with someone you hardly know?" She frowned down at him, shaking her head. "That's awful. Terrible. Fate's own twisted little joke. No commitment, no affection, no great feeling. That is the very definition of bad."

His eyes rolled up and his expression darkened. "I never said there was no affection or great feeling."

She went back to walking around his chair, tapping her chin as she thought everything through. "Hmmm? Forget that. How do you know? I mean about the mate business. I'm assuming there's something, but what is it? What was it about me that you decided meant I was your mate?"

He leaned up, still staring at her. "Your scent, love."

"Right." She jerked her head in a sharp nod, and then shook it. "You've got to be kidding me." Oh, this was *awful*! She'd been picked out of the hospital because of the way she *smelled*? Did life get worse than this?

"And there's no chance there's another mate out there for you? Or maybe there'll be someone else who smells the right way?"

"No."

"No? Just like that? Okay, how about this?" She nervously pushed a few loose strands of hair behind her ear and exhaled. "You and I are going to put some distance between us. No more sleeping together, no more intimacy. We're going to be really, really good. And we're going to go out, and see if we can't find someone else who smells right."

His head moved slowly, back and forth. "Come here. I have something else I want to tell you"

She went to him and knelt beside his chair. "Eben, I'm not trying to be mean, here. I have no doubt that for you and yours, declaring someone your mate is a very important thing and all that, but I don't think you've got the right person. I'm flattered and everything, but—"

He grabbed her and jerked her onto his lap, his easy expression suddenly gone, replaced with something far more feral and harsh. "I don't fuck around. Not about anything, and I certainly wouldn't with you. *You*," he snarled, "are my mate. My only. *And I didn't make a mistake, Gwen. Not about this!*"

She swallowed painfully and shook her head. "Eben—"

His mouth came down on hers, not hard, not painful, but soft, gentle. And Gwen opened hers and welcomed him, because no matter how much she liked to argue with him, the sexual response was there whether she wanted to admit it or not.

"Please," she whispered, her tongue sliding over his, stroking it, massaging it for more pressure. All those feelings of confusion and worry joined and boiled down into old-fashioned lust. "Eben, *please!*"

He pulled up slowly, his eyes looking into hers. "I do love you. You may not want to hear it, but don't think that this is nothing but a physical attraction. I do love you."

She laid her head against his chest and gave up the fight. "I believe you."

He settled back in the chair again, his arms around her.

He didn't make love to her that night, which Gwen thought a little strange, but it sort of felt right. Her emotions were too raw, her insecurities too fresh to handle that type of intensity. Instead, he held her all night, keeping her at his side or spooned in front of his chest. Warmth didn't even begin to describe the amount of heat that came off the man's skin.

She woke up wrapped around him, one hand on his nape, and the other lying on his hip. And Lord, was it comfortable.

"You're awake," he said, his voice sleep-roughened.

Gwen blinked her eyes open and stared at his chest, which was less than an inch from her face. Ahhh. Perfection in the morning. Was there a better way to wake up? Slowly, she rolled away, stretching, a soft squeak escaping from her throat as she did so.

He smiled and pulled her back to him. "I was hoping you'd help me with a problem."

"Oh. Sure. What's up?"

He pulled the covers back, revealing his cock, hard and throbbing. "I am." His eyebrows rose in question. "You can tell me no. I won't like it, but I'll abide by it."

Gwen looked at his glorious body, bare to her eyes, and couldn't quite manage to bring herself to actually say it. The word just wouldn't seem to form in her throat. Her eyes traveled up his body, and stayed on his face. She felt the desire in her body, pooling quickly in her loins, already dangerously close to the breaking point.

"*Yes.*" She lunged for him, her hands itching to touch him, her lips seeking the pressure of his. "Eben…"

"I know baby, I know." He pulled her mouth to him and latched onto her, sucking and swiping his tongue inside, his hand already on her breast. Teasing, stroking her nipple. It stiffened immediately.

She wiggled with impatience across his chest, her own hands exploring down his body, across his chest, his sides, down his hips. He was so wonderful to touch, she'd never be able to get enough. And because there was so much of him, she doubted that would be a problem.

"What do you want?" he whispered against her mouth. "What can I give you?"

She stopped her hand's caress over his thigh, confused over his question. "What do you mean?"

He pushed her hair over her shoulder and leaned up, pressing a kiss to her forehead. "I mean, how do you want it? What are your fantasies? What have you dreamed of?"

"You know where I was. In that place, I didn't dream. I had nightmares, and that's it. As far as this type of thing goes," she shook her head, "I'm a blank slate. I just want. I don't know specifics."

"You want," he repeated, his hand returning to her nipple and gently squeezing. Gwen sucked in a breath and closed her eyes. "I want you," he whispered. "One day, in the change, but for now, I'll settle for skin."

She barely heard him. His mouth immediately latched onto her other nipple, and his mouth pulled at the flesh, rhythmically using pressure to make her squirm. She slid her hands into his hair and held him there, thrusting her chest out, hoping he'd take the hint and keep going.

He did.

"The other," she breathed. "Eben, please…"

He let her nipple slide from his mouth, and when he did, she saw his eyes, changed as before. "Have your breasts always been this sensitive?"

"Jesus, you expect me to think *now*?"

A rough laugh escaped his throat even as he took her neglected nipple into his mouth and gently caressed the other, plucking it delicately between two fingers. Gwen cried out from the barrage of sensation.

She was content for a while, but soon her whole body was shaking with fire. It flooded her veins, traveled into her skin, but most especially down to her sex. She dripped with need, and at any other time probably would have been embarrassed. But with him at her breast, and his lovely body before her, she didn't have room for embarrassment, and gave herself up to the desire.

He pressed on her lower back, until Gwen could feel his cock, swollen and hard against her stomach. She moved, sliding against him gently, and his mouth opened wide, releasing her nipple as his head went back and his eyes closed.

"Christ."

Gwen took his mouth with her own, thrusting her tongue delicately at him. His hand fisted in her hair, anchoring her head while his other hand kept pressure on her back.

He growled and thrust his hips against her. Gwen moaned and ground her mouth against his, needing more. The feel of dampness against her stomach keyed her in to the fact that he was just as needy as she was.

"I know," he whispered roughly. "I know." He kissed her, and then abruptly rolled them over so that he was on top. "Are you ready?"

Ready for what? The heat in his eyes said it was something different, but what exactly he had planned, she didn't know. But then, she didn't really care, either.

He got up on all fours and crooked his finger at her. "Come here, beauty. We're going to try something new right now."

She stayed where she was for a second, stretched on the bed, her legs separated and her breath coming in little pants. *He wanted her to get up now?*

He smiled tightly, but helped pull her to her knees, and then pushed her down so that she was in front of him, on her hands and knees.

Gwen looked at him over her shoulder, even as he pressed down on her spine, which caused her butt to dip up. Very embarrassing, she thought, but he seemed to be in rapture.

"Beautiful," he murmured, his hand sliding down her spine. "Spread your legs, Gwen love. Ahhh. Lovely."

She let out a shuddering breath—to hell with embarrassment. The way he was staring at her, she was the equivalent of a meal in front of a starving man.

"I'm going to take you like this now. But, one day, I'll have you like this in the change."

She opened her mouth to refute his declaration, but nothing came out except a moan as he delicately slid his fingers through her folds, rubbing against her clit just barely, but enough to make her want to scream.

"Would you stop teasing me?" She glared at him over her shoulder.

His finger entered her fully, pushing in and sliding out. A second later, he pushed two fingers in, and Gwen's eyes rolled back.

"I think you're ready," he said, pulling his fingers out and sucking them clean. He grasped his cock and rose up on his knees, already pressing the head at her opening. "Gwen?" he growled.

"Please," she begged, rocking backward, the feel of him as smooth as silk.

He surged forward, burying his cock deep inside her. "Good?"

"Ummm." She closed her eyes and hummed as the feeling of him entering her, again and again, took over her body. For her, there was nothing else except him, the curve of her back, the feel of his chest lying against her, and his cock, constantly moving, constantly burrowing inside her. It was like nothing else. Certainly nothing she'd ever felt before.

His hand came around her body and fondled her breast, squeezing and plumping, until everything was too much, and Gwen cried out, her body tightening around him.

"Do you really doubt me, mate?" he taunted, his lips so close they brushed the shell of her ear. "Do you really doubt that I'd know my match, my woman when I saw her?"

All the air whooshed out of Gwen's lungs. She didn't care what he said, his cock was huge, and hard enough that she could feel every little bump and ridge as it plundered her body. So hard, the taut skin so velvety, he kept moving rhythmically inside her, over and over, slowing getting stronger and rougher with each thrust of his hips, until at the end, she was damp from head to toe with sweat, and Eben's chest slid lightly against her back and absolutely every cell in her body was tied up and twisted in a painful knot, just waiting to be released. And then he stopped.

He panted against her back and bit down gently on her shoulder. Gwen shivered and tried to thrust her hips back, except this time he didn't allow it.

"Uh-ah. Not yet."

She squeezed her eyes closed and tried to concentrate on the rioting, pulsing lust deep inside her. Everything throbbed. Everything felt swollen to about twice its size. No doubt she'd orgasm if he so much as let her legs move.

His right hand slid down her arm and covered hers where it supported her weight on the bed. "This. Between us. It's proof we're mated." His free hand rubbed her nipple, plucking at it with just enough pressure. "I love how it feels when I'm inside you. So tight, so hot. You squeeze my cock like nothing else, Gwen."

"Oh God." She tilted her head back and canted her hips forward the tiny millimeter he allowed. "Just—just finish, Eben. Please, finish."

She actually screamed as he suddenly pounded inside her, and her body went up in flames. The rippling started immediately, and went on even after he stiffened and came inside her.

They crumpled to the bed together, both of them too satisfied to speak. Gwen smiled in satisfaction and finally broke the silence. "If I'd known you'd have this kind of effect on me, I think I would have climbed into your bed the first night I was here."

He pulled her against him and curled his body around her back, his chest rumbling. "I wouldn't have turned you away."

She smiled. Life was very good.

She woke up finally around noon, and spent the day in the studio with Connor, who insisted they get some of the portrait done. Gwen argued, pouted, bitched and cried, and she still ended up half-naked and posed in the chair as Connor painted.

They broke just before five, with Connor wanting to get dinner on. Gwen dressed, and then went down to the kitchen, picking at the specks of paint Connor had accidentally splashed over her arms.

The boys were already in the kitchen. Connor had a bottle of wine open and a glass half-filled with the dark red liquid at his elbow. Christian toasted her lightly with his glass as she came in. Eben stared at her and quietly sipped, somehow making the act of drinking seem obscenely graceful. Especially for a big man.

"Good evening." She ducked her head and scooted into the room.

"Glad you could join us." Christian tipped his glass up and emptied it.

"Would you like some?" Connor asked, chopping onions at a furious rate.

"No. Thanks. What do you want me to do?" For a second, she was actually dizzied by his speed. It was impossible that his hands were moving that fast. She watched, entranced as he pulled a large onion forward, halved and quartered it, and then went to work. Ten seconds later, it was cut into fine, perfect little pieces, and he was already working on another. His eyes were still glossy with tears, though, which made her feel a little better. At least being a werewolf didn't mean you weren't affected by onions like everyone else.

"Christian has declared that he needs a steak, and since I have some lovely ones, just delivered yesterday, in fact, I bowed to his lesser judgment. But," Connor held up his knife "you can wash the potatoes if you don't mind."

She busied herself first with the potatoes, then went out and started setting the table, her mind on other things as she placed the plates and silverware. Foremost in her mind was Eben, because lately she just couldn't seem to get him *out* of her mind. What in the world she was going to do with him? Sure, history was filled with women being stuck with men they didn't want, but if she was being honest with herself, she had to admit that she really, *really* wanted him. She wasn't necessarily in love with him, but there was a definite pull in her heart, and it was growing stronger every hour he was around. Especially when he was all dark and brooding, which was how he was now.

Both Christian and Connor were speaking easily. She kept waiting, expecting Eben to cut in sometimes, but he didn't. He just kept up the silent glowering, most likely directed at her, since she was ignoring him. She could practically feel the weight of his eyes on her back, which was just weird. And what exactly did he have to be pissy about? He'd gotten everything he wanted. She was in his bed, they'd had great sex, and now it was dinner time. Steaks, no less. He should be ecstatic.

She surveyed the table critically, and after she was sure everything was there, returned to the kitchen and leaned against the doorway, watching as Connor removed a huge package of steaks from the refrigerator.

"Now," he said, looking at each of them in turn, "Eben, you'll eat three, Christian you'll probably have the same. I'll have two, and Gwen…" He turned to her and held up a huge piece of beef. "One?"

Her brow crinkled as she stared at the meat. "Jesus. What are those? Like twenty ounces? Yeah. One will definitely do it."

"Don't worry," he said, throwing the steaks into a pan and heading for the door to the porch. "Someone will finish it." He popped the door open and entered the cold, not even bothering to get a jacket.

"He's grilling?" She turned to Christian and pretended not to see the way Eben's eyes were narrowing. "Grilling in below-zero temperatures? Is he *insane?*"

"What can I say, the man likes his steaks, and he doesn't fuck around when cooking them." Christian shrugged his shoulders.

"Apparently."

Connor came back in, bringing a rush of cold air with him, his pan absent of raw steak but streaked with watery blood. He hummed softly as he went over and rinsed the plate off, and Gwen got an idea.

"Do you use gas or charcoal?"

He almost sneered in his oh-so-proper accent, "Love, anyone who cooks worth a damn knows that gas is a poor substitute for charcoal. I'm appalled you suggested that I would even *think* to skimp when it comes to something as important as cooking steaks."

"Sorry, I was just asking." She waited until he was occupied again before calmly bending down and digging through the cupboard. The marshmallows were in the front, right where she'd left them.

"What are you doing?" Connor's brow furrowed as he eyed the bag of marshmallows with suspicion. "You aren't going to make those awful cracker things, are you?"

She looked up from the cabinet, a pack of chocolate bars in hand. "Yeah. So?"

He shuddered delicately. "They're so messy."

She stared at his paint-covered pants but politely remained silent on the issue of messiness. "But they're good."

"You can make one for me," Christian offered, leaning on his elbow against the counter. "I haven't had one of those things in years."

"You can make your own." She set the grahams alongside her other supplies and stood up, her work done.

After the steaks and potatoes were finished, she and Connor set the food on the table while Christian filled glasses.

"Wine?" he asked Eben, who had followed him into the room.

"Please."

"For me, as well," Connor said, coming through the door with a basket of baked potatoes.

With his eyes sparkling, Christian turned to Gwen, his eyebrows raised. "Okay, let me guess. Apple juice?"

"You are such an ass." She shook her head at him and rolled her eyes, already turning back toward the kitchen. Apple juice indeed. "I will have you know," she told him over her shoulder, "that I will progress to harder substances when I feel ready. After four years on tranqs and God only knows how many sedatives, it's probably a good idea that I take it slow, don't you think?"

His laughter stopped and he tilted his head. "Oh. Actually, that makes a lot of sense."

"You're still an ass." Just before she got to the doorway, she was pulled to a halt. Strong arms wrapped securely around her and pulled her to the side. Eben's arms hooked around her waist and held her completely still.

"What are you doing?" she whispered, struggling against him. Even as she tried to get away, she saw Christian smile and shake his head, passing them as he went to the refrigerator. "It's not really necessary for them to know absolutely every detail. I'd like to keep *some* things private."

"I don't like being ignored." His head lowered to the curve of her neck and he inhaled deeply. "You smell good."

A blush crept up her neck and face. She wanted to groan when Connor smiled over at them as he took his seat at the head of the table.

"It's called soap. Marvelous invention. Eben, stop."

"Why?" He shifted her closer and kissed her neck softly.

"Because!" She pulled her head back, glaring at him. "They'll think that we're…" She widened her eyes in an effort to get her point across.

"They know we're mated, Gwen." His eyes were steady and pale, tilted exotically at the corners. Lord he was lovely. Even when he was being a pain.

"It's not like it's a secret," Christian added, coming out of the kitchen with the milk in hand. "We're not human. I can smell him on you." He held the jug up for her perusal. "Any complaints with this?" He went over to the table, whistling as he filled her glass.

She groaned and wished the floor would open up and swallow her on the spot, but it stayed stubbornly firm beneath her feet. "That's not what I needed to hear."

"Kiss me," Eben ordered, pulling her chest flush with his. "And I'll let you go." He didn't give her any time to maneuver away, and lowered his mouth to hers, making his lips soft and sensual.

Almost helplessly, she responded to him, forgetting about her embarrassment as she slid her arms over his neck and held on for all she was worth.

Eben pulled away and nuzzled below her ear. "Now you can go." He released her and took his seat at the table.

Christian smiled coyly as she sat in her chair still in a daze. She made no comment as the food was passed around, not even when someone dumped a huge steak on her plate.

Halfway through the meal, the doorbell rang. Connor wiped his mouth and set his napkin beside his plate as he got up. "I'm sure that's Jacques. He wanted to speak with you tonight, Eben."

She heard the door open, and then low voices talking. Connor came back to the table with a younger man, around Christian's age, following close behind. He was shorter than both Christian and Eben, and thinly built, but with the promise of greater mass as he aged. His features were plain but pleasant, his hair a lovely auburn in the light of the dining room. The minute he saw Eben he nodded respectfully, his eyes downcast. "Eben."

Eben stood up and gave him his hand. There was no shaking, but their hands clasped together for a moment before Eben released him and motioned him toward a chair. "Join us."

Jacques took the seat across from Christian while Connor went to get an extra setting.

"Here." Christian forked over one of his steaks once Jacques had a plate. "You can have this one since Gwennie's going to give me most of hers anyway."

Jacques looked over and smiled at her, nodding his head just slightly. "It's a pleasure."

"What do you have?" Eben asked.

Jacques braced himself. "Theron is speaking to pack members, spreading rumors about a challenge you refused."

It was like a wave of arctic wind suddenly blew into the room. The men were so still, Gwen wasn't even sure if they were breathing. And once again, she was in the middle of a conversation about challenges, except this time she had a better idea of what they were talking about. And Theron. That name kept popping up, too, and every time it seemed to be worse and worse. She wasn't sure what exactly a challenge was, but it didn't sound good.

"Really?" Eben murmured softly, laying his fork and knife aside and sitting back in his chair.

"Yes. Most don't believe it, knowing you well enough, especially after your last challenge. But there are a few who would be happy to see you thrown from the pack for a refusal." He looked between Eben and Connor, and then down at his plate.

Christian whistled. "They've got to be idiots to believe that one. They'd have better luck trying to take him down themselves."

Connor inclined his head and stared at Gwen, steel in his voice as he said, "Why don't you tell us what you know about Theron, Gwen."

She sucked in her breath as they all turned toward her. Four sets of inhuman eyes settled on her and waited expectantly. She shook her head. "I don't know what you mean."

"What *do* you mean?" Eben questioned softly. His head tilted in that feral way they all had. "What do you know, Gwen?"

Her eyes flew to Connor, and narrowed. He raised his brows. "She asked me about him two nights ago while you were on a run. She *claims* to have heard the name from you and Christian."

"I did," she argued. "You talked about him at the pub." Christian elbowed her side. She turned and glared at him. "Knock it off."

"Why are you protecting him?" Christian shook his head at her. "I don't get it. Just tell us what you know and it's done. We can take care of the rest, Gwen."

"Are you going to kill him?"

Christian looked to Eben, and Eben remained stoic, his eyes still locked on her. "Does it matter?" he asked, his tone easy and smooth.

She wanted to laugh hysterically. *Of course it mattered!* "All I want to know is what he's done that's so terrible." *He tried to have you kidnapped,* her mind screamed, but Eben had done that himself, taking her from the hospital without a thought to what her wishes were, or that of her mother. Thomas had even admitted that rape wasn't part of his order from Theron. That had been his choice, and he'd paid for it with his life.

"What are you looking for, Gwen?" Connor's eyes searched her face, trying to see her secrets. "What do you need to know before you'll tell us how you know about Theron?"

The men's attention was like a lead weight tied around her neck, dragging her down. She exhaled slowly and bowed her head, bracing herself. "*If* I tell you, and you kill him, it'll be my fault."

No one spoke for a moment, and the uncomfortable silence grew. She looked up, seeing the intent in each of their eyes as they stared at her.

Christian was the one who broke the silence. "Gwen, Eben *will* have to fight him. And," he added, his eyes so dark they were almost black, "he's going to kill him. It's only a matter of when."

A half gasp, half laugh escaped her. "*That's supposed to make me feel better?*"

Eben got to his feet and leaned on the table with his hands on each side of his plate. He watched her, his eyes menacing and glittering with violence. "You will tell me."

She shrank beneath the force of his glacial anger. Inside, every little piece of bravery was shriveling on the vine of courage, dying under the ice of his demeanor. She took a deep breath and raised her eyes to him, flinching slightly, and clung to the last bit of backbone she possessed. "No."

His nose flared slightly. "No?"

"No," she repeated, her voice no more than a whisper. "I'm sorry."

His hand crashed down on the table, so hard the heavy table jumped from the pressure. Two dishes broke and leaked vegetables over the tablecloth.

"Gwen," Connor said soothingly, "we need to know how you know his name. It's important."

She shook her head. "I'm sorry, but I can't. If you'll please excuse me." She threw her napkin on the table and pushed her chair out, practically leaping away and running from the room.

They watched her go in silence. Connor turned back to his plate and sighed heavily. "Try and find out as much as you can."

Jacques nodded and picked up his fork, finishing his steak quickly, obviously eager to be gone.

Eben went to the side-bar and poured himself a healthy shot of brandy, downing it almost in one swallow. "I want to know how she knows his name."

"We did talk about him in the bar," Christian said dully.

"Yes, and if she'd been curious then, she would have asked. She knows something about him, somehow." Connor tapped his chin in thought as Eben resettled himself at the table and started cutting his steak in controlled, vicious movements. "Jacques, see if you can find out if Thomas was aligning himself with anyone. Eben, we need to be sure about this if you're to call Theron out before the next full moon."

"I'll see what I can find," Jacques said. "But Thomas was pretty solitary. It may be difficult to find anyone willing to talk about him."

"Do what you can." Connor turned to Eben, his eyes dark with memories. "You know how Gina died. If this goes the way I think it will, you'll be forced to make the same choice. Remember—it's better to have her angry with you, even horrified and scared, rather than dead in the hands of your enemies."

"I won't live with that bastard threatening my life and family every other month," Eben snarled. "He dies."

She was shaking too much to sleep when she got to the room. Adrenaline was running amok in her system and made her too jumpy and hyper to even hope for sleep, so she took a bath in the wonderfully large, claw-foot tub. After filling it up nearly to the brim, she climbed in and reclined against the end, sitting as far down in the water as she could.

It took forty minutes, but eventually her body slowed down to normal speed, and she stopped feeling like her heart was going to jump out of her chest. She was left feeling utterly exhausted. Wasted away to nothing.

She got out when the water cooled, drying herself off with an almost detached air. It was like her body didn't even belong to her anymore. She was apart, floating freely above everything, untouched and safe. Except it was a lie. Nothing was safe.

She cried herself to sleep.

"Wake up, Gwen..."

She opened her eyes groggily and blinked into the dark.

Eben leaned over and kissed her softly. Still sleep-muddled, she opened her mouth to him immediately, inviting the seduction of his tongue. As the kisses deepened, her hands ran over his stomach, loving the feel of his hard silkiness.

"I want you," he breathed against her lips, sucking lightly on her bottom lip. He laved it with his tongue, then bit down, using his teeth to wring a moan from her.

Everything below her waist was suddenly wide awake and wanting him. She clutched at him, digging her fingers into the heavy muscles of his chest as the desire built. Under her hands, his muscles flexed and jumped.

He stayed on all fours above her, bending down every time he sucked her skin or lapped at her nipple. He buried his hand in her hair, angling her head better, allowing his tongue deeper access. His breathing became harsh with the thrusts of his tongue in her hot mouth, growing deeper and wilder until Gwen was sure she was going to go out of her mind if she didn't get him inside her.

"Give me more," he ordered harshly, his face savage in the shadows.

Gwen blinked slowly. She trailed her fingers up, along his sides, feeling the bumps of his ribs, the hard muscles of his chest, and the slight contraction of his nipples as she attended them. She swirled her fingers around them until he hissed and groaned.

She pushed herself up on her hands and kissed the column of his throat. When he rumbled in pleasure, she gently nipped at his skin, trailing lower to his collarbone.

His breath whooshed out like a steamer. "Lower," he gritted, pushing at her shoulders gently. "Please, love. *Lower.*"

Gwen moved down his body, sliding her legs between his, licking and kissing his chest. She stopped at his nipples and laved the hard nubs with her tongue, over and over until his body shook with tension. His whole body was like that of a statue, hard with tension, but hot to the touch. There was nothing cold about him. Sometimes he may look it, but it was a mirage. Eben ran hot all the time.

His teeth gritted. "*Lower.*"

Taking a deep breath, her hand captured his cock, squeezing it gently before she wiped the pre-cum off the tip. "Here?" she whispered, fondling his testicles softly with her free hand.

He lowered his head, watching her, his eyes filled with wild things she couldn't ever hope to understand. "*Do it.*"

She was a wimp, a coward. She wasn't the kind of girl who did things like this. It was the last thought that had her beating the fear down and going for broke.

She lay beneath him, curved up at the waist, and licked his penis, the first swipe of her tongue shy and curious. The taste of him burst in her mouth, slightly salty but spicy, just like him.

"God, Gwen!" His breath hitched in his chest as she took him in her mouth, sucking on his length. Her hand crept up and wrapped around the base of him, moving in time with the pulsing of her mouth.

"Deeper," he grunted, as he thrust his hips slightly. She took it, but gasped. "Relax your throat," he gritted out, and flexed his hips again.

She closed her eyes and let her body feel, without the visuals, and then she found she *could* take him deeper. It was easier for her—her brain wasn't able to analyze and say *Run for your life!* at the sight of his cock. And her reactions to him got stronger with just the feeling of him moving in and out of her mouth. It made it more sensual, special even. It made it easier to hear every gasp and groan that came from his throat, made it easier to feel every thrust of his hips, every bunch of his buttocks. She realized how much more there was to desire and sensuality than just the visual.

She heard the sheets tear as she swirled her tongue beneath the head of his cock. He gasped, the sound so deep she wasn't sure what it was at first. "I'm going to come. And you're going to take it." His hand threaded into her hair and held her head to him. Her hands clenched against his thighs, and with a shout, his seed shot from him, the spurts hitting the back of her throat.

Gwen held onto him through his release, obediently swallowing all he gave her. When he was done, she let his cock slide from her mouth, licking the head just before he pulled away. She slid back up to the pillows, not sure if she should be shocked with her behavior and hide her head beneath a pillow, or brazen it out.

He was on his knees before her. His head stayed bowed and his eyes closed. "Was I too rough?"

"No," she whispered. "It was nice." She rolled to her side and curled in on herself, wondering where her pajamas were. *Probably on the floor.* She glanced behind her just to check.

"We're not done," he said, his voice almost vicious.

She shivered slightly. "I'm fine. You don't have to—"

"I want to fuck. Hard, long, all night."

She stared at him for a minute. "But, you just finished. Don't you need to wait?"

His hand reached down and grasped his cock, already hot and hard again. He sat back on his heels and masturbated for her, his movements slow and methodical. His head fell forward again as he watched her from under his brow. "I don't need long. I'm good all night, and I want to fuck you *now.*"

He tugged her forward, lifting her onto his lap. His mouth searched for hers, found it, and plundered, seeking her tongue. His hand manipulated her higher until her heat rubbed against his cock, over and over until she was out of her head to have him.

"Do you want me?" he asked her harshly, pulling away.

She couldn't speak, every nerve in her body was too fired up for her to get a word out. In answer, she slid her hand to his nape and tugged him back down to her, needing some part of him inside her. She gasped against his mouth, demanding his attention.

He groaned and kissed her, pulling her legs around his waist as he positioned her. His jaw clenched a second before he pulled her down over him, impaling her in one fast motion.

The scream died in her throat as Eben used his hips brutally, pulling her off before he jerked her down again. Gwen gasped and her eyes closed as she absorbed the sensations of his aggressive manipulations. Her hips rocked against him, searching for more stimulation, rubbing closer and closer against his smooth skin with every surge of his hips.

"Do you like that?" he asked, abruptly stopping the movements. She cried out, frustrated and wanting. With a hard smile, he slid a finger over her clit, rubbing the fevered flesh delicately, once, twice, and then he stopped.

"What are you doing?" she whispered, her whole body left wanting. She needed *more*. Not much, just enough that it released the tension and she went over. And she needed it *now*!

He stared at her, all menace as his jaw clenched. "Who told you about Theron, Gwen?"

She sucked in a breath and rolled her eyes to the ceiling, trying to get herself under control. "Don't," she groaned. "Don't do this to us. *Don't ruin this!*"

"I want the person who told you about Theron," he ordered, his eyes icy orbs in the darkness of the room. He pushed his hips at her slightly, enough to make her shudder, then he stopped again. "Where did you hear that name?"

She gasped and closed her eyes, needing the peace of darkness under such a painful onslaught. "The…pub," she said through gritted teeth.

"Don't lie!"

He threw her off his lap and onto the bed. She landed with a bounce, and he came down on top of her a second later. He pulled her arms over her head and locked them there with one hand. "Now," he said through gritted teeth. "Tell me."

Gwen breathed slowly, in and out, and felt the remnants of the pre-orgasm in her body, still there, but cooling with each breath. She closed her eyes against him and turned her head, taking the only escape she could. "No."

He settled himself between her thighs and brushed his cock against her heat. "I want to know."

Slowly, she shook her head against the pillow and whispered, "I'm sorry."

"Tell me!"

"I can't," she cried, tears escaping from beneath her eyelids.

"Damn you," he said darkly, and in one move, he slid inside her, moving quickly as he fucked her, his mouth clamped shut and fury in his eyes. A single tear escaped from the corner of his eye, only to be brushed away as he pressed his lips to hers, desperately seeking her tongue.

Gwen's eyes flew open the moment his cock touched her, and he began moving with harsh, jerky thrusts. She tried to pull her hands free, but he kept them prisoner.

"Don't stop," she begged, pulling her mouth away and winding her legs around his hips in an effort to keep him inside. "Don't leave me like that again."

"Shut up," he hissed, and surged into her harder, enough to make her gasp. His free hand crept down and caressed her clit, then dipped slightly lower, massaging her gently.

It was so good. *So good!* Stronger than anything else, sweeter, yet also more bitter. She couldn't speak anymore, and concentrated on the feelings sparking through her body, like fireworks during a Fourth of July display. It was so hot, each buildup to her orgasms sending her higher and higher, until she couldn't take it anymore.

She burst suddenly, crying out with it. Eben removed his hand, and grasped her hips, pulling them higher over his arms as he continued thrusting through her orgasm. He grunted with each move, then shuddered over her and buried himself one last time, as deeply as he could, gritting his teeth as he came in long waves. He let his head fall to her shoulder, and lay still.

The silence lay between them, uncomfortable and foreboding. He pulled away from her and settled on his side. "I want to know who told you about Theron."

Gwen turned away from him, a tear running down her cheek. "I heard it in the pub."

He turned, snarling and deadly. "Stay silent, I don't give a fuck, but *never, ever lie to me again.*" He got up and jerked his jeans back on. The door slammed behind him as he left.

The silence surrounded her as she tried to make plans. One thing was certain—mate or no, it was time to leave.

Chapter Eleven

ஐ

Eben returned to bed at two in the morning. He didn't touch her or say anything as he slipped under the covers and fell asleep. Gwen waited two hours before she got up. She dressed quickly and threw a few things into a plastic grocery bag. She let herself out of the house without a backward glance.

She stole his keys off the hook by the front door and used them to unlock the garage. Once in, she flipped on the lights and surveyed the possibilities.

She wasn't a very good driver. Her father had taught her on a tractor once, but it was over six years ago. She just hoped she wouldn't screw up too badly.

There were only two cars in the garage, Eben's SUV and a small compact. Off to the side was Christian's motorcycle. Guilt tugged at her heart for taking one of their cars. Of course she planned on parking it somewhere for one of them to pick up once she got to a bus station, but still, it wasn't a nice thing to do. Sighing, she took the compact, rationalizing that it was the least expensive, and in the case that something *did* go wrong, she wouldn't be paying for it the rest of her life.

Is this a good idea? she asked herself, sitting in the driver's seat. Her immediate answer was an emphatic *No!* But no matter how she tried, she couldn't see any other options. Eben wouldn't stop pushing, prodding and manipulating her until he had the information he wanted, and then he'd go on a rampage and Theron would die, all because she couldn't keep her mouth shut. And a death on her head wasn't something she could live with.

Taking a breath, she started the car and backed up.

Driving was easier than she expected, although after she thought about it a bit more, how difficult could it be with only two pedals? But the snowy roads gave her a bit of a problem, and the first time she hit one that had a large drift covering it, she ended up driving over the fluffy white snow slowly, wincing as her tires spun. But she didn't slide, and she convinced herself it was a sign. A good one.

She'd be okay, and it would all work out. She'd find a nice little town and get a job at a restaurant or a bookstore, maybe. She would even get her mother to send her birth certificate and Social Security stuff so she'd be legal. And then maybe, after she was settled and secure and a comfortable amount of time had passed, she'd go and see Eben again. She shivered at the thought. Maybe not.

Theron watched as the little white car went by at a staid speed. The small form hunched behind the wheel was easily identified, and made his heart sing.

He pulled out his cell phone, hit speed dial and waited until it was picked up. "Get your ass up. His bitch is going to be driving past your place in ten minutes."

There was silence on the other end, and then the voice said, "You got it."

He slid the phone back into his pocket and smiled, watching as the car disappeared slowly over the hill.

The ringing was driving him crazy. Christian reached out for the phone blindly, desperate to make it stop. "Hello?" he mumbled.

"Christian!" Jacques yelled. "Christ, man, get up and find Eben. We've got movement from Theron's end. I think they've got his mate."

Christian lay still for a second, and then the sentence registered in his brain. He shot up in bed and was out of his room and down the stairs in seconds. He barged into Eben's room, his eyes wild and searching.

"Fuck!" She wasn't there.

He threw the phone at Eben, who turned and caught it in his raised hand. "Get up you son of a bitch!" Christian shoved his hand through his hair and glared. "Your girl's flown the coop." He whirled around and ran up the stairs to get dressed.

Twenty seconds later, Eben's howl shook the entire house.

Gwen looked at her position in the road, or more accurately, in the ditch. It wasn't her fault the car slid into a bank. It was the squirrel's.

She leaned back against the seat with her eyes closed and called the squirrel every inappropriate word she could think of, ending with the mother of all words, fucker. It felt good to say out loud, so she did for about thirty seconds, ending by slamming her hands against the steering wheel. The car gave no reaction.

"Need help?" someone shouted through her window.

She looked over and saw a large truck stopped just ten feet behind her. A bearded man with a Grizzly Adams appearance stood beside it, his form shrouded by a heavy leather coat. He was smoking a cigar as he leaned on his truck.

She opened the door and got out, shooting a look of disgust at the car. She was a disgrace, a failure, not even able to drive more than an hour without getting stuck. Eben would probably chain her to his bed for the rest of her natural life.

"I'd appreciate it," she said, looking over at him and trying to appear competent. "I was trying to avoid hitting a squirrel."

For some reason, he laughed at her, so hard tears streamed from his eyes. He had to wipe them away with his leather gloves, twice.

"Well," he wheezed, finally standing up straight, "I appreciate it. That's the best laugh I've had in about three years." He reached out a hand to her. "My name's Matthew Granville, hon."

Gwen shook his hand. "Nice to meet you. I'm Gwen Branson."

His hand closed over hers for a moment, and then she was yanked forward, her arms wrenched behind her back.

She gasped with the sudden pain of it, and then shrieked as something cold was tightened around her wrists, locking them together.

"Sorry to do this to you, Gwennie," he said easily. "My Alpha's called on me, and I don't like to disappoint him."

She tried to run, but he just kept a hold of her arms. "Eben told you to tie my wrists together?"

He snorted. "Eben, no. I don't got nothin' to do with that asshole. I'm talking about the true pack leader, Theron. He'd like to meet with you for a while." He pulled her toward his truck and tossed her in before climbing up behind the wheel. The engine roared to life as he cranked the wheel, turning around in the road. "You should have stayed safe, locked away in that house of Connor's. But it's their bad luck, and good for us."

"Why?" She tried to twist her wrists free. It hurt, but less than it should have. The feeling was already leaving her fingertips. It would only be a matter of time before she wouldn't even be able to bend her fingers.

"It's going to throw the asshole off for a while. He's going to come charging to the rescue, unprepared, and try to take you back. I can't wait. I'm going to rip out his fucking spine." He chortled over the thought.

The easily said threat froze her blood in her veins and the image of Eben dead solidified in her head. They were all crazy. It was the only explanation that made any sense. "He's not going to come for me. He doesn't even like me right now." It was the truth, and would only become more so after he learned she'd left him.

He looked at her incredulously. "I can smell him on you, puss. That prick's fucked you less than eight hours ago. No use lying 'bout it." He winked at her and turned back to the road. "Yup. It's a strange thing to be Were, although I don't really have any basis for comparison, you understand. We used to be mighty. Predators among sheep, you might say. Anything in our woods, we'd kill. Didn't matter if it was little Suzy from daycare, or a stray cow from the farm down the road. If it was walkin' on a full moon night, we took it down, and damned the consequences. We always made a good meal of it.

"We had one guy," he continued, ignoring the look of horror on her face, "a real old-timer. He liked to skin them first, while they still squirmed. Only afterward would he eat them."

Her mouth fell open and bile rose in her throat. "Stop."

He smiled over at her. "Don't ever confuse us with your humans. Other than the appearance, we're nothing alike. Our brutality is too dominant. I'll have to kill Eben, and if not me, then Theron, because if Eben's left alive, he's going to fuck us six ways to Sunday for touching you. Don't get me wrong. I don't blame him for it. That's as it should be. He's Were, and he'll react like one. None of this write-your-congressman bullshit for us, thank God."

She sat stunned, her bound wrists forgotten. His words echoed in her head, so awful she couldn't get them out. But they served as a reminder—she'd forgotten what they all were. She'd made a mistake. They looked and talked like humans, but they weren't. They were animal, far more than they were human, and she couldn't ever forget it.

"I want to go home," she announced, staring straight ahead.

"Sorry," he replied, sounding anything but. "We're going over to Angie's house. Theron's meeting us there. Besides, she wants to see the bitch who took her out of the running for Eben's bed."

It hurt to think of another woman in Eben's bed, more than she wanted it too. "Does she love him?" she asked softly.

He snorted. "Fuck no. She's a strong bitch. She wants the power that goes along with fucking him. Angie was kinda pissed when she found out he had a little human to do."

"Why does Theron want me?"

He glanced at her, his lips twisting slightly. "It seems you've a history with him. He met you a few years back. Don't know why he didn't take you out then."

It took her a minute to put two and two together, but when she did, a whole new horror surfaced, and stared at her with murderous eyes.

"Oh God."

"Yup. For you, anyway."

She stayed silent the rest of the drive, trying to come up with anything that would get her free. Matthew Granville happily continued chattering the rest of the way, recounting the most horrible stories she'd ever heard, and laughing ever time she flinched during the telling.

He pulled up at an old homestead with dilapidated barns. He got out of the truck and dragged her behind him, making her stand still as he looked at her restraints.

He whistled. "Damn, you did a number on your wrists." He leaned down and jerked her hands up at the same time, which made her yelp as her shoulders were stretched in a way that was painful and not entirely possible.

When she felt the wet lap of his tongue on her forearms, she tried to jerk away. He retaliated by roughly pushing her down to the ground, keeping her still with a knee in her back. "Don't move," he ordered, his voice deep and rough, all amusement gone.

His tongue licked her wrists, moving below the ties in long swipes. She cringed, trying not to think about what he was doing or why he was doing it, and thankful that everything below the restraints was numb.

"What are you doing?" someone screeched from the right.

Gwen lifted her head from the snow, gasping as she was dragged to her feet by a rough hand on her bound wrists. A woman was striding toward them, tall and pretty, with a narrow frame and sleek muscles. She had cruel eyes, and they practically snapped with hate as they stared at her.

"This here is Eben's little bitch," Matthew said happily, absently wiping the blood from his mouth with the back of his hand. "She's sweet, too. No wonder he keeps her around."

The woman, Angie, Gwen assumed, came forward, a sneer on her face as she studied her. "She's a runt. Christ, what's he thinking taking a little piece like this?"

"Maybe it's not just her blood that's sweet," Matthew suggested lasciviously, smirking and wiggling his eyebrows. Gwen shuddered and looked away from him.

Angie cocked her jaw and narrowed her eyes. Quick as lightning, her arm shot out and her fingers gripped Gwen's jaw hard, jerking her head to the right, and then the left. "What's he see in you, human girl? What makes you so special?" Angie leaned forward and drew Gwen's scent deep into her lungs. "Christ," she sneered, "you still smell like him. He probably fucked you just a few hours ago, didn't he?"

Gwen shrank back from the woman's resentment, but not quick enough. All at once, Angie's hand came out and slapped her, so hard her ears rang.

Stars exploded before her eyes. She fell back and was about to go down when Matthew caught her and jerked her back to her feet with a vicious tug on her restraints. "Knock it off, Angie," he growled, holding Gwen up with one arm. "She's still got marks from that fuck-up Thomas. She doesn't need any more beatings."

"Fuck you," Angie bit out angrily. "The little whore doesn't need your protection. Do you think I'm going to let her fuck Theron into making her his mate?"

Matthew snorted. "God you're a dumb cunt."

Suddenly Angie screamed furiously, her hands reaching to scratch his eyes out. Matthew laughed and pulled Gwen behind his back and still managed to keep Angie away with one arm.

"Knock it off, you bitch." He pushed her lightly and she fell back, only to spring to her feet and charge toward him again. Grabbing her by the hair violently, he threw her to the ground and smiled evilly. "I said," he enunciated clearly, "knock it off."

He turned to Gwen and she saw his eyes, changed and inhuman, pale yellow and spooky. "And you. Theron wants you ready in the barn."

"If he's going to fuck her, I want to fuck her!" Angie sat up, blood dripping from a gash on her chin.

"He may or may not," Matthew said lazily. "But she dies either way. She saw him eating some bitch on a road a couple years back. Don't know why he didn't knock her off then."

Angie wiped her face with the back of her hand, spreading blood along her cheek. "I don't care. I want her first. I want her *now!*"

"You said she wanted Eben." Gwen's eyes went back and forth between them. She was about to meet the thing that caused her father's death, but she couldn't even focus on that while faced with these two. She looked harder and harder between them, trying to decide who was the greater threat, but she couldn't do it. Angie was downright crazy, but Matthew's maniacal hilarity was just as dangerous.

"No," Matthew drawled, "I said she wanted the power fucking him would give her. I don't think she even likes dick."

"Give her to me," Angie ordered, her hands out, her fingers curled like claws.

Matthew folded his arms across his chest, forgetting Gwen for a minute. "I want to watch."

Gwen didn't think twice. She shoved her shoulder into the small of the big man's back, turned around and began running for her life. Her feet couldn't move fast enough as she heard Angie laugh at the sky, the sound more of a high-pitched bark, and Matthew's bellow and snort as he joined the chase.

She headed for the trees, knowing it would be no contest and figuring the cover would help. She couldn't get away, but she could try to make one of them angry enough to kill her outright. Death didn't scare her—rape and torture did.

She ducked between trees, dodged around bushes, and all in all zigzagged as much as possible. She looked behind her, and saw no one, looked again, and saw the flash of a dark hide. Her heart immediately plummeted—they'd changed their skins.

Everything suddenly jerked to a halt as she tripped over a tree branch and fell onto her chest, so hard her breath whooshed out. Nothing moved for a second, and then the woods exploded. One of them landed on her back, heavy claws digging into her flesh. She screamed and tried to buck it off, but the creature stayed, already growling and drooling on her neck.

"Little bitch," Angie said gutturally. Gwen shuddered beneath her, ready to try and kick her when another form came from the woods and plowed into the female Were. They went tumbling, and Gwen didn't wait around. She clumsily got to her feet and started running again, the sounds of their fighting drowning out the heavy pounding of her heart.

It was only thirty seconds before she saw another flash of dark in the pale morning light. This time, it didn't come from behind, but from the side, and Gwen was forced to veer right. Only then did she see the other Were, already waiting. It pounced, and she went down.

It snarled, its cock hanging out, red and ridged, ready to rip her apart. Matthew's laugh came from the animal's throat, deeper and far more terrifying than before.

"Pretty bitch," he said through his Were mouth. "Gonna eat you up." His clawed hand ripped at her shirt and scratched her breasts. Gwen tried to twist away, only to be stopped by Angie, who stood ready at the side, a wide gash open along her stomach.

She panted and drooled as she stared at them. "*Give me a tasssste...*"

Matthew snarled back at her and leapt off, guarding Gwen with a snap of his muzzle. Angie danced away, then circled and rushed him, locking onto his hind leg, tearing and clawing at him. They fell, both dominant and strong, and Gwen huddled against the snow, trying to get air into her lungs as she watched the horror play out in front of her.

They were evenly matched, she thought, turning on her side and watching through glazed eyes. Matthew was larger, but Angie was meaner, and in the end, with her muzzle coated in blood, she ripped his eye out with one swipe of her claws, and Matthew was left bleeding heavily, gasping through the pain as he fell aside.

"Now," Angie said, slinking over to Gwen with her breath puffing out, "I'll have my taste."

Gwen kicked at her, and connected solidly with the Were's muzzle. Angie's head snapped to the side, a sharp bark of pain escaping from her throat.

When she turned back, her body trembled with rage. Her lips lifted in a warning snarl, and then she struck, latching onto Gwen's calf, her teeth sinking into her flesh.

Gwen felt nothing except the intense pressure of the creature's jaw. She held her for a moment, then jerked her entire body. Angie dropped Gwen's leg and fell back, howling.

Gwen's breath froze in her chest as she watched the Were. The creature's head lowered again as her tongue came out and cleaned her muzzle. She eyed Gwen like she was a juicy roast, then her body collected, readying to strike.

Gwen tried to steady herself, and when Angie lunged, she closed her eyes and waited for the pain to start. It never came.

A new snarl, this one deeper and meaner, echoed in the woods. Gwen opened her eyes and inched back, staring as Eben leaped onto Angie, his hands deadly with claws, ripping her apart with little effort. The female Were growled and changed her attack, aiming for him, only to be caught in mid-leap, her head clenched between his hands. With one quick twist, her neck was broken. Eben roared and threw her to the side like so much trash.

"Come on!"

Gwen flinched away, but it was Connor, bending down and hurriedly lifting her in his arms. "We need to leave, *right now.*"

He ran from the woods with her clutched to his chest, looking behind him every few seconds. Gwen couldn't help but stare at the massacre that was Eben as he laid the other Were dead, opening Matthew's body from pelvis to neck with a vicious roar. Matthew put up little fight and died, blood streaming from his empty eye socket and his intestines spilling from his open abdomen.

"Don't watch," Connor ordered sharply, stopping next to the SUV and shoving her in the passenger side.

Jacques was there behind the wheel, revving the engine. "Come on! He's already on the chase."

Another roar shook the forest, this one so much deeper, containing ragged pain, forcing birds to suddenly depart their branches as they feared for their lives.

"Go," Connor gritted out, jumping in behind Gwen and pulling the door closed. Jacques threw the vehicle in gear and they roared off, leaving the old farm behind. Gwen watched out the back as it grew smaller and smaller.

The drive seemed to take forever, when in reality it couldn't have been more than twenty minutes. When they stopped the car, neither of the men moved. "What's wrong?" she asked.

"*Shhh.*" Connor held his hand up, quieting her. Then after a minute of silence, he said softly, "Shit," and threw his door open.

He helped Gwen out just as Jacques came around, ready to help.

"He's close," Connor said, picking her up and running to the front door.

Christian was there, holding it open and motioning them inside with a desperate wave of his hand, yelling, "Hurry!"

As soon as they were in, he slammed the door shut, locked it, and shoved three deadbolts home. Gwen watched through glazed eyes as he tugged over a huge trunk and started piling bags of what looked like sand against the door.

"What's wrong?" she asked groggily. "Why are you acting like we're about to be attacked?"

Christian added more bags, stacking them until they nearly covered the door. "Go take care of her," he said, heaving another bag over. "Jacques and I can finish this."

"Let me know if he tries to come through," Connor ordered.

He took her through the living room, making sure to stay away from the windows, and carried her upstairs. As soon as he set her on the bed, Gwen rolled to her stomach. "Can you loose my hands?"

Connor went to the bathroom and came back with scissors. Once the bands were broken from her wrists, it took a few minutes before her circulation came back to her hands. When it did, the pain was worse than anything she'd experienced. She couldn't help but cry as her nerves tingled back to life.

"Christ, you're all messed up," Connor muttered. He got a towel from the bathroom and pressed it to her wrists. "Hold still. I'll be right back."

He was gone a minute before returning with his medical supplies. He already had the bandages and gauze pulled out, and immediately set to work, cleaning up her wrists and applying antibiotic ointment.

"It's ugly more than anything," he said, peering into the wounds around her wrists. Gwen looked away and gritted her teeth until it was done.

After her wrists were bandaged, he looked at her back, which was heavily bruised more than anything, and then at her leg, which wasn't nearly as bad as she'd feared. There were two puncture wounds, but they were clean and relatively small. The worst of the damage was heavy bruising, that went up nearly to her knee.

"Well, at least we don't need to worry about rabies," he quipped, taping a bandage over the wound, his eyes going to the window for a second before returning to her leg. "You'll heal."

Glancing at the window, Gwen asked, "What's wrong?" Just then, the cry of a lone wolf cut the night. "Eben," she whispered, answering her own question. Connor nodded.

He was close, close enough she knew she could see him if she looked out the window in the living room. His howl was long and lonely, and sad, she thought. It broke off, and then there was a minute of silence. When a heavy weight hit the house, making the walls vibrate from the force, Connor hung his head and whispered, "Shit."

She stood up and whirled in a circle, trying to decide which side he was hitting. "What's he doing?" she asked in a hushed voice.

"He's trying to get you," he said, following her nervous movements. "He fought for you and won, and now he wants you as his prize."

"Wants me how?"

He stared at her, his eyes glittering. "He wants you in his pelt. He wants to mate. It's imbedded in us, just like in other species that fight for mates. That's why we got you out of there. He didn't want you to have to take him like that, because he can't help himself."

"Oh, God." She leaned against the wall for a minute, absorbing the idea. Eben was dominant and aggressive as a man. She couldn't even think about what he'd be like in his changed form.

"He's not going for the windows. Why?" she asked, as another hit racked the house.

"They're specially made, reinforced. A bullet couldn't even get through those windows, and he knows it, so he's aiming elsewhere, hoping to break through."

The house shook again from the force of his body. Christian came running up the stairs panting. "He's trying to get through the south walls."

Connor surged up. "*Dammit!*" he said, and they both left the bedroom.

Gwen felt the vibrations of another hit, and her body shuddered along with the house. The south wall—that would be the living room, or maybe the study. Actually, it was the direction their shared bedroom faced. That's where he was trying to come through.

After a minute, silence reigned again, and she couldn't help but hold her breath, expecting another hit with every second that passed. Needing something to do, she undressed and used a washcloth to wipe away the worst of the dirt. Afterward, she pulled on her sweats and stood by the window, needing to see.

There was hardly anything there to see, other than trees, snow and darkness. The sun wasn't up yet, and she realized it wasn't even midmorning. It seemed funny to think she would have been eating breakfast with Conner right now if not for the mess she'd created.

From the trees loped a huge, black form easily visible against the snow, its body covered in thick hair the color of midnight. It ran, increasing its speed until it was nothing more than a blurred shadow, and crashed into the side of the house. Gwen couldn't see the damage he was causing, but from the shaking of the structure, it had to be substantial. Pieces of siding already littered the snow as evidence of his previous efforts.

She turned away from the window and winced. Her calf hurt every time she put weight on it. It was strong enough to use, but the pain made it difficult as she walked downstairs to find the men. They were all in the kitchen, standing around the counter, their eyes wary and their bodies tense.

"I'm sorry," she said as she joined them. Tears burned her eyes, but she fought against them and tried to keep a brave face. "I'm so sorry. I didn't know what else to do except run."

Connor sighed and dragged her into his arms, burying his nose in her hair. "It's not your fault, love. You're young and impetuous, and we've forced you to accept major changes in your life."

"Is he going to break in?" she asked against his shirt.

He didn't answer right away. "I don't know," he said truthfully. "I've never seen him like this. And he's so strong. This house is supposed to be safe, but..." He shrugged and left it at that.

"Will he kill me if I go out there?"

"You're not going out," he automatically replied, tightening his arms around her. "He asked me to keep you in until the rut leaves him."

The house shuddered again, then again. There was silence for a minute, and then another long howl. Christian's eyes closed, and an almost dreamy look came over his face. She watched him, realizing that he wanted to be out there, running wild with his brother.

The house settled around them, each of them too nervous to speak in case the noise attracted him again.

"What happens if he gets in anyway?"

"Then we're all fucked," Christian said bluntly, his eyes opening.

"I'll go out," she said quietly.

"She should," Jacques said immediately, only to flinch from Connor's answering snarl.

Gwen put her hand on his chest and pushed away from him. "I made this mess. If it takes me going out there and dealing with him to fix it..." She sighed. "I'm terrified, but I don't want you to get hurt protecting me."

"We'll wait," Christian said. "We'll see if he's going to bust through. If it looks like he's going to make it, you can go out. But not before, Gwennie. He's lethal right now. He wouldn't kill you, but..." He shrugged, leaving the rest to her imagination. Unfortunately, she had a vivid imagination, and all sorts of images popped into her head, not all of them distasteful, which worried her almost as much as Eben.

Connor nodded in agreement. "We'll wait, preferably in the living room so I can drink a brandy. Gwen, be careful with your leg. I don't want you making the wound worse."

He stayed at her side as she hobbled to the living room, forcing her to take the chair nearest him. After she was seated, he elevated her damaged leg on pillows before seating himself and pouring a large brandy. For a few minutes nothing was said as they all waited, on edge and jumpy. Then Eben hit again, and the house shook. Every time he hit the house, Christian flinched, looked over his shoulder toward the window, and muttered, "Fuck." Jacques just shook his head and looked sympathetic.

The time passed slowly. Connor attempted to read, Christian and Jacques played chess, and Gwen sat in her chair and stared out the window. The attempts to break in got more desperate as the afternoon progressed, and finally culminated in a frantic two-hour period of almost solid hits against the house. Then it stopped completely.

"It's been an hour since he's done anything," Christian said, glancing at the clock as he moved his bishop. "He's over it."

"I don't know," Jacques said, moving his queen forward. "I wouldn't put it past him to stop just to get you to open the door."

"We wait," Connor said sharply, looking over the top of his book. "When he's all right, we'll know."

At quarter to eleven, he knocked on the door.

Chapter Twelve

Connor went to let him in and took a step back at his appearance. "My God, are you all right?"

Eben brushed past him, his eyes still changed but the rest of him back to normal. He gave no answer as he stalked into the house and went to the kitchen. He pulled a glass down, filled it with water, and drank it down in one gulp. He refilled the glass twice more before he was satisfied.

"Where is she?" he asked through gritted teeth, his hands clenching on the rim of the sink.

"Eben," Connor said cautiously. "She didn't mean to hurt you."

"I'm here," Gwen answered, limping to the doorway and staring at him. He was nude and covered in dark bruises and cuts. They seemed to cover almost his entire body, painting it in a wide array of blues and greens.

His head turned toward her slowly. "Get upstairs."

She opened her mouth and looked to Connor for help.

"No!" Eben flew at her, pinning her against the wall with his body. *"You* will *obey me in this or I'll fuck you right* here!"

She stared at him, fear lancing her body. Gulping, she nodded her head. "All right."

He released her and she slid across the wall toward the steps, her movements slow and painful, like an old woman with arthritis.

"Eben," Connor tried again.

"Don't tell me how to treat her," he said sharply, staring at the steps where she'd disappeared.

"She's young," Connor cautioned carefully. "She didn't leave to hurt you. Be careful with her, Eben."

"Stay out of it." With one last look, he left the kitchen and climbed the stairs, his cock already hard for her.

Gwen couldn't make herself get into the bed. For one thing, she was sure she was going to be ill the moment he stepped through the door, and wanted to be ready to run to the bathroom if needed. For another, he was already at his peak as far as rage went. She wasn't risking anything by not being in bed, so she stayed near the window and waited. She tried not to think about the other emotion that was running rampant, but it was there all the same, and nearly as strong as the fear. Guilt. The sucker of all emotions, and possibly the most damaging.

He came into the room silently, closing and locking the door behind him. He was already aroused and ready as he stopped next to her and jerked her hands up for his inspection. He stared at her bandaged wrists for a second, and then dropped them without a word. With stiff movements, he pulled and pushed until her sweats lay in a pile on the floor, and she was as nude as he was.

"What are you doing?" she asked, staring up at him fearfully.

He crowded her against the wall, using his chest and arms as a cage. She leaned back against the wall, her stomach plummeting.

"You ran from me," he bit out, sliding his hips closer to her until he was pinning her lower body to the wall. "You ran away from *me!*" He breathed hard as he faced her, his eyes still wild.

Gwen looked away and tried to ignore the feel of him against her, so large and hard. She would have missed it. The feel of him. The scent of him. It would have hurt to be separated from him. "I needed to get away for a little while."

"You're a fucking liar," he snapped, abruptly stepping away from her and going to the bed. "Did you really think I'd let you leave?" His head cocked to the side, his pale eyes staring at her, already fucking her. "Did you think you could get away from me?" he sneered.

"Yes," she said honestly.

He inhaled sharply, his anger growing from her answer. "Get on the fucking bed."

Gwen got on the bed and lay down, stiff as a board.

He crawled to her, his muscles shifting unnaturally, as inhuman as his eyes. She realized how close he was to changing again, and vowed to do everything he told her.

He jerked her legs apart. "I'm going to lick your cunt, baby. I'm going to eat all that cream out of your pussy and make you come again and again until you're begging for my cock. And you *will* beg, do you understand?"

She gave a brief nod and inhaled, shuddering.

He pulled one of her legs over his shoulder and went at her as if she was a meal and he was starving. His tongue licked her all over, starting at the bottom and going all the way up to her clit. Every fold of skin was touched, examined and then licked again. He went as deep as he could go, tongue-fucking her through an orgasm, and then moved up and sucked her clit until she had another. He did it over and over, wringing climax after climax from her, in between drawing her juices out and drinking them down. Then he'd return and make her orgasm again.

He went on forever, without giving her recovery time, forcing her to take it. As she became more and more sensitive, he began to use his teeth, biting her clit gently, which sent her spinning and made her scream and lose her breath. After, he used his fingers and began thrusting them deep into her while he nibbled at her outer lips. Gwen was so sensitive all over she nearly came from it, but he held back, biting at her inner thigh for a minute while she cooled down. Then he went back to her pussy and did it all over again.

It went on and on. She lost count of how many times she came, but with each one, her body felt emptier and emptier, as if he was licking her soul away and eating it down with her heat. By the time the clock struck one, she felt as boneless as a rag doll, and just as lifeless.

"Eben," she whispered hoarsely, his name coming out as a plea. He raised his head, his eyes still Were and his lips twisted in a snarl. "Please." She pulled at his shoulders.

He thrust his fingers back into her pussy and lowered his mouth to her clit, becoming more forceful with his tongue.

She stiffened, and with a cry, came. "Eben, please!" She shuddered, wanting more, needing to be filled.

"Tell me what you want," he urged roughly, coming up over her, still pushing his fingers inside her.

"Anything," she gasped, arching to get closer to him, but it did no good. She wanted his body against hers, his chest, his legs, his stomach. She wanted to feel his body heat and the smoothness of his skin. But he held himself away from her and watched her writhing, a bitter smile on his lips. He didn't touch her except where his hand was buried deep within her.

"Tell me you want my cock, Gwen, my love. Tell me you want it deep."

"I do. Please, Eben. Please come inside me."

He leaned closer and whispered against her lips. "Promise you'll never leave me, Gwen. Promise it, and I'll fuck you until the sun comes up."

She nodded, her hands holding his head still so she could kiss him. "I won't," she whispered against his lips, urging him to respond, but he just held still as her tongue flitted over his mouth. "I'll never leave you," she promised, then sucked in a deep breath as he jerked her leg over his shoulder and forced his cock into her, all at once. She screamed from the shock of the invasion, but her hips immediately picked up his rhythm and joined him there.

"More," she panted, squeezing her inner muscles around him. He thrust harder, grunting each time, his pace quickening until it was inhumanly fast, the piston movements of his hips sharp and punctuated.

Neither of them lasted long. Gwen came with a cry at the same time Eben did. He hissed and flooded her body with his seed. She tightened her loose leg around his hips and tried to hold him inside her. She looked deep in his eyes, and saw all the pain there. Pain she'd caused.

He only gave her a minute before he began moving again, pushing in jerkily. "Take it," he gritted out, and pulled her leg tighter against him as he continued. "I want you again."

Gwen sucked in air as she tried to fight her body's ultra-sensitivity. She needed a break from the sensory overload, but he rode her through it, his face twisted with anger and lust and bitter hurt, forcing her to accept him and his attentions.

He took her through two more orgasms, flipping her to her stomach for one, then afterward making her stand so he could take her against the wall. Gwen cried through it, imploring him to let her rest, but he was relentless, and her body didn't really want it. It wanted to come, no matter what her mind said.

"Do you know how good your body holds me?" he taunted against her ear, breathing hard with every plunge of his cock. "It's the tightest little pussy I've ever felt, and it's all mine, Gwen. All mine. I'll never let you leave me, do you understand?"

His words pushed her over the edge, and with the next orgasm, her body didn't recover. It stayed ready at the peak, just waiting for one more time. Feeling her readiness, Eben slid his hand down to her clit, and with each penetration, his fingers had an answering motion against her hot flesh.

She came again, so hard and fast her vision wavered for an instant, her heart nearly bursting from the rioting sensations. Eben thrust three times more before he came, the last push of his hips so strong it brought her feet off the floor and pinned her to the wall. His body shook against her, and his cock seemed to jump inside her as it spurted, covering her womb with seed.

When he pulled out, her legs gave and she crumpled to the floor.

"Saddle-sore?" he asked sardonically, with one eyebrow raised, a mean twist on his lips.

Gwen pushed herself up on shaking legs that felt like they had more in common with noodles than they should. She watched him warily—he was still furious.

She fell against the wall, barely managing to conceal a moan of pain. He reached out for her, and she recoiled from him. "Don't."

His hand dropped to his side, his accent was suddenly crisp and hard. "Then get into the shower, if you can."

She turned her head away from him and pushed against the wall, determined to make it to the bathroom unaided. She managed to stand upright, was even able to ignore the way her legs screamed in protest, but wasn't able to take that first step, and after a minute she tipped to the side until her shoulder was once again leaning against the wall.

"Stupid fool." He scooped her up and carried her to the bathroom, his jaw clenched hard and his eyes sparkly, like cold diamonds. "It'd serve you right if I left you in there, too weak to even help yourself."

"I'm fine," she said, refusing to look at him. But she held onto him, her arms tight around his neck as he carried her.

He sat her on the toilet and pulled her chin around in his hand, forcing her to stare at him. "Don't fuck with me," he growled, rubbing his thumb across her kiss-swollen bottom lip. "You owe me big for this last stunt, and I'm going to collect."

She jerked her chin from his hand. His fingers loosened and let her go, but she knew it was because he chose to.

He turned the shower on, adjusted the temperature and crooked his finger at her. "Get in."

She held out her wrists. "I need these off first."

Although he appeared to be cruel, when he removed her bandages, his hands were all gentleness. For some reason, it made her cry as she stepped into the shower.

After five minutes, she was shaking too much to stand. Eben pulled her against his body, and Gwen rested against him thankfully, taking comfort from his strength. He cleaned her with a soft rag and copious amounts of soap, careful around any new cuts and bruises. He washed her back, her stomach, her breasts and between her legs, being especially careful there. She was still sensitive, and jerked against him from the soft abrasion of the cloth.

She held onto him as the shower beat down on them, the warm spray doing wonders for her body and aching muscles. "Thank you," she whispered, moving closer to him and hanging onto his shoulders, needing the feel of him against her, strong and dependable. "Thank you for finding me. Thank you for not letting them get me."

He didn't say anything, but he held her and rubbed her back as she cried.

When they got out, he dried her off just as carefully, and then carried her to bed.

Gwen watched him go back to the bathroom and then come out with a bottle of oil, which he set on the table near the bed.

"You're not done," he said coolly, as he joined her on the bed, pulling her body toward him. "Now, spread your legs like a good girl."

She was going to refuse him, was about to do so when his hand pulled her thighs apart, widening them. He left her like that for a second, and then his hands were back, rubbing lightly over her inner thighs, spreading warm oil over her skin.

He seemed content with just rubbing her thighs for a while, but gradually, his hands moved farther and farther in, until he was working the oil into her sex, rubbing her delicately with his callused and scarred hands, as if she were a piece of spun glass.

She couldn't help the heat that started to grow to life in the pit of her stomach, but she resented it. She resented how her hips angled for him, making his petting easier, resented the fact that she could still get hot, even after the multiple orgasms her body already had.

"You're so soft," he marveled, tracing a finger down her slit and letting the tip rim her sex lightly. "And pretty. So pink, so lovely."

Gwen bit her lip to keep from moaning, but her hips betrayed her and tilted up, searching for his finger, wanting more depth.

"Is this what you want?" he murmured, letting his finger sink into her several times before pulling it out.

Her head thrashed on the pillow as she fought the desire for him. What had she become? Because of this man, she couldn't even control her reactions or her body's unstoppable needs.

He leaned down and licked her cunt, groaning against her clit as his tongue dug into her deeply. "God, you're good. I can taste myself on you, Gwen," he purred, letting his tongue burrow into her further.

She cried out as her body clenched around his invading tongue. It was hot and slick, but she needed more.

His tongue flicked upward, paying homage to her clit before he clamped down on it and sucked the nub of flesh. Gwen jerked beneath him, her body needing completion. "Want more?" he asked, raising his head and letting his finger push into her again.

She didn't say anything, and just breathed heavily with her head turned away. "You have to say it," he growled at her. "Tell me you want my cock, Gwen."

Tears fell down her cheeks, burning across her skin. "I want your cock, Eben."

It came out as nothing more than a whisper, but it was enough. Carefully, he lifted her hips and positioned his penis at her entrance, pushing forward so slowly she mewled with it. When he was halfway in, he surged forward until he was fully seated, stopping for a minute and just breathing in her scent.

"So tight," he marveled, pulling out and sliding back smoothly. "God your pussy is tight."

He held himself up with one arm, and let the other caress her breasts, using his fingers to pluck at her nipples, to make them peak and beg for his attention. She cried out, arching closer to his hand. Still thrusting, he leaned down and took one into his mouth, sucking hard in time with his thrusts, flicking his tongue over the bud.

So gently he moved, every motion of his hips was smooth and slow. It drove Gwen crazy. She needed to come. The need was there, like before, just as strong, just waiting. But he kept denying her, keeping his penetration shallow and lazy the closer she got.

Although her orgasm built slowly, she was held at the top for a long time. She breathed heavily with her eyes squeezed shut as he sucked on her nipples and played with her clit. When she was ready to scream, needing to come so bad she was going mad, he finally dug his cock in all the way, sharply and violently, sending her over the edge on a piercing shriek.

She came down with no memory of him coming, but she could tell he had. She was wet with it, could feel it flooding her core. He was still leaning over her, propped up by his elbow with his hand caressing her breast.

He leaned down and kissed her deeply, letting her taste herself on his tongue and in his mouth. When he pulled back, his eyes flashed at her, full of foreboding. "If you ever run from me again, Connor won't be there to protect you. You'll have to take me, in the change, and I'll fuck you until you can't move. Do you understand me?"

She nodded.

Chapter Thirteen

ဆာ

She was lethargic and morose when she woke at midday. She didn't get up. Her body was too heavy, like it sensed the tension in the house and prepared for it accordingly by making movement hard. She hadn't even stepped out of the bedroom, but she could feel the strain in the air, like a noxious perfume that clung to everything in a one-mile radius. She stayed in bed as long as she could, and went downstairs for dinner.

She knew she looked terrible as she walked into the kitchen, and it was reinforced by the double take Connor did when he saw her.

"Are you all right?" He came around the counter, wiping his hands on a towel and helped her to a stool.

"I'm fine," she lied. "Where's Eben?" She needed to know that. To know he was close.

Connor nodded his head toward the study. "In there, doing some research on his latest commission. Do you want me to get him?"

"No."

He stood away from her, studying her form. She was pale and wan, her hair limp, and she looked like she was about to fall over. He wasn't one to worry incessantly, but her appearance was enough to cause concern, that and the difference in her scent. Just to double-check, he inhaled deeply when he stood next to her — it was there, a subtle change, but a change all the same.

"Why don't I get you some coffee, and then we'll look at your wounds, hmm?" He filled a mug, added plenty of sugar and handed it to her. Gwen took it and held it with two hands while he went off for his medical bag. She set her mug aside when he returned and held out both her hands.

After cleaning and bandaging the lacerations, he went back to preparing dinner. He kept it simple and prepared a salmon, all the while looking over his shoulder at Gwen to make sure she was still sitting up.

Dinner was uncomfortable. No one spoke, which was bad enough, but Eben seemed set on being as overbearing and demanding as he could possibly be, staring at her woodenly throughout the meal, and frowning as she picked at her food. Gwen became so uncomfortable she kept her eyes pasted to the tablecloth.

"She's not to leave the house until I've taken care of Theron," he said, turning to Connor. "She can't be trusted not to run, and she's too vulnerable outside."

"Eben, stop it," Connor said, his eyes gleaming in warning. "She's suffered enough. There's no point in torturing her."

"She's mine," Eben bit out, turning his head toward her. "Apparently that's all the reason he needs to take her."

Gwen choked and coughed as a pea lodged in her throat, the memory of Matthew's taunting ringing through her ears. Christian pounded her on the back until she held her hand out, begging him to stop.

"That's not why he took me," she gasped, reaching for her water and drinking it down.

"Are you going to tell us how you know of him?" Connor asked, setting his fork down. "I'm assuming you don't object to his dying after this last episode. Matthew was Theron's uncle. There's no doubt about the connection this time."

She finished her water and set the glass aside. She bowed her head and played with the napkin on her lap, not sure how to start. "I *did* first hear that name at the pub. You guys were discussing him at the table."

"But that's not why you asked about him," Eben said sharply.

She shook her head. "No. I heard his name from Thomas, the night he shot Christian. He spoke of Theron."

Eben leaned back in his chair lazily, but she wasn't stupid enough to ignore the menace in his cool gaze. "Really?" he murmured.

Connor watched him for a second before turning back to Gwen. "And you still didn't tell us? Why?"

"Theron didn't tell that man to hurt me," she said lamely. "He just wanted him to take me somewhere. I knew you were going to kill him when I told you, so I didn't."

"Bloody little fool," Eben spat. "He almost killed you."

"But then Matthew talked about him too," she continued, wrapping the napkin around her fingers tight enough to make the tips purple. "And he admitted Theron wanted me dead."

Connor nodded. "So now you tell us," he murmured. "Child, he's like that. He's the type of man who takes advantage of anything he can. He wants you dead for no other reason than to hurt Eben. It's not fair to you, but that's how Theron operates."

She lifted her head. "You've got it wrong. He wants me for a different reason, at least according to Matthew Granville he does."

"What could he possibly want you for?" Christian asked, frowning. "He doesn't even know you."

"Actually he does. He's the—"

"—Were you saw the night your father died," Connor finished for her, realization dawning.

Gwen nodded. "Yes. At first I wondered if it was true, but if it wasn't, how would he even know what I saw?"

Silence reigned for a few minutes. "He's been gone for a few years," Christian said finally, propping his chin on his hand. "And no one seems to know exactly where he was. The only answer I ever got was in the States somewhere."

"When did he return to the area?" Eben asked.

"I don't know." Christian shrugged. "Maybe two months ago."

After another minute of silence, Connor said, "So you can call him out before the full moon." He looked at Eben, and nodded slowly. "He killed a woman as prey. You have a witness to testify to that. That's all you need."

Christian whistled. "That's heavy stuff, though. You better be pretty sure about everything before you announce it to the pack. There're going to be some who object to the charge."

"You can have Gwen speak," Connor argued, tapping his finger on the table for emphasis. "Any member of the pack will be able to scent a lie."

Eben's eyes went from Christian to Connor, finally settling on Gwen. "Christian, call Jacques and tell him. I want this fucker out of commission within a week."

Christian pushed his chair back and nodded. "Right." He headed to the den to use the phone.

Eben left the table, calling over his shoulder, "She's to stay in the house until this is finished."

"Where are you going?" Connor frowned at his back.

Eben yanked the door open. "For a run."

Late that night, Gwen fell asleep to the sound of howls echoing through the woods. She had nightmares.

The next morning she felt even worse. It was bad enough she sat on the toilet with her head in her hands, ready in case she needed to throw up. Nothing came of it except an hour of true misery, and Eben's large form, frowning as he stood in the doorway.

"Go away," she whispered.

"You're ill?" He leaned down and pressed his hand to her cheek. "You don't feel warm."

"Just go away," she said again, rolling her eyes up at him. "The last thing I need right now is for my lover to witness my utter humiliation as I throw up in the toilet. Please, Eben."

He leaned in closer and inhaled sharply. She thought about pushing his head away, but it would require too much effort, so she ignored him, even when he jerked back, his eyes suddenly wide as he stared down at her.

"I'm going to get Connor."

She groaned but let him leave, happy just to be by herself in the cool bathroom. It was surprising how much of a comfort the cooler temperature was. She'd never been in a position to actually suffer through nausea. Usually, she just vomited up whatever was in her stomach immediately. But, this time, she had time to think through it and analyze what made the nausea worse, and what made it better. All in all, she preferred the instant vomiting—the absence of suffering was extremely appealing.

Connor came rushing into the room, his silky striped pajamas perfect on his sleep-tousled form. Even his beard seemed slightly mussed, Gwen thought as she stared up at him.

All businesslike, he dampened a washcloth with cold water and held it to her forehead. "God, that feels good," she moaned, leaning into the coolness of it.

"We'll do this for a minute, then I'm taking you downstairs and we'll see if we can't get some tea and saltines into you. That may help."

She didn't argue with him, too happy with the washcloth to bother.

As it turned out, the tea and crackers did help, and an hour later, she was feeling fine. With renewed energy, she went back to the bedroom to change and prepare for her morning.

Eben was still in bed, lying on top of the covers with his body stretched out and taking up three quarters of the bed. Gwen admired him for a minute before going to the dresser and pulling out her clothes for the day.

"You're feeling better?"

She made a noncommittal noise.

"I mean it," he murmured. "You stay in the house."

She paused in the act of pulling her jeans on. "I understand."

He turned over onto his back and watched as she finished dressing. Gwen blushed through it, but she didn't rush away and hide, figuring that he'd seen everything there was to see already. Except any vomiting, thank God.

"I know I said this last night, but thank you for coming to find me," she whispered softly, as she tugged a shirt over her head. She kept her back turned to him as she said it, not wanting to see his face tighten with anger at the reminder.

"Why'd you leave?"

She thought for a minute to organize her reasons before she answered. "I don't ever want to be the cause of another person's death." She pulled the shirt down over her stomach.

"Even if he threatens your life?" Eben questioned, propping himself up on an elbow.

"*I* tried to end my life," she pointed out, looking at him over her shoulder. "That's not a very good argument."

"Then why now?" he asked, his tone becoming rough. "Why tell us about him now?"

"He killed that woman."

He swore and fell back on the bed, covering his eyes with his arm. "I don't understand you."

"Then we're even," she replied, walking over and sitting beside him on the bed. "Because I don't understand you either."

After the first day of being cooped up, Gwen was ready to rip her hair out. She was surprised at how accustomed she'd become to going around the property as she pleased, taking walks along the trails, visiting the barns, even helping shovel snow. She'd become accustomed to the physical activity, and now her body craved it.

She'd spent the first half of the day in the study, drawing. When she actually stood back and looked at the finished product, she realized the Were was Eben and not her monster of nightmares. She shook her head over it, but put the picture aside for later.

By midday, after going through her normal routine of activities, she needed something different, and she went in search of Connor.

He was in the kitchen, baking pie shells and looking like one of those serious baking people the cooking magazines always talked and raved about.

"Can I at least shovel off the porch?" she asked.

"No." He pulled a perfectly browned shell from the oven and set it aside, examining it as critically as if it was one of his paintings.

She leaned on the counter and sighed. "I need something to do. Like right now, or I'm going to go insane."

"You've done that already," he quipped. "Choose something a little more original."

She pursed her lips in thought and pictured the drawing of Eben. "Has Eben ever posed for you nude?"

He dropped the pie pan he was holding and stared at her like she was wearing a cellophane bra. "Nude? Eben?" He propped his hand on his hip and shook his head, marveling at her. "Do you realize how much stronger you've become since you've been here? You *never* would have asked me a question like that a few weeks ago."

"I'm not sure if that's a good thing," she said, slouching slightly. "So, has he?"

He bent down and picked up the pie pan, setting it in the sink as he turned on the tap. "Eben doesn't do nude."

She thought about that for a minute before attempting to put the idea away. But it was difficult—she couldn't quite get the image of him out of her head.

Jacques stopped by later in the afternoon. Connor ushered him into the house and led him to the kitchen.

"Gwen," he said, pouring a cup of coffee and handing it to Jacques, "would you please call Eben and tell him Jacques is here? The number's beside the phone in the den."

Her eyes flew to Jacques for a second and then she nodded. When she rang Eben from the den, she said simply, "Jacques is here."

He sighed on the other end. "I'll be over."

When she returned to the kitchen, Christian had joined the other two men, and sat beside Jacques at the counter. She leaned against the doorway and zoned out as they discussed the problems that would arise from the charge.

Jacques stayed through the evening and went over strategy and the wording of the official challenge with the men. Gwen tried to listen, but after a minute, her eyes started drooping. The next thing she knew, she was being carried up the steps.

"I'm sorry," she murmured against Eben's chest, wiggling closer. "I didn't mean to stop your meeting."

"We were done, and you're tired," he said.

He carried her to their bedroom and laid her on the bed, shaking his head when she tried to shed her clothes herself.

"Let me." He pushed her hands aside.

"Okay," she whispered, and let sleep take her.

She woke up early again, her stomach as unhappy as the day before. She sat on the floor of the bathroom for a half hour with a wet washcloth on her forehead. When she felt marginally better, she headed for the kitchen, where she served herself tea and crackers.

Christian came down an hour later. Gwen was so shocked she double-checked the clock just to make sure she wasn't mistaken about the time.

He slumped onto a stool and leaned against the counter, bleary-eyed and ragged, with dark shadows under his eyes and his face covered in yellow-blond whiskers.

"Why are you up?" She searched his face for any sign of life, but there was little there. Christian was definitely one of those people who shouldn't be up before noon, much less eight in the morning.

His lids cracked open, revealing bloodshot eyes. Without prompting, she got him a cup of coffee, leaving it black. His tired flesh briefly lifted in a weak smile of thanks before he grasped the mug and held onto it for dear life.

He seemed to go into a trance for twenty minutes before he actually lifted the cup to his lips. After that, he began to wake, although from the looks of it, it was a long and painful process.

"Better?" she asked, refilling his mug.

"Mmm." He sipped and winced from the hot liquid. "I feel like shit."

"You kind of look it, too." She studied him with a worried frown. "Do you want me to get you anything? Maybe an aspirin or something?"

"Yes," he groaned, holding his hand out desperately.

She got him the tablets and smiled as he looked at them as if they were the Holy Grail before popping them in his mouth. He ignored the glass of water she'd set next to him and swallowed them dry. "Thank you."

She resumed her seat beside him and chewed on another cracker. "Want to tell me about it?"

"It's nothing serious, babe," he sighed, opening his eyes fully for the first time. Absently, he snagged one of her crackers and popped it in his mouth, grimacing as he chewed. "God, these are awful. Anyway, it's just Connor. He's getting nervous about the fight coming up. He always does this when Eben's going into a serious battle. I think he just went to sleep about a half hour ago."

Gwen motioned to the pies and cookies lining the counters. It looked more like a bakery than a private home. "Is that why he's been doing all the baking?"

"It's how he copes," Christian said. "He bakes. And then I'm left to eat everything. I'm probably going to gain ten pounds by the time the damn thing is actually over."

He sounded so morose over it, she smiled. "Has Eben ever lost one?"

"No. But there's always that possibility. It's a brutal thing to watch the man you know as your brother rip the head off some guy you grew up with. The first time I saw him in battle, I was thirteen. I had nightmares for a month."

She flinched as his words dragged up the image of Eben killing Angie and Matthew. It *had* been brutal, worse than anything she'd seen before.

"He's not like them," he said softly, reading her expression. "He'd never hurt anyone just to hurt them, and he's never drawn out the pain and torture because he could. Every kill he's made has been quick and clean. He's lethal, Gwen, but he isn't evil."

And that was the big difference, she supposed. He'd never hurt her, as angry as she'd made him, he'd never harmed her. He'd yelled, raged and threatened, but he'd never done anything to suggest that he would ever do anything more than that.

Frowning in thought, she stared at the counters and let the ugly thoughts and memories drift away. "Why is there nothing with chocolate?" she asked, straightening her spine and really examining all the desserts. Her stomach clenched in hunger, and suddenly she needed chocolate.

"Brownies in the morning? What's wrong with you?" Connor frowned at her. A large pan of brownies sat in front of her, three rows already gone.

Gwen ducked down slightly in embarrassment, but still looking at the brownies covetously. "I'm sorry."

"And you, Christian! I suppose you're part of this as well?" he huffed.

Christian shoved the last bite of his brownie in his mouth and chewed thoughtfully. "She put tart cherries in them. Said it cut the too-much-chocolate thing. They're really good."

"It does," she said earnestly.

"Breakfast," Connor enunciated, "requires breakfast food. Namely eggs, cereal, bacon, fruit. Something of that nature." He pointed to the brownies with a shudder. "Those are not part of a morning meal. You realize, of course, that breakfast is the most important meal of the day. And look what you've wasted it on."

Lazily, Christian reached over and pulled the pan toward him, cutting another large square and scooping it out with a wink and a smile. Gwen followed the brownie as if her eyes were physically attached to it.

"I can't believe this," Connor muttered with disgust, turning to the stove and twisting the knob to the burner viciously, clearly vexed.

"If you were a nice person, you'd give me that brownie," Gwen said, sidling closer to Christian.

He took a bite of it and said through the brownie, "I'm not a nice person."

She sighed and cut one for herself, slightly bigger than Christian's. When she held it in her hand, all moist chocolate and frosting, she had a sudden feeling of satisfaction. Brownies were the underdog in the dessert world, completely underrated as a quality dessert.

And then it was plucked from her hand by a nasty old man with a temper. He whisked the brownie far away, several feet at least, and held it aloft as he scowled at her. "Go get dressed, Gwen. When you come back, I'll have a proper breakfast started."

"I need that," she pleaded, but he just shook his head.

"No, you've had enough. Now go."

She looked at him mutinously for a minute, then at the pan still sitting on the counter, within reach.

"Don't even think about it."

She turned and stomped from the kitchen, her angry expression enough to let him know she was cursing him under her breath.

As soon as she was out of earshot, he turned on Christian. "How could you? Don't you realize how delicate she is right now? She needs *healthy* food, not chocolate and sweets!"

Christian shrugged and took the brownie Connor still held in his hand. "Hey, she wanted chocolate. Who was I to stop her?"

"She's pregnant. The first months progress faster than a normal human pregnancy and she needs nutrition, not chocolate! You're going to be an uncle. Act like it!"

Christian raised his hand in the air, like a student in elementary school. "Speaking of which, when is Eben going to tell her? And when is he going to *marry* her? Does he realize by human law his kid's last name is going to be Branson unless he does the deed?"

Still irritated, Connor whipped out a pan and slapped it on the stove. "It's not my business to interfere in his relationships."

"Bullshit, old man. Why don't you try telling another one? Maybe something a little more believable?" Christian prodded.

Connor turned his head toward him and raised his brow. "Eben took my grandmother's ring to be sized."

Christian halted in the act of biting his brownie and whistled. "Yup, that'll do it."

"It better," Connor grumbled, cracking eggs into the pan.

Chapter Fourteen

ဢ

The tension in the house was palpable, thick enough to cut with a knife and serve with coffee. Gwen was pretty sure it was cinnamon flavored.

It would have been easy to use it as an excuse, but when she woke up nauseous and sick, again, she knew she had bigger problems to worry about than the anxiety the men were feeling. She was pregnant. And it so far wasn't progressing normally, or at least, she didn't think it was if she was experiencing morning sickness so early on. But then, Eben wasn't exactly human, so that kind of made sense.

"Oh bloody fucking hell," she moaned, leaning her head against the cool tiles on the bathroom wall. It was even better than a cold washcloth. When one spot got too warm, she just slid her head over and she had a brand-new cold tile to use.

She remembered her mother complaining about how sick she'd gotten when she was pregnant. It was always one of the complaints she issued, like Gwen owed her for suffering through four months of morning sickness. For the first time in her life, Gwen felt a measure of compassion for her mother, because it *was* horrible.

After a time she got up and hurriedly dressed, making sure to be quiet so as not to wake Eben. She went downstairs after, anxious for the tea and crackers that seemed to be her cure-all. She wasn't sure what she was going to do. It was still a little early to take a pregnancy test, she thought, since her period wasn't due for another week or so, but it did seem a little obvious. Of course, it wasn't all her fault. Eben was older and wiser—at least he was supposed to be. It didn't negate her own responsibility, however. She certainly should have thought about protection before she'd engaged in carnal activities with him. And because she hadn't, she now had to suffer the consequences. It seemed her mother had been right after all.

Connor already had the pot on the stove and a cup prepared for her. She thanked him with a weak smile as she sat at the counter and pulled the box of crackers over, still trying to figure out what to do. She wasn't sure how Eben would react. He didn't seem like the type to be furious. Instead, she could easily picture him becoming even more protective and domineering. He'd make her life hell.

"You look sad," Connor commented.

She shrugged and bit into a cracker, chewing it slowly. After swallowing, she said, "I'll be fine." And she would be.

She slept through the afternoon. On the couch, no less.

She hadn't started out wanting a nap. She'd planned to page through a magazine, but the next thing she knew, she was cold and shaking, with images of sharp teeth coming at her. She woke up crying.

Connor came to the door of the kitchen, worry on his face. "Gwen?"

She sat up, heartsore and cold and looked around the room, slightly surprised to find herself in the living room. "Where's Eben?"

"The study. Honey, are you all right?"

She slid off the couch, her shoulders hunched as she wrapped her arms around her waist. "I'll be fine," she said over her shoulder, already heading for the study.

Eben looked up from the papers on the desk when she pushed the door open and stepped in. His eyes were clouded, as if he'd been focused entirely on what he was reading.

She didn't give him any time to even question her. Gwen crawled into his lap and curled up with her arms around his neck. When his arms wrapped around her back and held her to him, she sighed and closed her eyes.

"I had the worst dream," she breathed. "Just awful."

"Did you?" He threw his pen down and nuzzled her hair.

She nodded. "But I don't want to talk about it. I just want to sit here for a little while, if that's okay."

He leaned back in the chair. "It's okay." He rocked gently.

She closed her eyes and rested against him, absorbing his strength, his protection. What a funny thing it was to think that she'd never have met him if not for the loony bin. Possibly the worst point in her life, yet it had given her so much. "You're really a wonderful man, you know. Even though you try not to be."

"I'm glad you think so."

"I do." She smiled against his neck and let out a little sigh. "Eben, what is all that on your desk." She lifted her head from his shoulder and stared at the papers spread across the surface of the desk. They looked official, sort of. With stamps and seals, but none like she'd ever seen before.

He pulled a manila folder forward and handed it to her. His voice was deep and devoid of emotion as he said, "These just arrived an hour ago. It seems a pack in southern Illinois had a problem with a rogue Alpha terrorizing the human population nearby. Three kills, each were blamed on one of its members even though they knew it wasn't one of theirs."

She opened it and immediately gasped at the horror of the pictures inside. They were ghastly, the people in them torn into no more than scraps of flesh and bone with blood splashed here and there. She slammed the folder closed and threw it back on the desk. "Those are awful."

"Look at the last photo." He opened the folder and pulled the back picture to the front. It wasn't as grotesque as the others, but it was terrifying in its own right. A figure from her nightmares stood on it, his deep red fur easily identifiable under the garage light as he chewed on the arm of some poor soul. His eyes were just as empty as she remembered.

"That's him," she whispered, her hand going to her throat.

He replaced the picture and closed the folder, tossing it on the desk. "The pack leader is a man who used to run with us up here. He recognized Theron's scent, even though he'd met him just once before. This will add to the case against him."

Gwen returned her head to his shoulder, the image in the picture make the one in her head solidify and match it. "Do I still have to go to your meeting?"

"Yes."

"And then you have to fight him." She didn't like that. At all. "Aren't you worried?"

"I'm not stupid," he said softly, wielding the end of her braid like it was a paint brush. He made one swipe, and then another against her cheek. "I know what I can take and what I can't, Gwen. I can take Theron." He dropped her braid and cupped her jaw with one hand, tilting her head so she had to look in his eyes. "I do know."

"But have you ever met anyone you couldn't take before?"

His eyes looked into hers, completely impassive. "No."

"So you don't really know, then," she argued earnestly. "Eben," she grasped at his hand desperately, "this doesn't make me feel any better."

"You worried?"

"Well, you're going to be fighting a great big huge man-beast thing with really big claws and a terrible temper. There're going to be people watching and cheering, I suppose, although I never did understand that part." She marveled over the brutality of man and Were for a second. "You're going to be trying to kill him, and he you. *You* should be worried, too."

He smiled slightly, just the barest curve of his lips. "Why should I, when I have you and Connor doing it so well for me?"

"This isn't funny," she whispered.

He tilted his head and studied her. "No, it isn't. But it's how we settle charges like this. He is guilty—you've seen him, and now so has another. He has to die because he won't stop, Gwen. He's endangering us all by taking down humans like this."

"Then I guess you have no choice," she answered dully, hating it. Hating the situation. Why it had to be Eben, she didn't know, but it seemed unfair to saddle him with so much responsibility.

"No," he agreed. "There is no choice."

She looked over to the side for a minute, searching for something to study in the room. It was a nice room, with dark wooden furniture and some pretty antiquey-looking things on shelves along the cream-colored walls. It was a masculine room, and she could just imagine Connor and

Eben sitting at the desk, going over whatever business they had.

"Are you still angry with me?"

The half smile disappeared. "Do you really want to know?"

She nodded. "Of course."

"No."

She pursed her lips and waited for more. When there wasn't any, she raised her eyes to his face. "*No?* That's all?"

"Don't be pushy," he growled. "You'll get more than you've bargained for."

"Jesus." She slid off his lap and carefully straightened her pants. "Fine. Forget that. But I want you to know I'm complaining. Officially. I don't like this situation with that…that…person." She pointed accusingly at the folder on the desk. "I don't like it at all."

"Don't worry." He pulled her down by the end of her braid for a quick kiss. His other hand absently rubbed against her hip. "Don't worry, sweetheart. I promise everything is going to be all right."

"You can't promise that," she pointed out. "And I can't seem to stop worrying."

"You could try."

She sighed and pulled away from him, already missing his warmth as she headed for the door. "And you could pose nude for me, but that's never going to happen either."

He suddenly straightened in the chair. "What?"

She finished her day by playing video games with Christian. He was inordinately pleased that she agreed, and soon they were in front of the television, each mashing on the buttons of their controller, trying to arrange colored blocks in the right positions.

"Fuck," Christian grumbled. "You're better at this than I expected."

Gwen got her rows of blocks to go down farther, and watched in glee as Christian's went up. "Serves you right," she said.

"Goddammit!" He threw the controller at the TV and sat fuming. "This is jacked up!"

Gwen hit the pause button and folded her hands. "Don't get all grumpy because I'm better at this than you."

He attacked her, his hands tickling her stomach and back. She fell over, laughing and giggling, and actually felt happy for the first time since she woke up. Her fear and nervousness for Eben was forgotten, even if just for a short while.

Eben came to bed that night after midnight. Gwen rolled over groggily as he slid into the bed, reaching for him. "What time is it?"

"Shhhh," he whispered, biting her neck gently.

Her desire roared up. She was desperate, wanting the feel of him deep inside her where the yearning burned. The need for him was so strong, she could hardly wait.

He kissed her hard, his lips forcing hers to open as his tongue took over, making her groan and cry with wanting.

"Eben, I need you." She arched as his hand cupped her breast and rubbed over the nipple.

"Shh." He slid up, his cock huge and pulsing against her stomach. He lowered his hand and cupped her heat, pushing a finger inside her to test her readiness. "You're wet, Gwen. So wet."

She cried out, her voice harsh and rough with arousal, telling him how much she wanted him. With his teeth bared, he pulled his finger out of her. "Good enough to eat," he growled. "But that's later. Right now, I'm going to love you, my beauty." He positioned his cock and with a slight thrust, sank halfway into her depths, only to pull out again, and sink in the rest of the way.

Gwen was breathing hard, the heat burning her from the inside out as he pushed inside her, whispering against her ear, telling her how beautiful she was, how tight she was, and how hard he was going to come. He touched her with his hands, his mouth, each caress starting a little fire along her skin until her whole body was ablaze.

"So beautiful," he murmured again, and he swooped down, taking her mouth firmly.

"I'm close," she whispered, shuddering as he increased his speed and depth.

He caressed her neck with his fingers and dragged his hand down, tracing the center line of her chest, through the valley of her breasts. He smiled when her breath locked in her lungs, and lunged into her harder until he felt the answering spasms of her tight inner muscles.

She came hard, harder than ever before, each shudder wringing a soft moan from her throat. It went on forever, lasting through his orgasm, and then some. Even afterward, she felt a shadow of the climax as she lay in bed, clinging to him because she needed his closeness.

He rolled off, taking her with him as he settled onto his back. Content, Gwen cuddled into his side, her body completely boneless with satisfaction.

"I want to marry you."

She lifted her head from his shoulder and blinked the sleep away. "What?"

He turned toward her, his eyes pale. "I want to marry you."

A wave of cold swept her body, causing her to shiver suddenly. "I don't think that would be a good idea." She pushed away from him and sat up against the pillows.

"Why?" he questioned, his voice tight with tension. "Because I'm not a Christian?"

She pushed her hair behind her back and shook her head absently. "No. Actually, I didn't even think about that. I'm more worried about the normal stuff. We haven't been together long enough, Eben. And no matter what you said before, you are still angry with me."

"I love you. You know that. What else is there?"

Her heart palpitated slightly as his words sank into her soul. "Well…" She bit her lip in thought and tried to get back on track. "I guess the everyday stuff that most couples face. Generally, people date for years before getting married, and there's a reason for that. They figure out everything about each other before getting married so they're sure. I'm not going anywhere. There's no reason to rush this."

He sat up on his knees, facing her. "I *want* you to marry me, Gwen, and not in a few years. I need you to belong to me in every way possible. If you were Were, I wouldn't ask and I wouldn't push for this. We'd already be completely married in the ways of my people, but you're human, and I want that piece of paper that says you're mine."

"Eben, it's not necessary." She inched toward him cautiously, knowing she was causing him further pain by refusing. "I won't leave you again. I promise." She waited, but he said nothing. "Eben?"

"I'll bargain with you," he said finally, his tone biting. "If I win the challenge against Theron, you marry me. If I lose, you don't."

She blinked in the dark for a minute, hoping she'd heard him wrong. She hadn't. "Uh, if you lose, you're dead. This isn't such a good bargain."

He slid closer, his face just an inch away. "Are you saying you don't want me dead, my beauty?"

She felt like hitting him, but she wasn't that brave yet. "Don't be silly," she said breathlessly, as his lips brushed against her, feathering kisses along the line of her jaw. "You know I don't want you dead. I've never even said anything *close* to that."

"Excellent," he murmured. "Then we have a bargain. When I win, you will agree to marry me."

"I'm a modern woman. I don't need to be married." She'd always thought about it, wondered, actually, but this was beyond anything she'd ever come up with. God. Marriage. And by the tone of his voice and the determination in his eyes, he wouldn't stop until she said yes. And for some reason, that caused her both fear, and a strong sense of elation.

"*I* want marriage," he replied darkly. "And because of that, I'll have your promise tomorrow, after the challenge."

"*Tomorrow?*" she practically shrieked, marriage completely forgotten as the fear of losing him rose up strong. "Eben, so soon?"

He brought his mouth to hers, and kissed her shock away. "Tomorrow," he repeated softly, as he spread her body beneath his. "Now attend my needs, Gwen my love."

He gave her no option other than to please him, and with the approaching dawn, she became desperate for him. He could die. Her heart fluttered with the knowledge, and she clung to him as he entered her, knowing it could be her last time with him.

Early in the morning, she opened her eyes to find him looming over her, his face taut and his eyes wild.

She touched his face reverently, lovingly. "You're leaving."

He nodded and leaned down, pressing his lips between her breasts. The feel of his cock jutting was impossible to resist. Knowing where he was about to go, Gwen sat up and pushed him to his back. He rolled over and pulled her on top of him.

"I know you," she murmured sleepily against his neck, rubbing herself against his erection and humming softly with pleasure. He felt so good against her. She'd miss that if he didn't survive. "Sometimes it scares me how well I know you. Better than anyone else, I think."

"We're mated," he crooned, grasping her hips and increasing the pressure as she slid over his cock. "This is how it is for us. This is how it will always be."

Gwen spread her legs even wider and moaned, feeling the tip of his cock teasing her entrance. She shifted just so, and when he next rubbed her up his length, she canted her hips, and sighed as he slipped in fully. And then because she had to, she kissed him, licking his mouth as delicately as she could manage. When he growled and sucked at her tongue, she laughed and sat up, loving the feeling of so much heat and strength inside her.

"I'll miss you," she breathed, lifting and lowering her body in a steady rhythm. So good. *So good!*

"Harder, love. Jesus!" He held her up longer, and then thrust his hips up as she was coming down, making them both gasp, and causing the tightening deep in Gwen's belly to suddenly tighten a lot more.

"Do it again," she breathed, lifting up. He thrust, and she went down. The tightness grew dangerously tighter.

She leaned down, flicking her tongue into his mouth as she clung to him and rocked, loving the way he felt deep inside her. More and more and more, until finally she couldn't stand any more. His cock, so deep, hit just the right place, and suddenly she stiffened and cried out, her muscles pulsating against him, pulling at him. Milking his cock.

Eben swore and roughly clasped her, jerking her hips up and down until his eyes changed and his mouth twisted with tension. He went over with a sharp cry, with his head thrust back and his body stiffened. Deep inside, Gwen felt the resulting pulsing of his release.

She sank down on his chest, breathing hard. A light coating of sweat gleamed dully on his skin. So beautiful, he was.

He reached up, his hand moving to the bedside table. Gwen groaned and fell to the side, still holding onto him. "Don't go yet," she said, snuggling up against him. "Just a little longer."

"Shh," he murmured, taking her hand in his. "I have some time."

"Okay," she whispered, and fell asleep.

She woke later that morning, and he was gone. She was forced to stay in the bathroom longer than necessary, partly because of the nausea, partly because of the terror she felt over losing him, but also because of the ring she'd discovered on her finger. It was no big diamond or anything flashy, but old, and finely made in white-gold, with a small green stone at the center of a woven-vine band. It was simple and elegant—perfect. And it fit.

She stared at it for another minute, marveling at him. And she'd thought he was getting ready to leave when he'd reached over to the nightstand. Tricky man.

Feeling brave, she left it on while she dressed. He'd given it to her, after all, and it *was* just a ring, even if it was on the designated ring finger. It didn't carry a sign of flashing neon to attract everyone's attention. Besides, she didn't want to hurt him by refusing his gift, so it was only right that she wore it.

After her bout with nausea in the bathroom, she shuffled downstairs and encountered Connor in the kitchen. He looked as miserable as she felt, but he perked up when he saw her.

He slid a cup of tea over as she sat down, then cocked his hip and smiled smugly. "Excellent. He's finally asked." He stared pointedly at the ring on her finger, completely missing her T-shirt, which she'd donned in his honor. She wore it over a long-sleeved white shirt, which emphasized the black material and the colors of the British flag that were painted across the front.

"You can relax," she said tiredly. "I haven't agreed to anything yet."

"But you will. He's not exactly one to accept no as an answer," he said knowingly. "And you're wearing it. That must mean something, don't you think?"

She studied the ring for a moment. "Was it your wife's?"

He shook his head. "No. She favored a more contemporary style. I have hers still, and when Christian chooses, I hope he'll use it. That particular ring," he nodded at her hand, "belonged to my grandmother. She was a fine old lady, unlike any I've ever met. Eben felt this would suit you best."

"It does," she murmured. "It's perfect." She looked up at his face, studying him. "You should have told me the challenge was today."

He flinched slightly and refilled his coffee cup. "Yes. But none of us wanted to worry you. I won't lie to you—this could very well end with Eben dead. Theron's strong. But then, so is Eben, and he's just as ruthless and vicious as any I've known. It'll be a close fight."

Her heart did its fluttering thing again, and she felt weak with it. He could die. How would she survive it?

"What time do we leave?"

He glanced at the clock. "In two hours. The Elders will want to question you, and they'll need time to do so. And I always prefer to be there early rather than late."

She tapped her fingers on the countertop, trying to picture the gathering, but her mind wasn't up to it. There was still one more aspect she needed an answer on.

"Are they going to be changed?" she asked carefully.

"Some will," Connor said. "Some won't. Eben will be in the change of course, as will Theron. Other than that, it's a personal choice. Christian will change, he always does. I won't."

"Thank you."

He bowed his head slightly. "It's my pleasure, Gwen."

She dressed heavily for the meeting, putting on as many layers as she could manage under her jacket. Conner came prepared for cold weather, but Christian only wore a heavy flannel.

At her raised eyebrows, he only shrugged. "Our body temp goes up when we change."

The drive was tense. Connor seemed especially agitated as he drove to their destination, and replied tersely to Christian's questions. Gwen wisely chose to stay quiet during the drive, and watched silently as the sky darkened to the constant night of winter.

Connor pulled into someone's driveway. At least, Gwen *thought* it was a driveway. It was so old and overgrown it was difficult to tell at first. As they drove down, she saw an old house, abandoned by the look of it, and two outbuildings, although they were in disrepair. Everything else was just trees and woods and empty spaces. Connor pulled in next to the barn and turned off the car. There were already what looked to be thirty other vehicles there.

They got out, and Gwen immediately felt the sharp cold. Christian didn't seem to be bothered by the icy breeze that was blowing, but then, neither did Connor. Both men looked directly toward the woods, their focus on the coming battle and the gathering of their pack.

"Come on," Connor ordered, no longer the nice older gentleman she was so fond of. He was domineering and autocratic, powerful enough to hold position as pack leader for years. Gwen couldn't help but feel a tingle of alarm as she followed them into the woods. He let Christian lead, and stayed next to her the entire time, keeping her safe and pointing out obstacles in the path as they walked. Occasionally he'd nod to other pack members, but he was intent on his purpose, which was keeping her healthy and whole.

The forest they entered was ancient, with huge trees, and vines growing around and through the branches, wild and curled everywhere. It was like a completely separate world, Gwen thought. It reminded her of being in church. The feeling of inferiority was the same whether facing God or his greatest creations, and it comforted her. This place of all places was right, untouched and wild as it was intended.

The path grew more and more narrow, and thicker with snow as they went. She had trouble more than once, only to be saved by Connor's strong arms lifting her out of a drift or over a thick branch. No one else seemed to have that problem, but no one else seemed to even see that she did. Even Christian was totally focused on moving forward.

They finally broke from the path and poured into a clearing, overhung completely with trees so that it formed a sort of dome that opened in the middle. The sky was visible through the hole in the canopy, dark and heavy with clouds. Gwen stared up at it for a minute, wondering how they knew when the moon was full if they couldn't see it.

"Stay by my side, child," Connor cautioned, as they stood at the back.

Gwen nodded, feeling her heart beating too quickly. No one had changed yet, but she could feel that wild energy that seemed to surround those who were Were, and she took it seriously.

"Christian," he ordered. "Let Eben know we're in."

Christian nodded and loped off to the other side of the clearing. She followed his movements and saw him stop before three older men, bow regally, and then move off to the side, where Eben stood alone, large, dark and imposing.

"God, he's beautiful," she murmured.

Connor's heart melted at her whispered tone. "Have you told him you love him?"

She looked over at him, an almost panicked look on her face. "What?"

"You love him," he said simply. "He's always been lacking in love. His mother abandoned him when he was young, and I think that left a scar. He needs love, Gwen, perhaps more than anyone I've ever known."

She turned away from him and wrapped her arms tighter around her waist. "I don't know him well enough." Yet her words from early that morning echoed in her ears, as if to refute what she'd said.

Connor tilted his head and watched her, noting her worried expression and the pain in her eyes. "I knew my wife for one day before I fell in love with her, and she was my heart. When she died, I knew there was no use trying to replace her. I love her still, and I will until I die. It's not always like that, mind you, but with Eben, I have no doubt he will love just as fully as I did."

Just then, a young woman came through the crowd. She was tall, near six feet, with long blonde hair and deep brown eyes. She bowed regally to Connor, then looked at Gwen. "They will see you now."

Gwen reached for Connor. He grasped her hand tightly and followed her through the crowd as Gwen followed the other woman. She kept her head down, didn't look at the others as she made her way, and tried to figure out what, exactly, she was going to say.

The woman stopped them before the three old gentlemen. Each one looked like he was over eighty-five, and each one had hard eyes, full of memories of the glory of youth.

"This is the woman?" the one on the left asked, turning his head to Eben.

"It is," he answered, staring coolly at Gwen.

"She's rather small, isn't she?"

Gwen frowned at the old man. "You're not terribly large, either." And he wasn't. They were all three shrunken with age. It seemed rude to her for them to point fingers.

"True," he sighed. "But I haven't always been like this."

Gwen let that go and waited. It didn't take long.

"We wish to know about this Were you saw," the one in the middle said, his voice breathy with age. "Tell us of that night."

Behind her, Connor squeezed her hand reassuringly. She started out haltingly. It was difficult to recount such a personal tale to utter strangers. At some point, she found herself watching Eben, and from that point on, she grew more comfortable, and finished the story without crying.

"And you're sure Theron was this Were, this animal you saw that night?" a man asked from the side. He had a hostile look in his eyes, like he blamed her for the proceedings.

She frowned but directed her answer to the Elders. "I thought about this also," she said. "I drew several pictures of him after it happened, so his image has remained fresh in my mind. But also, I'm sure because of what Matthew Granville said several days ago, during a botched attempt to kidnap me."

"We've heard the tale," the middle one said. "So you didn't pinpoint Theron as your attacker of that night."

"No," she said. "But I believe it is him. I recognized him in the pictures Eben showed me."

The old men all nodded in tandem. One of them said, "You are dismissed." The man at the side took her place in front of them and started arguing fiercely. Gwen didn't wait around to hear what he was saying, and happily let Connor lead her away.

The people looked ordinary, even boring, she decided as she looked over the gathered crowd as they passed through. Some were tall, others weren't. Some were heavy, and others weren't. Some were men, some were women. She would have never picked any of them out as werewolves, but in the clearing their combined energy was familiar, and reminded her of the night in the pub. That had been what was off with them. It wasn't anything visible, just a sense, and it grew stronger when they gathered together.

Gwen and Connor were on one side of the clearing when suddenly there was a huge indrawn breath from the crowd. She stood on her tiptoes, trying to see over everyone, and caught sight of a tall nude form striding around the circle left bare in the middle of the clearing. He was tall and lanky, with muscled arms and chest, and red hair and beard. He was attractive, if a little boring with it.

He bowed low to them all. "My people," he said in a rich baritone voice, a smile on his lips. Then he looked through the crowd at Gwen, and pressed his lips into a kiss.

She stumbled back and turned to Connor. "Did he do what I think he did?"

Connor's eyes were hard as he turned to her. "He did," he growled low.

There was another collective breath, and then she saw a shadow move forward, large and bulky and dark. Eben seemed to glide, his steps were so smooth. He too was nude as he stepped within the circle, and the differences between the two men were obvious. Eben, too, was muscular and tall, but he was thicker, and built heavier. He was built for endurance, where Theron was more high-spirited.

Eben didn't bow at all, but looked around the crowd, like a king viewing his subjects.

The three old men stepped forward, almost a single entity in their unity. The one in the middle seemed to be the speaker for the other two as they faced the pack and meted out their decision.

"We hereby declare this challenge binding and subject to those laws that govern the pack. Theron Granville is hereby censured by the Elders, and turned over to the formal challenge of pack leader."

And that was it. The minute they were done speaking, the battle between the two men started.

A long howl suddenly cut through the clearing. Gwen jerked her head over and saw Eben, in the center of the circle with his head thrown back, his arms held out at his sides. His flesh rippled, and like some horrible experiment gone wrong, he began to change before her eyes, his muscles and bones shifting with painful cracks and groans, his nose and mouth elongating, making room for rows of sharp teeth, and his legs bending and breaking, only to reshape themselves as he fell to the ground on all fours. All along his body, thick, black hair sprouted, and soon his skin was entirely covered. In Were form, he was just as huge as she'd remembered, and just as frightening.

Others in the crowd began to change, although it certainly wasn't everyone. Those who did fell to all fours and completed their transitions as if it were nothing unusual. And it wasn't, she supposed. Not one person looked at them oddly.

More and more howls joined the first, until the forest was filled with their sounds of joy and sorrow as first Eben, and then others rose, completely shifted over to their Were forms.

She took a step back as the creatures got up, suddenly taller and larger than she could scarcely believe. Different colors of pelts were mixed in with the other human forms swathed in heavy jackets, from the blackest of blacks, to the palest creams. Size differed from creature to creature, but every one dwarfed her and was armed with lethal claws and fangs that were sharp enough to kill in a single bite.

"Relax," Connor said beside her, his face unchanged and as kind as she remembered. "None of them will hurt you. It's simply a shift in skin. Their hearts and personalities remain the same, even if they do become a bit more wild."

She nodded. "Right," she breathed, trying to convince herself. Then the fight started, and she forgot everything else. "Come on. We need to go forward. I want to see everything."

They went through the crowd, moving slowly through the sea of bodies. Gwen kept her eyes on the ring in the center, wincing and looking away every few seconds, but unable to not witness the fight. Theron attacked Eben first, coming so quick and strong that Eben was thrown to his back, forced to fight the other Were off with claws and teeth. Gwen was crying within minutes.

He screamed in pain as the red-pelted Were scraped his claws down his side, and then he roared and threw him off. He flipped to his feet, and prowled around the circle, ignoring the chanting of the crowd surrounding him.

"We've got to get closer," Gwen gasped, even as Connor tried pulling her back. She shook her head at him and pushed forward, searching for a better vantage. When she saw a spot just outside the ring, she took it, pulling Connor in close behind her.

Theron attacked again, aiming low, but this time Eben was ready, and swiped at him with his claws. Theron grunted, but gave no indication he was hit as he jumped back and prepared for another attack, circling slowly.

He fell to all fours, and stood completely still, his lip lifted in a snarl. Eben lowered himself, and just as his front legs touched the ground, Theron attacked, charging forward and plowing into Eben, taking him to his back.

They snarled fiercely, clawing and ripping at each other. Theron stayed on top, holding Eben down, his muzzle just inches from his throat. When he finally lunged forward, Eben turned just slightly, but enough. Theron latched onto Eben's shoulder, his teeth going deep even as bone snapped and tissue tore through.

"Eben!" Gwen yelled, her heart stopping in her throat as the terrible noises reached her ears. It was like nothing she'd ever heard, awful crunching and gurgling as blood collected in Theron's throat. She would hear that sound in her nightmares.

Theron growled deep and clenched his jaw even tighter. Eben's head fell back as he screamed with pain, even as his hand came up and smashed against Theron's side, jarring both of them with the impact. There was another snap as Theron rolled away, the jerk of his teeth breaking another bone in Eben's shoulder.

Theron was already up, waiting for Eben to roll to his feet. When he did, he wavered slightly. His eyes went over the crowd quickly, and when they landed on her, they stayed for a minute. Gwen's knees nearly gave out.

He turned back to the center of the ring, his one shoulder useless, his side ripped open from Theron's claws. He stood there, looking beaten down like she'd never seen him look before. Broken.

"You can yield," Theron muttered thickly, stalking forward. "But I'd still kill you."

"Then fight, and finish it."

They charged, and somehow Eben managed to throw Theron off, so far he bowled into the crowd, knocking over pack members, causing some of them to yip in fright and pain. With a savage curse he got to his feet, scraping his claws over the chest of one who didn't move, snarling at the rest in warning. Then he turned back to the circle, his eyes glinting evilly in the pale light. His head fell back in a howl, and then he ran forward, diving toward Eben, who moved back at the last second, and swiped his claws down Theron's back.

"Connor," Gwen said worriedly, her eyes locked on the scene in front of her. "This is not going well." She squeezed his hand as the Weres went for each other, once again meeting in the center. Again, Theron went down, but it was close this time, with Eben nearly losing his balance and falling onto his damaged shoulder. "Connor—"

"I know," he said hoarsely. "I know."

In the circle, Theron got up slowly, his back open nearly to the bone. His breathing was hard, and his head hung low for a second. Then he moved sideways around Eben, who stood still in the center of the circle. When Theron moved again, it was too fast for Gwen to even see. He dodged low, his claws going for the soft tissue of Eben's stomach. Eben snarled, and didn't allow it.

He lunged forward, snapping at his opponent's throat. But it was his clawed hand that did the most damage, wrapping around and digging through the already flayed layers of skin and muscle of Theron's back until he connected with his spine. He shoved his claws through it, shattering nerves and vertebrae, and with a vicious tug, he severed it completely, dragging out a length of the shiny bone and leaving it to sparkle dully in the night.

Theron's body stiffened in shock and pain, his eyes going wide for a minute just as a scream of defeat poured from his throat.

And like that, it was over. Eben leapt away from his opponent, scraped and bleeding, but the victor. Theron crumpled to the ground and lay still, gasping for breath, his eyes rolling to the back of his head. After a minute, his body gave up the fight, and he died.

Gwen didn't know at what point she fell, but suddenly she was being hoisted up by Connor and carried forward. He said nothing to the other pack members as he entered the circle with her securely in his arms.

Eben's head swung around and he growled, his lips lifting in warning. Connor stopped just inside the circle, every muscle tight with tension. "I'm bringing her to you, Alpha. I'm bringing you your mate."

When he took another step, Eben's growl deepened, but his eyes were on Gwen. "Put me down," she whispered, loosening her hold on Connor's neck as he let her feet touch the ground. Carefully, she walked forward, tears running down her cheeks as she reached for him. The minute her fingers touched his body, she collapsed against him. His uninjured arm curled around her back, holding her to him tightly.

Every fear she'd ever had about being terrified of him while he was changed completely slipped from her head. She clung to him, wrapping her hands in his thick pelt as she felt for herself that he was well and healthy, if a bit beat up. His arm and shoulder were a complete ruin, as was his side, but he seemed otherwise to be well. From the crowd, one of the Weres howled. Eben's head fell back and joined in, and Gwen couldn't do anything except wrap her arms around his thick neck and hold onto him for all she was worth.

The call went on and on, and then suddenly the crowd was surging forward, bowing to him, wishing him prosperity and many cubs. She hid her head farther in his neck and waited for it to be over, wanting nothing except to go home and sleep.

"You're hurt," she whispered against his chest, once the changed Weres had run off, and the unchanged were intent on changing and joining a hunt.

"I'll live," he growled out, his changed mouth working oddly to create the words.

She wiggled enough that he released her, but she stayed near his side, watching him in case his loss of blood and injury suddenly took its toll. "Where's Connor?" she asked, searching the crowd for his familiar form. "We need to get you home. You're going to need stitches, I think."

But he didn't hear her. His eyes were staring through the woods, his body tensing as the sounds of the Weres crashing through underbrush and chasing God-only-knew-what reached his ears.

"Eben?" She brushed her hand against his chest, and nearly screeched when his head abruptly turned toward her. "What's wrong?"

"I have to go."

"But—your injuries." She stared pointedly at his shoulder, at the blood that was running freely down. "Eben, you're hurt."

A high-pitched yip filled the air, and he quickly dropped to all fours, his head pointing in the direction it'd come.

Gwen held onto his fur, grasping it thickly at his back. "Eben, don't. Please, don't leave me like this."

He turned to her briefly, but he was ready to go, his body thrumming with energy. "I'll come for you tonight. Christian!"

Her fingers loosened on him just seconds before he ran from her, his large body rippling with muscle as he ran through the woods, faster than anything she'd ever seen. Just before he disappeared from sight, he met up with a similarly large, blond Were. Together, they chased into the trees, and then they were gone.

"They can't help it," Connor said, coming up behind her, a funny smile on his face. "I raised both of my boys to embrace their dual natures. I believe I succeeded, but perhaps a bit too well."

She shook her head, her worry still too fresh. "His shoulder. Connor, he's hurt. He almost lost. He probably has broken ribs to go along with the shoulder, and his side was ripped up, too."

"He'll heal. And I doubt that he was quite as weakened as he appeared. He's a smart man. He'd make an advantage out of an injury if it suited his purposes."

"Are you sure?" She looked at him pleadingly before returning her stare to the trees they'd disappeared in. "Can he get help if he suddenly goes down?"

He smiled. "The entire pack is with him, Gwen. He's safe. Now, you and I are heading home. There's an excellent cherry pie waiting for us, and a strong cup of tea. After this week, I need it."

She took the arm he offered and reluctantly walked away from the clearing, the excited sounds of the Weres hunting ringing in her ears.

Chapter Fifteen

෨

Near midnight, she was wide awake, her eyes pasted to the window leading out to the front. So far, there was nothing, but she felt sure that he'd show.

"I was wondering on the type of wedding you'd care for me to plan? I was thinking of something simple and elegant, with just a few friends and family." Connor frowned and looked up from the notepad he was scribbling in. "I do hope your mother won't be able to make it, however. I absolutely fear meeting her. What do you think?"

She turned her head. "Hmm? What was that?"

"The wedding. Your mother. Fear of meeting her. What are your thoughts on all this?"

"Oh God. Please tell me you're not going to start in on all this." She turned back to the window, sure she'd seen something move. But there was nothing. Just a partial moon and an empty yard. "You're supposed to be on my side for this. There's no reason we have to rush getting married."

"Oh, you'll marry him for sure. And sooner than you realize. Now, as I was saying, it won't be more than a hundred people. We'll have to speak to someone immediately about a dress for you, and of course a florist—"

"Connor," she said, swinging around and pinning him with her coldest stare, "The most he's going to manage to do is get me before a justice of the peace. I'd dye my own hair green before I do a wedding, as I'm sure you already know."

He smiled in satisfaction and leaned back in his chair. "Just so you realize you will be getting married. It's a shame really, though. I do so enjoy a wedding, and I know so few humans. I wish the Weres had adopted the practice."

She let his voice drone on and turned back to the window, anxious to see something. Anything. Eben had promised. She just hoped he didn't wait until four in the morning to fulfill it.

Her eyes wandered over the yard, and after a time, she turned back to the living room, her eyes getting heavy as she stared at the crackling fire. Connor smiled at her and turned back to his notebook, a fresh glass of brandy at his elbow.

Minutes before the clock struck one, Connor's head lifted, and his eyes got that faraway look that he adopted when his wild side rose.

"They're back."

Gwen got slowly to her feet and looked out the window. There, just in the distance, a shaggy form stood, pale yellow in the moonlight. And just beyond him, there was another. Darker, larger and more fierce.

"I'll get your coat," Connor said.

The air was beyond brisk, beyond cold. It was fucking freezing.

Gwen stopped just beyond the porch and stared out into the woods even as Eben's dark body slinked forward. He was still on all fours, his back bent as his body hunched down.

"Eben?"

He trotted forward, coming at her quickly. She started to scream even as he halted in front of her and buried his head in her stomach. Gwen's knees gave out and she sank to the ground, the frozen snow and wind completely forgotten.

"Are you okay?"

He hunkered down with her. Even lying on his stomach as he was doing, his head was almost level with hers. It made her feel ridiculously small, as if she were a child playing with a German Shepherd Dog.

"We hunted."

She leaned down and laid her head against his neck, her hands digging into his soft fur. "What now? What do we do?"

"You will marry me."

She held her breath, and then let it out slowly on a sigh. "Yes. I will marry you."

"I want the words, Gwen."

She lifted her head and looked into his odd eyes. She knew what he was asking for, knew it because she wanted to say them as much as he wanted to hear them. "I do love you," she whispered.

A rumble came from his chest as he laid his head in her lap, his clawed hands clenching gently against her legs as he inhaled her scent. "I want to love you. Like this. In my pelt."

"Now?" She looked around, but saw no one. It was still unnerving, though. The house was right there, and she knew Christian was somewhere close. "Eben, they'll see."

"Now." He got up on all fours, his fingers slipping into the waist of her sweatpants and pushing them down. "I need you," he growled.

Gwen shook, but she allowed him to remove her pants and underwear. He left the rest of her clothes alone, although she suspected that was more for protection against the cold than any desire on his part.

He positioned her knees on her discarded sweats, and pushed her to her hands, already rising up behind her. His cock brushed against her bare legs. She shivered, but not from the cold.

"It's going to be fast," he snarled, pushing her legs wider. "And hard."

Gwen nodded, watching him over her shoulder. She should have been terrified. Here she was, about to screw around with a creature that rightfully belonged in her nightmares, yet she couldn't seem to get past the lust. It was there, as always, just beneath the surface, waiting only for the slightest hint from Eben.

Gwen wiggled her hips at him. "I'm waiting," she breathed.

He laughed throatily, the sound coming out more like a threat than something signaling amusement. Slowly, he pushed his cock forward. He didn't stop until he was inside her to the hilt.

He stayed still, his hands locked on her hips, the fur of his pelt rubbing against her thighs and lower back. "We're to have a baby."

Gwen closed her eyes, the cold of the snow barely even a thought compared to the heat of him deep inside her. "I know."

And suddenly, he started fucking her, and just as he'd promised, it was rough and fast and hard. Gwen loved every glorious minute of it.

Enjoy an excerpt from:
DREAMS ECLIPSED

Archer joined them to form an intimate circle. Liam's chest brushed her arm on the left, Archer's on her right. She found her new position arousing. Slightly distracted by the blended masculine scents, Janet fought to keep her focus on the conversation.

"Here's where we're at," Archer began. "When your Dream shuts down the Zodiac, the information about what caused the system failure doesn't reach long-term storage. The only way to get the answers we need is for someone extremely knowledgeable about the Zodiac's operation to be with you when the disconnect happens."

"We already tried that, remember?" She did, especially the part where he was warming up in the shower. That was going to play a big role in her private fantasies for months to come. After all, turnabout was fair play. "You didn't get the information you need then?"

"Actually, last time I made a lot of mistakes. Not only did I fail to please you, but the approach I selected made it impossible to get the critical data."

She pushed against him with her shoulder until he gave her enough space to retreat behind her desk. She needed some extra breathing room. "And to fix that oversight, you're telling me I have to have VR sex with you again?"

"Or me," Liam offered. "Or anyone else on the project team for that matter. Who gets that honor is entirely up to you."

Janet bit her lip. She longed for a man who would generate the kind of primal heat in her that forced the rest of the world to disappear every time they kissed. Could either of these two men give her that feeling? She doubted it. The only place she'd ever met that kind of man was in the pages of a romance novel.

"Does it have to be a real person? Can't I pick one of Houston's Dream dates like I did before? There's got to be a way for you to play voyeur."

Archer explained, "I know I mentioned that possibility before, but honestly the best way to observe this kind of situation is to be right on top of it—no pun intended. If I'm even ten feet away or looking through a lens, or any one of a hundred other things I could be doing to spy on you, I may miss the critical clue."

"What if the glitch occurs only when I'm with a Dream lover?" Janet asked.

Archer waved off her argument. "We could debate what-ifs for months. The only way we're going to eliminate possibilities is to conduct more experiments."

"And I can pick anyone on the project team?"

Archer and Liam shared a long look, but it was Archer who replied, "That's what Dr. Bartel said and I guarantee whoever you choose will happily cooperate. However, brain boy and I feel the best chance for success is with one of us. I know the system better than anyone, and Liam knows all about how your mind works."

"What about Houston?" she asked them. The dark-skinned man from Chicago had a luscious body and a warped sense of humor that could make her laugh when she thought even smiling was impossible.

"Houston crossed his entire team off the list. Said they'd be too distracted checking out their handiwork from the inside to treat you right," Archer told her. "Frannie scratched her name off too. Apparently she already knows she's not your type. That leaves me and Liam as the most senior members, unless you have a thing for older, balding PhDs."

Janet chuckled. The thought of her and Dr. Bartel bumping uglies, even virtually, was very amusing. She had a great deal of affection for the old scientist but not in a way that would help here. "No, I think Dr. Bartel's virtue is safe from me."

Liam smiled. "Then all you need to do is pick which of us you think has a better shot at getting you to that trouble spot."

"It's not as easy as you make it sound," Janet replied.

"Go with your gut instinct," Liam encouraged her.

Her gut was too preoccupied with a bad case of butterflies to impart any useful advice. She looked between them. "Isn't there another option?"

"Not right now, no." Archer softened his voice. "It's a simple matter, Janet. Just choose which one of us you'd rather see in your bed."

While Janet admitted his advice was sound, she didn't find either man suitable for the job. From a purely physical point of view, she knew, and approved, of what she'd be getting with Archer, Mr. Tall, Dark and Handsome. However, she'd already been down that road once with him, and despite his explanation, she wasn't eager to leap back into bed with him so soon.

Liam, on the other hand, appealed to her more in that respect. She couldn't imagine any woman being disappointed by his blond, All-American good looks. However, Liam tended to coddle her, often treating her like a fragile glass sculpture he had to protect from a cold, cruel world. He wasn't controlling or demanding, just persistent about easing her way through life. That didn't usually translate into hot sex.

Maybe she was selling these two men short. Maybe both of them were capable of being the type of lover she most desired under the right set of circumstances. A successful outcome hinged on figuring out what those circumstances were and how to ensure they'd achieve them. Until now, that had largely been left to Houston and his team. They wrote the scripts, she just followed along.

"What scenario did you plan to run?" Knowing that much would give her some idea of who would be better suited to the environment.

They exchanged a look which said they hadn't gotten that far in their discussions. Figured.

"We, uh, thought we'd leave the time, place and position up to you," Archer ad-libbed.

"Speak for yourself," Liam said, glaring at the crude terms. "I'd be happy to craft a romantic environment for us."

Liam's suggestion triggered a bright moment of inspiration. "Excellent idea," Janet said. "Go for it. Both of you."

Archer frowned. "Both of us? I don't understand."

Janet relaxed against the back of her chair, feeling as if she'd just found the key to solving world hunger. "You each possess qualities I find attractive. Lest that go to your little heads," she said as they perked up, "neither of you is perfect. To determine which man is right for this job, I have to consider how all three elements—who, where and how—will work together."

"So what are you proposing? A competition?" Archer asked.

"Exactly. Come up with a concept of what you think it'll take to get the job done. The scenario I like best will be the one we use, along with the man who wrote it." Janet picked up her ruined purse, deciding she'd have lunch, after all. With Frannie. As she sailed out the door, she said, "Good luck, gentlemen. I think you're going to need it."

Why an electronic book?

We live in the Information Age—an exciting time in the history of human civilization, in which technology rules supreme and continues to progress in leaps and bounds every minute of every day. For a multitude of reasons, more and more avid literary fans are opting to purchase e-books instead of paper books. The question from those not yet initiated into the world of electronic reading is simply: *Why?*

1. *Price.* An electronic title at Ellora's Cave Publishing and Cerridwen Press runs anywhere from 40% to 75% less than the cover price of the exact same title in paperback format. Why? Basic mathematics and cost. It is less expensive to publish an e-book (no paper and printing, no warehousing and shipping) than it is to publish a paperback, so the savings are passed along to the consumer.

2. *Space.* Running out of room in your house for your books? That is one worry you will never have with electronic books. For a low one-time cost, you can purchase a handheld device specifically designed for e-reading. Many e-readers have large, convenient screens for viewing. Better yet, hundreds of titles can be stored within your new library—on a single microchip. There are a variety of e-readers from different manufacturers. You can also read e-books on your PC or laptop computer. (Please note that Ellora's Cave does not endorse any specific brands. You can check our websites at www.ellorascave.com

or www.cerridwenpress.com for information we make available to new consumers.)

3. *Mobility.* Because your new e-library consists of only a microchip within a small, easily transportable e-reader, your entire cache of books can be taken with you wherever you go.

4. *Personal Viewing Preferences.* Are the words you are currently reading too small? Too large? Too... ANNOYING? Paperback books cannot be modified according to personal preferences, but e-books can.

5. *Instant Gratification.* Is it the middle of the night and all the bookstores near you are closed? Are you tired of waiting days, sometimes weeks, for bookstores to ship the novels you bought? Ellora's Cave Publishing sells instantaneous downloads twenty-four hours a day, seven days a week, every day of the year. Our webstore is never closed. Our e-book delivery system is 100% automated, meaning your order is filled as soon as you pay for it.

Those are a few of the top reasons why electronic books are replacing paperbacks for many avid readers.

As always, Ellora's Cave and Cerridwen Press welcome your questions and comments. We invite you to email us at Comments@ellorascave.com or write to us directly at Ellora's Cave Publishing Inc., 1056 Home Avenue, Akron, OH 44310-3502.

THE
✝ ELLORA'S CAVE ✝
LIBRARY

Stay up to date with Ellora's Cave Titles in
Print with our Quarterly Catalog.

TO RECIEVE A CATALOG,
SEND AN EMAIL WITH YOUR NAME
AND MAILING ADDRESS TO:

CATALOG@ELLORASCAVE.COM

OR SEND A LETTER OR POSTCARD
WITH YOUR MAILING ADDRESS TO:

CATALOG REQUEST
c/o ELLORA'S CAVE PUBLISHING, INC.
1056 HOME AVENUE
AKRON, OHIO 44310-3502

erridwen, the Celtic Goddess of wisdom, was the muse who brought inspiration to story-tellers and those in the creative arts. Cerridwen Press encompasses the best and most innovative stories in all genres of today's fiction. Visit our site and discover the newest titles by talented authors who still get inspired - much like the ancient storytellers did, once upon a time.